CW01497230

Fiona Leitch is a novelist and s
past. She's written for football
childbirth videos and mail ord
raves in London, been told of
during a studio debate; and was the Australasian face of a
series of TV commercials for a cleaning product. All of
which has given her a thorough grounding in the
ridiculous, and helped her to write funny stuff.

facebook.com/fionakleitch
instagram.com/fionaleitchauthor

Also by Fiona Leitch

The Nosey Parker Cozy Mysteries

THE CORNISH CHRISTMAS PANTOMIME MURDER

A Nosey Parker Cozy Mystery

FIONA LEITCH

One More Chapter
a division of HarperCollins*Publishers* Ltd
1 London Bridge Street
London SE1 9GF
www.harpercollins.co.uk
HarperCollins*Publishers*
Macken House, 39/40 Mayor Street Upper,
Dublin 1, D01 C9W8

This paperback edition 2025
2
First published in Great Britain in ebook format
by HarperCollins*Publishers* 2025
Copyright © Fiona Leitch 2025
Fiona Leitch asserts the moral right to be identified
as the author of this work
A catalogue record of this book is available from the British Library
ISBN: 978-0-00-875468-6

This novel is entirely a work of fiction. The names, characters and
incidents portrayed in it are the work of the author's imagination. Any
resemblance to actual persons, living or dead, events or localities is
entirely coincidental.
Printed and bound in the UK using 100% Renewable Electricity
by CPI Group (UK) Ltd
All rights reserved. No part of this publication may be reproduced, stored
in a retrieval system, or transmitted, in any form or by any means,
electronic, mechanical, photocopying, recording or otherwise, without the
prior permission of the publishers.
Without limiting the exclusive rights of any author, contributor or the
publisher of this publication, any unauthorised use of this publication to
train generative artificial intelligence (AI) technologies is expressly
prohibited. HarperCollins also exercise their rights under Article 4(3) of
the Digital Single Market Directive 2019/790 and expressly reserve this
publication from the text and data mining exception.

Important Note from the Author

For those of you unfortunate enough (or fortunate enough, depending on your point of view) to not have experienced a pantomime before, please allow me to explain how they work. You need to know this stuff.

Linguistically, the word 'pantomime' comes from Ancient Rome, where it referred to a dance based on myths and legends by a sole performer who took on all the roles of the story. However, when it comes to the traditional English pantomime we know and love today, its roots go back as far as the 1600s (maybe even further), with travelling players who would go from town to town performing plays based on well-known folk tales, and it was heavily influenced by the Italian theatrical form *commedia dell'arte*. All of which sounds like it should have a certain gravitas, and could fool you into thinking of it as a highbrow intellectual experience.

It isn't.

Modern pantomimes are usually based on fairytales, but

with some pretty hefty liberties taken with the plot, normally in order to shoehorn in a bit of topical humour and maybe a cover version of a completely irrelevant pop song. Audience participation is a major part of the panto experience, and there are certain phrases that are included in every performance, with the crowd responding with their own time-honoured lines. Let's use *Jack and the Beanstalk* as an example.

Jack's Mum:
(*to audience, as Jack himself lurks right behind her, out of view*)
Where's that useless son of mine?

Audience: He's behind you!

(*Cue Mum walking around in a big circle, with Jack following close behind, so of course she STILL doesn't see him.*)

Jack's Mum: Oh no he isn't!

Audience: Oh yes he is!

It ain't Chekhov.

The 'principal boy' – the young male lead character – is played by a pretty young woman, clad in a short tunic and tights, who struts around the stage slapping her thigh and being irritatingly perky. The female lead character, who is normally the love interest, will also be played by a pretty young woman, which these days is all well and good, but it does make you wonder how previous generations could accept this whilst still getting het up about same-sex marriages.

There will always be a villain – possibly with a bit of racial stereotyping thrown in – and he will always be a right evil bugger whilst also being completely ineffectual, a bit like Nigel Farage. Comic relief is provided by a pantomime dame, otherwise known as a fat bloke in an outrageous dress, massive wig and the entire contents of the makeup counter at Boots. He'll usually have either a gruff Northern accent or a falsetto voice that's shrill enough to make the fillings in your teeth vibrate, and will say stuff like 'lawks', often while cracking jokes that are *just this side* of inappropriate. The dame will play a character like Jack's mum or a random washerwoman, or maybe there'll be two of them in *Cinderella*, playing the Ugly Sisters, whose names will always be something like Syphilydia and Chlamysilis.

Casting is a big part of panto, depending on the size of the theatre and their budget. If you go to a professional production the cast will be made up of soap actors, *Love Island* contestants and H from Steps, but if you go to an amateur show like the one in this book you'll have to make do with Denis from the estate agents and that surly-looking woman who works on the till at the Co-op. You know, her with the chin.

And of course any amateur dramatic theatrical

production is rife with rivalries, frustrations, thwarted ambitions and illicit love affairs, so it's the perfect setting for a spot of murder.

READER:
Oh no it isn't!

ME:
Oh yes it is!

See? You're getting the hang of it already.

Chapter One

'So where's my leading lady, then?' Tony Penhaligon, my oldest friend in the world and erstwhile thespian, stood on the doorstep, stamping his feet to warm up. 'I won't come in, we're already late. Is she ready?'

'Yes she is,' I said, wrapping my cardigan tighter around me. Having the door open was letting all the cold air in. At my feet Germaine, my Pomeranian fur baby (a phrase I'd started using ironically and now couldn't stop), gave a little bark, wondering why Tony – one of her favourite people – was waiting outside and not coming in to make a big fuss of her, like he normally did.

'Oh no she isn't!' cried Mum, coming through the connecting door from her granny flat (not that we were allowed to call it that) into the hall behind me.

'Oh yes she is!' cried Tony enthusiastically. Germaine barked happily in agreement.

'No, she ain't,' said Mum. 'I can't find me script anywhere.'

Daisy came down the stairs, wrapping a scarf around her neck with a resigned expression on her face.

'Nana, it's the dress rehearsal in two days,' she said. 'You're supposed to be off-book by now.'

'It ain't a book, it's a script,' said Mum. 'And I *did* know it, until *somebody* went through and changed half of it.'

I cringed inwardly. Daisy had agreed to help the local amateur dramatics group, the Penstowan Players, ostensibly as the line prompt for their annual Christmas pantomime, but really she'd been drafted in to rewrite the script. It seemed to have originally been written sometime in the 1970s by Benny Hill or Bernard Manning – the sort of comedian who relied on mother-in-law jokes and racial stereotypes – although it had actually been penned by one of the founder members of the group, back in the 80s, who swore it had been performed at the time to great acclaim. We only had his word for it, though, as most of the members who'd been around then had either moved away or died. A couple of Daisy's friends were in the chorus and, backed by some other cast members, they'd felt that the script was (understatement alert) 'mildly problematic'. Knowing that my daughter was a fledgling political activist – she'd staged a very visual protest against deep sea oil drilling during our local mermaid festival a couple of years ago, and a sit-in at the school canteen when they'd refused to include a vegan lunch option – they'd 'strongly suggested' (threatened to go on strike) that the director bring her in to rewrite the worst bits of the play. He already knew it had major issues but, as a newcomer not just to the Players but to Penstowan itself, he'd been a bit worried about changing it and potentially ruffling a few feathers. Feather ruffling was, however, one of Daisy's favourite pastimes, so he'd gladly handed it over to her.

I was very proud of my daughter.

'There's no way they could keep the joke about the black rabbi, the gay priest and the transgender nun,' said Daisy, reasonably. 'It was racist, sexist, homophobic, transphobic, misogynistic, Islamophobic, *and* antisemitic.'

'And it didn't have anything nice to say about the Irish, either,' I said, shuddering at the thought of it. 'Or the French.'

'It's true, Shirley,' said Tony. 'The best you could say about the original script is that it was written by an equal opportunities bigot.'

'It offended *everyone*,' I said. 'It was omniphobic.'

'It was still funny, though,' said Mum stubbornly.

'Not to anybody under seventy,' muttered Daisy. 'Good comedy should punch upwards, at those in power, not downwards. Taking the piss out of minorities isn't comedy, it's bullying.'

Mum opened her mouth to speak again, but thankfully we were saved by Nathan arriving home from work.

'What's this, mothers' meeting?' He leant in and kissed me on the cheek, smiling around at everyone else and then stooping to pick Germaine up before she went crazy with joy at his return.

'Tony's here to take Mum and Daisy to rehearsal, only Mum can't find her script,' I said. Nathan frowned and pointed the dog towards the hall table Mum was hovering in front of.

'It's behind you,' he said. Daisy groaned.

'Don't you start. December is going to be a *looong* month.'

We watched them get into the car and drive away, before I shut the door and pulled my husband into a big hug, making Germaine whine in alarm. *My husband.* I was still getting used to calling him that, but I loved it.

'No regrets?' asked Nathan. I looked at him in surprise, startled out of my thoughts.

'About what?'

'Being in the panto. Or rather *not* being in the panto. You could've been principal boy, striding around the stage in a pair of tights, slapping your thigh and doing all the "oh no he isn't!", "oh yes he is!" stuff.'

'There's enough of that going on in here,' I said. 'But you like the idea of me strutting about in a pair of tights and slapping my thigh, do you?'

'Well, yeah, but let me get my coat off first…'

Of course, with Mum and Daisy (and Tony, and what felt like half of Penstowan – I was starting to wonder who would be left to sit in the audience) involved in the panto, I hadn't been able to get away completely scot-free. As well as going through the script with Daisy (and helping her edit it heavily), I'd somehow allowed myself to be coerced into catering the after party for cast and friends on opening night. One of the leading lights of the Penstowan Players, Tim, just happened to be married to Maurice, the mayor, who *just happened* to be looking for a caterer for a big civic bash he was holding in the New Year. And, said Tim, this would be a good opportunity for me to showcase my culinary talents in front of him. I was gracious enough not to mention that I'd already catered a couple of functions at Penstowan Town Hall, or indeed that Maurice had already told me I was top of his list of chefs for hire. As long as they paid for the ingredients, I was happy to put everything together and set up a buffet if it guaranteed that they wouldn't pester me to be in the chorus or something.

'What exactly is Shirley doing in the show?' asked Nathan later, as we sat in front of the TV with a cup of tea and enjoyed the rare peace that came with both Mum and Daisy being out at the same time. Even Germaine was making the most of it, snoozing on the sofa next to me, although to be fair that dog could snooze for Great Britain.

'I shudder to think,' I said, and he laughed. 'She was in the chorus, but she couldn't keep up with the dance routines, so they gave her the part of the old washerwoman.'

'Lots of scope for overacting and chewing the scenery there, I'm guessing?'

'Put it this way, there'll be more ham on that stage than on the deli counter at Sainsbury's.'

5

'What about Tony? I can't see him being happy with anything less than the lead role.'

'Well, Aladdin himself is being played by Kirsty someone or other. She used to be a teaching assistant at Daisy's school but she left under a bit of a cloud, I think. I don't know what she's doing now.'

'I know her, she works in the One Stop round the corner from the station,' said Nathan. 'Nice girl.'

'So he had to settle for the other really big role, the villain, Abanazar the evil magician…'

'Oh, I bet he *loves* that,' said Nathan. 'I've always thought it must be much more fun to play the bad guy than the hero.'

'That's because you're a hero in real life,' I said, snuggling into him. He laughed.

'Yeah, I've been a real hero lately. The worst we've had to deal with over the last couple of months is old Joey Trevally persistently parking his tractor in the Co-op car park and taking up too many spaces.' He shook his head. 'We never had *that* in Liverpool.'

'Don't tell me you'd prefer a nice juicy murder to get your teeth into?'

'I wouldn't go *that* far, but it would make my job more interesting.'

'You'll probably be able to arrest Mum for crimes against theatre, comedy and humanity in general at the performance,' I said soothingly.

At about ten-thirty we heard the front door open and

shut, and two pairs of footsteps come into the hallway outside.

'Night, sweetheart,' we heard Mum say, somewhat tersely.

'Night, Nana,' said Daisy, in an equally measured tone. Nathan and I exchanged looks. Even Germaine looked slightly perturbed.

'Uh oh,' I said. At least the door hadn't been slammed shut the way it had been a couple of rehearsals ago, hard enough then to make the newly erected Christmas tree shake and all the baubles rattle.

Daisy came in and flopped onto the sofa, reaching out a hand to stroke the dog.

'How did it go?' I asked, carefully. Daisy let out a big, exasperated sigh.

'Honestly, how hard is it to learn your lines?'

'Nana?'

'Not just her. All of them, apart from Tony and Kirsty. Half of them have only got about five words to say and they can't even get *them* right. At one point Colin was hyperventilating so much I thought he was having a stroke. He had to take himself off for five minutes' soul searching and meditation.'

'Who's Colin?' asked Nathan.

'Colin Sweeney. The director.'

'The name rings a bell. Have I nicked him?'

Daisy scoffed. 'Colin? I can't imagine him doing anything that interesting. Unless you can arrest someone for being ostentatiously spiritual.'

'Poor Colin,' I said. 'He's not *that* bad.'

'Yes he is. Even Jocasta says he's a bit much.' Jocasta was the stage manager, and one of Mum's best friends. She had the world's biggest collection of pashminas and clanking ethnic beads, and wafted around in what I had assumed was a cloud of patchouli but actually turned out to be Jo Malone Pear and Elderflower eau de toilette. She had, after all, spent her entire working life as a high-powered (and well paid) lawyer before retiring to Cornwall and becoming the nearest thing Penstowan had to a spiritual guru. If Jocasta said you were a bit much, you probably were.

'I know I'll be going to bed in a minute, but have we got any chocolate?'

'Oh dear, that awful, was it?' I said sympathetically. 'Will Jaffa Cakes do?'

'Well, I'm assuming there's no weed in the house, what with him—' she nodded at Nathan '—being a copper.'

'No, sorry,' said Nathan. 'We smoked it all while you were out.'

'Oh, ha ha ha, you're *soo* funny… Jaffa Cakes it is, then,' she said, heading for the kitchen followed by a hopeful Pomeranian who refused to believe that chocolate was toxic for dogs. 'December is going to be a *looong* month…'

'Do you think you should check on Shirley?' asked Nathan, in a quiet undertone.

'Who, me? You've got to be joking. I'm not getting involved.' But he kept looking at me, so I heaved myself off the sofa and padded along the hallway to Mum's annexe. I knocked.

'You all right, Mum?' I called. Daisy came out of the kitchen, clutching a packet of Jaffa Cakes, and shot me a look of utter betrayal. 'I'm not taking sides,' I whispered to her, 'but she *is* an old lady.'

'Who you calling old?' demanded Mum, opening the door.

'Well not you, obviously. You've got the hearing of a bat. Just checking everything was okay, as you didn't say goodnight.'

'You want me to tuck you in?'

'No need to be sarky, woman,' I said, rolling my eyes. At least she couldn't complain when Daisy or I were sarcastic to her; it ran in the family. 'Can I remind you both, it is Christmas, and the baby Jesus would have something to say about... whatever this is.'

'General unpleasantness,' said Nathan, joining me for moral support.

'What he said.' I nodded. 'He was brung up Catholic and all, so he knows. Jesus didn't go in for... for...?'

'General unpleas—'

'General unpleasantness, yes, that was it. Not on his birthday, anyway.'

'It's not his birthday yet,' said Daisy stubbornly, but she was fighting to keep a smile off her face.

'He doesn't like nitpicking either,' said Nathan, reaching out and tickling her. She burst out laughing and squirmed out of his reach, but not before he'd grabbed the packet of Jaffa Cakes from her.

'Oi!' she cried. Mum laughed.

'I'll have one of them too,' she said. Nathan handed her the packet, and she immediately returned it to Daisy with a wink.

'Thank you, Nana,' she said.

'Thank *you*, sweetheart, for taking the time to help me learn me lines. I promise I'll do better at the dress rehearsal.'

'That's okay,' said Daisy, and I felt a huge surge of relief that two of my favourite people in the world were friends again – not that I could really imagine them ever being anything but. We all kissed each other goodnight (we are a very kissy family), then Mum went into her granny flat and Daisy and the dog headed upstairs after offering both of us a Jaffa Cake.

'Crisis averted,' said Nathan, nibbling at the chocolate coating.

But the real crisis was yet to come.

Chapter Two

'Has anyone seen my boobs? I put 'em down earlier and now I can't remember where I left them.'

Now that was a sentence that would've been out of place anywhere but here – backstage on the opening night of the panto. Tim, for someone who ordinarily looked like Idris Elba's older brother, made a surprisingly feminine pantomime dame, even without his enormous false bosoms. He hitched up his voluminous skirts and rushed off into the backstage maze without waiting for an answer.

'I tripped over them on my way in,' I called after him, plonking down the box of buffet food I was carrying on a battered old sofa in the corner of the storeroom. I say 'buffet food', but what that really equated to was half a ton of sausage rolls. It seemed to be my lot in life – in catering life, anyway – to never be too far from a plate of them. Every blooming catering job just wanted the standard buffet of sausage rolls, quiches, finger sandwiches and that 70s classic, the cheese-and-pineapple-on-a-stick-stuck-into-half-a-grapefruit hedgehog. My teachers at catering college would be rolling in their graves if they were dead. All that effort spent learning how to make a croquembouche, wasted.

It was pretty cramped behind the scenes, with 'backstage' being made up of a myriad of different rooms and storage areas for props, wardrobe, and random stuff that no one had got round to throwing away yet. The theatre was in an old building – parts of it over three hundred years old – which had originally been a village hall, and bits had been tacked on here and there, creating loads of little rooms and odd-shaped spaces that were almost unusable. There was no proper green room, just a very small kitchen area with a kettle and a couple of chairs, so after the performance the buffet would be set up on a long table at the back of the auditorium, and cast, crew, friends and family would all help themselves. Nathan joined me, carrying not just the last box of buffet food but also, slung over his shoulder, what looked like a canvas bag with a couple of footballs in it.

'Tim's looking for those,' I said, as he dropped the bag on the floor.

'I did wonder where they'd fit into the buffet,' he grinned. 'I thought maybe you were going to do the old cheese-and-pineapple-on-cocktail-sticks hedgehog but had run out of grapefruit.'

'Dolly!' cried Tim, appearing in the doorway. 'Jolene! There you are…' He bent down to pick the bag – or bra, as I realised it was – off the floor. He straightened up and rearranged his bust.

'You've already got boobs,' I said, stupidly, and then hoped that they were another set of falsies and not unfortunate man-boobs. Moobs. But luckily Tim laughed.

'Oh *these*?' He gestured to his chest. 'These are my starter boobs. I call them my "storm in a C cup". There's a running gag that my bosoms keep getting bigger throughout the show. I start with these, then just before the interval I pop the girls on—' he hefted the bag in his hand '—and then by the end I've got my final set on, and they're enormous. I like to call those "dead heat in a zeppelin race".'

'You seem to be enjoying being dressed like that a bit too much,' I said. 'Are you sure there's nothing you want to tell us?'

'Love, I'm black and gay,' he said archly. 'I'm already enough of a diversity hire as it is.' He winked and headed back to the dressing rooms.

'He was born to play Widow Twankey,' noted Nathan.

'Definitely.'

'Where's my dame?' Colin, the director, appeared in the doorway of the room, making us both jump. He was a big man, in his early sixties; over six feet tall, and where he'd once been muscular and toned he was now soft and a bit squishy, but still powerful. Despite that he was gentle and trod lightly, able to sneak up behind you without you hearing him, although I didn't think he did that on purpose. And even though he was, as Daisy had said, occasionally a bit 'ostentatiously spiritual' – he did tend to go on a bit about aligning his chakras and greeting each day with a positive affirmation in order to manifest one's desires – he spoke softly most of the time, directing his actors with a smile and a suggestion rather than a firm hand. If he'd had a firm hand, Mum would've learnt her lines a lot quicker.

'You just missed him,' said Nathan. 'Did you not see him?'

'I must've lost him in the labyrinth,' said Colin with a smile, waving his arm behind him to indicate the quirky layout of the building before his eyes came to rest on the box in front of me. 'Is that the food for afterwards?'

'Yes, Jocasta said this was the best place to leave it because no one will need to come in here during the show,' I said. 'Is that okay?'

'Oh yes, if Jocasta says so it'll be fine.' He bestowed a calm, beatific smile upon us. 'I'm looking forward to one of your vegan sausage rolls when this is all over. Now I must go and prepare the cast.'

'Break a leg,' I said. 'See you on the other side.'

With all the food now brought in, all that was left for us to do was head out to the auditorium and take our seats. The performance space was small but perfectly formed, with room for perhaps eighty people in the audience, and every seat was taken. There was an excited babble of voices from the assembled crowd, still audible over the Christmas music that was playing over the PA system.

'Nice to have a full house on opening night.' Our seat neighbour, Carmen, was there in both her capacity as the vicar of St Botolph's church down the road – part of her job was supporting community initiatives and the like – and also as significant other to the villain of the piece, Tony.

'Is Tony nervous?' whispered Nathan. She shook her head.

'Not even slightly. He's been looking forward to getting out there and hamming it up.' She leant forward and tapped the shoulder of the man sitting in the seat in front of her. 'Sorry, can you take your Santa hat off when it starts? I can't see the stage.'

The last strains of 'All I Want for Christmas Is You' faded out as the man apologised and removed his hat. The lights dimmed and an expectant hush fell over the audience. And then, something weird happened. The actors came on, and… they were good.

Nobody forgot lines, or corpsed. I couldn't in all conscience say there was no overacting, but then it was a panto, and that was to be expected. The actors delivered funny lines with their faces absolutely straight, which of course made it funnier. The audience laughed, and booed in the right places, and joined in with 'he's behind you' and all that malarkey.

Tony was in his element as Abanazar, the villain. He stalked across the stage, slightly bent over, hunchbacked by the weight of the evil he was carrying. I looked at Carmen; she was watching him, mouth open in complete awe. Feeling my eyes on her she turned to look at me, mouthing, *'Oh my God!'*

'I know!' I mouthed back. The young woman playing

Aladdin, Kirsty, was also excellent, as was Princess Jasmine (who I recognised as Sarah, one of the lifeguards at the local leisure centre) and the Genie of the Lamp, who was being played by Sergeant 'Old Davey' Trelawney's eldest son, Louis. Davey was built like a mountain range, and twenty-eight-year-old Louis definitely had his father's genes rather than his mother's (Jen Trelawney was five foot nothing and weighed about as much as one of Tim's false boobs).

And Tim as Widow Twankey... well, if they ever decided to put drag nights on at the Market Arms, Tim would be the star.

And then there was my mum. She lurked in the chorus during Act One, but in Act Two she got her chance in the spotlight.

Oh God, here we go, I thought, as she waddled onto the stage dressed up as a washerwoman. I prepared myself to go rigid with embarrassment...

'Your mother is amazing!' In the row behind us, Bob the hardware shop owner (who had a bit of a thing for my mum) leaned forward and whispered to me and Nathan. 'She's a natural on that stage.'

'She is, isn't she?' said Nathan, sounding as surprised as I felt. He looked at me. 'I thought she didn't know any of her lines?'

'So did I. So did Daisy.' But Mum didn't put a foot wrong. She did her bit as the washerwoman with Widow Twankey and then, to the astonishment (and hilarity) of the audience, she threw off her costume and became a completely different character.

'Hold it right there, Twankey!' she cried. 'I'm Dunnit of the Yard.'

'Dunnit in the yard? Done what? What yard? My back yard?'

'Detective Inspector Hugh Dunnit, of Scotland Yard. At your service, ladies and gentlemen.' She bowed to the audience, who cheered, then pulled out a magnifying glass – I winced as I saw where she'd been hiding it – with a grin. 'And I detect that you, madame, are no ordinary woman.'

'Ooh, well, you've got *that* right,' said Widow Twankey, with a cheeky wink to the audience.

Mum studied Tim carefully with the magnifying glass. 'I suspect you are hiding something under that dress, Twankey.'

'You're right about *that* and all,' said Twankey. 'I suppose you want to frisk me now.'

Tim did a big star jump – as big as he could manage in his dress, anyway – and Mum started feeling over him. She reached his groin and turned to the audience, eyes wide.

'There's definitely something under there,' she said.

'You don't say,' said Twankey.

'Take it out, please, madame.' Tim went to lift his skirt up but Mum stopped him. 'Not in front of the children!' *Bit late to be thinking about THEM*, I thought. This bit of the panto had been a bit risqué, but then again that was part of the panto experience too. 'At least turn your back.'

Tim turned his back to the audience and started tugging at something under his dress. He seemed to be having trouble, as every now and then he'd look over his shoulder and grimace an apology to the laughing crowd. Mum did a big eye roll at the audience.

'Let me give you a hand,' she said. She went round to the front of him and also started tugging something. Hard. 'Good Lord, madame, you've got that tucked away tightly there.' She wiped her brow and tried again, turning to the audience and grimacing too. Everyone howled with laughter as Mum got on the floor and put her feet against the scenery to brace herself, hands above her head and tugging. Tim leant back, bracing his shoulders against another part of the scenery, and finally, with both of them pulling in different directions, the hidden item was freed, with a loud 'plop!'

Carmen wiped her eyes. 'Oh my goodness, Shirley and Tim are the perfect comedy double act.'

Mum held the item up triumphantly to the audience, and then her smile faded as she looked at it. It was a plastic chicken.

'Hang on – I thought you were hiding the genie and his magic lamp?'

'Magic lamp? Never heard of it,' said the Widow Twankey, with a big obvious wink at the audience. While Mum/Hugh Dunnit inspected the chicken, Tim Twankey sauntered across the stage and lifted up a flap in the scenery to show the lamp nestled inside. He pointed at it, making sure the audience had seen it, before dropping the flap again.

'What have you got there, madame?' cried Hugh Dunnit, crossing the stage.

'Nothing, nothing,' he said. He looked at the audience and did a stage whisper out of the side of his mouth. 'Say nowt.'

'It's behind you!' called some wag a few seats behind us, and everyone laughed. Tim rolled his eyes.

'There's always one,' he said. Mum reached over and lifted the flap. Tim Twankey braced himself, but—

'There's nothing there!' cried Mum. Tim did a big comic double-take.

'What...? I mean, of course it's not there!' He waited until Mum's back was turned and started searching the rest of the set, before opening another flap in the scenery. The lamp was in there. He gave a big sigh of relief, still holding the flap open. 'Well, it *is* magic...'

'There it is!' cried Mum.

'What? No, no it isn't it!' said Tim, reaching out to take the lamp and hide it under his skirt. He clamped his knees shut to trap it in place, then held up his hands to show that they were empty. 'See? Nothing here.'

But there *was* something – on, rather than in, his hands. Mum went to say something but stopped. Tim looked at his hands in surprise, his expression turning to one of horror.

'Is that – is that blood?' asked Mum. The audience had been laughing, thinking this was part of the joke, but as Tim frantically wiped his hands on his skirt and ripped the lamp out from under his clothes, the laughter began to trail off. Nathan and I exchanged looks.

'This isn't part of the plot, is it?' asked Nathan, as Tim inspected the lamp and then threw it on the ground in a reflex of disgust. But I didn't need to answer him, as the next line completely gave the ending away.

Sarah, the young woman playing Princess Jasmine, ran onto the stage, her face as white as a sheet and her clothes covered in blood. 'She's dead!' she cried, and crumpled dramatically to the floor.

Chapter Three

'Just what I like,' said Nathan with a sigh. 'A murder with about a hundred suspects.'

We were standing in the storage room, waiting for the Forensics team to arrive. In front of us stood the open door into the props cupboard, where the unfortunate principal boy, Kirsty, had been found, half rolled up in the not-so-magic carpet that was supposed to transport her and Princess Jasmine to 'A Whole New World' on stage, but had instead facilitated her journey out of this one. There was a small cut above her left eye, crusted with blood, but going by the pool of blood seeping out behind her, the real damage had been done at the back of her head, although of course we couldn't see it without rolling her over. A long smear of blood on the floor of the storage room suggested that she'd been dragged onto the rug and then shoved unceremoniously into the cupboard, although not deep enough into it to shut the door. Whoever had done this had soon realised they couldn't hide the body, but they could at least make sure no one would immediately stumble across it. Back in the auditorium, Davey Trelawney and one of my dad's old (and now retired) recruits, ex-desk sergeant Harry Adams (who unbeknown to me had been in the audience), had begun the task of taking everyone's name and contact details.

'You're not saying the audience are suspects?' I asked him.

'At this stage, I'm saying everyone is. We can't rule anyone out until we know when she was murdered.'

'During the interval,' said Daisy, joining us. Nathan diplomatically positioned himself in front of the cupboard door, so as to block the body from sight. 'She was in the last but one scene before the break. The first one after the break was the business with Nana and Tim. She was due to be on in the next scene, but she wasn't waiting in the wings so Sarah went to find her.' Daisy's eyes were drawn to the doorway behind Nathan, but I didn't think she could see anything.

'How long was the interval? Ten minutes?'

'Fifteen,' I replied, and Daisy nodded.

'Time for Tim and Nana to do a quick change, and everyone else to have a wee and a drink.'

'So she could actually have been murdered just before the interval,' Nathan pointed out. 'I'll need to talk to the cast and find out where everyone was.'

I pulled Daisy into a hug. 'Are you okay?'

'Yes,' she said, but her bottom lip began to wobble. I hugged her tighter as I felt rather than saw the tears start to come. 'Oh Mum, I was only a few metres away when she was being murdered! Why didn't I hear her call out or something? She was really lovely, as well.'

I patted her on the back, and then Nathan joined us for a family hug, stroking her hair.

'I'm glad you didn't hear her,' said Nathan. 'What would you have done?'

'Stopped whoever it was killing her, of course.'

'But then you might be dead, too,' he said. She stopped crying for a moment and looked at him, then started again, even harder. He looked at me in surprise and went to open his mouth, but I shook my head slightly. I knew he was trying to make her understand that there was nothing she could've done, but she now had to contend with the thought that she'd been close to a murderer, and who was to say that she wouldn't have been the victim if she'd been on her own? Nathan moved away as his right-hand man, Detective Sergeant Matt Turner, entered the room, followed by PC Chrissie Cardwell, one of Penstowan's finest and, coincidentally, Matt's girlfriend. Which explained why they always arrived at crime scenes at the same time. She took one look at the weeping Daisy and came over to hold her hand while Nathan caught Matt up on the situation.

'Probably best if you're not in here, Daisy,' said Chrissie. 'I hear your nana caused a bit of a stir earlier, is that right?'

Daisy managed a slight smile. 'She was magnificent,' she said proudly, 'until...' *Until her moment of glory was ruined by the discovery of the corpse*, I thought.

'I think she's probably in the auditorium with everyone else,' said Chrissie. 'Shall we go and find her?'

'That's a good idea,' I said. 'I'll be there too in a minute.' I kissed Daisy and gave Chrissie an unspoken *take-care-of-my-little-girl* look, which she returned with a sharp nod, and the two of them left.

'Blimey, that's a plot twist,' said Matt, peering into the cupboard. 'Poor girl. She works at the One Stop near the station, doesn't she?'

'She did,' said Nathan solemnly, and Matt looked stricken.

'Yeah, of course. Did.' He crouched down next to Kirsty's body, taking in the head wound silently. Nathan put a hand on his shoulder.

'Feels a bit different when it's someone you know, doesn't it?' he said softly.

Matt nodded but didn't look up at him. 'I only spoke to her yesterday. Went in and bought a packet of Hula Hoops for my lunch.'

'How did she seem?' I asked. 'Was she excited about the show?'

'Yeah,' said Matt, but he sounded uncertain. 'I dunno, actually. I *think* she was, but... I dunno, it was probably nerves. I don't want to read anything into it just because she's dead, if you know what I mean.'

'Yes, I do.' Nathan crouched down next to him.

'So obviously we can't be sure until the doctor looks at her, and Forensics get here, but it looks like blunt force trauma. She was hit on the head with a heavy object.'

Matt stood up and looked around the room. 'No sign of the murder weapon, though.'

'Ha, not here,' I said. 'It's out there, on the stage.'

'What?'

'Aladdin's lamp. It's a proper brass oil lamp, heavy old thing it is. Tim bought it at an auction for his antique shop, and when they were wondering what panto to put on it made him think of Aladdin.'

'How did it end up on stage?' Nathan mused.

'You were there, you saw it,' I said, surprised, but he shook his head.

'No, I mean, how did it get from here back to where it was supposed to be, on stage? Why would the killer do that? Why not clean it off and leave it by the body – which is what a sensible killer would do – or panic and hide it, to get rid of later? Which is what *most* murderers do.' He stared down at Kirsty, still dressed in her brightly coloured Arabian costume, as if she could tell him. 'Why put it back and risk being caught with it?'

'The show must go on,' I said. 'If the crew were poking around backstage looking for it, someone would probably have found Aladdin sooner.'

'Not a lot sooner,' said Nathan. 'She was due on stage in the next scene.'

'No,' I said, 'but maybe they didn't need much longer than that. Maybe they just needed enough time to put some distance between themselves and the murder.' I lowered my voice as an unwelcome thought occurred to me. 'Maybe they thought, if they were with a lot of witnesses when she was discovered, suspicion would be less likely to fall on them.'

'With a lot of witnesses?' asked Matt. 'Like in the audience?'

'Yes,' I said. 'Or on the stage…'

'But – the only people on stage were your mum and Tim,' said Nathan. 'I know Shirley's got a temper, but…'

'Oh, funny guy, you know I don't mean Mum,' I said. 'I don't necessarily mean Tim, either. I can't for the life of me think what possible motive he could have.'

'Doesn't mean he didn't have one,' said Nathan, and I had to agree.

'Yeah, I know. I guess I just don't want to think it was him. But it could also probably apply to anyone waiting in the wings, couldn't it? Like stage crew, or actors waiting to come on.'

'Where was Daisy?' asked Matt, and then held up a hand to ward off my indignation. 'No, I'm not accusing your daughter of murder, I just meant, could she tell us who was where?'

'It depends. She was waiting in the wings on the right-hand side. I don't know if she'd be able to see anyone in the wings on the other side of the stage. Or behind the scenery, for that matter. There had to be at least one person there, moving the lamp around in that scene.' I turned to Nathan.

'Let me ask her about that, will you? I don't want her upset.'

'Any more than I already have done.' Nathan looked sheepish. 'I'm sorry about that.'

'Don't worry, she'll be okay. It's just a big shock, something like that happening so near by.' I moved aside as the Forensics team started to arrive, the tiny room becoming even more cramped. 'Can I take those boxes of food out to the auditorium? If people are hanging around waiting to give statements, we can at least keep them sweet and cooperative by feeding them.'

'I thought I heard your tummy rumble,' said Nathan with a grin, and I couldn't deny it. I've seen too many murders for it to upset my appetite, unless they're really gruesome ones. And this one was more sad than gruesome.

Nathan helped me carry the boxes into the auditorium, and then had a word with Davey, who had very efficiently divided the assembled crowd into two parts – audience on one side, and cast and crew on the other. Colin sat with several members of his cast, his eyes closed, apparently leading them in some kind of prayer or meditation circle, watched by a bemused Harry Adams. Nathan turned to everyone and raised his voice.

'Thank you for your patience, ladies and gentlemen,' he said. 'If you were seated in the audience, once you've left your name and contact details with one of the officers, you can go home. We will contact you over the next few days to take a proper statement from you, but there's no need for you to stay unless you're waiting for a member of the cast or crew.' He turned to the pantomime members. 'We will need further information from all of you, so please remain in the auditorium until we get a chance to talk to you.' There were a few groans. 'I know you're all keen to leave, but I also know that by now the grapevine will have told you all what's happened. There has been a death backstage, and we are working quickly to establish the cause.'

'It were murder, weren't it?'

'Bashed in the head with the lamp, I heard.'

I looked around to see who had spoken, but I couldn't pick the culprits out of the sea of faces; some upset, some ghoulishly excited, but none obviously guilty.

'I would ask you not to speculate,' said Nathan, although stopping this lot gossiping would be like trying to hold back a tsunami with a paper towel. 'At this stage we are not ruling anything out.'

'They always say that,' said another bystander, and I had to hide a grin because they were absolutely right.

'You're letting the audience go?' I asked him quietly. 'Does that mean you think it was someone in the cast?'

'Or the crew. I think it's more likely, although there's obviously the possibility that someone from the audience could've slipped backstage during the interval. But we can't keep everyone here all night. I think we'll get more information from the people backstage than anyone who was out here.'

Nathan went back to the crime scene to talk to Forensics, and I found Daisy. She was sitting with Mum, Tony and Carmen, all of whom looked pale and shocked. I sat down.

'How's everyone doing?' I asked. 'Mum, you okay?'

'Better than Tim. He's desperate to wash his hands.'

'Oh God, yes. Forensics are here now, they'll take a sample and then he'll be able to scrub away at them to his heart's content,' I said, standing up again and looking around for Davey, so he could go and get someone from the scene of crime team, but there was already someone there – Robbo, who I'd got to know during my brief stint as a detective (an official one, anyway) in Penstowan a couple of years previously. I watched as Robbo gently swabbed Tim's hands, which were trembling, and gestured towards his dress; they'd need to take that, as well, to match the blood he'd wiped on it to the wound on Kirsty's head. Tim immediately stripped off down to his boxers, his eagerness to be rid of the bloodstains outweighing any embarrassment, although from what I knew of him he wasn't easily embarrassed anyway. But he was shivering, more from shock, I suspected, than cold. His husband, Maurice the mayor, stood close by, watching carefully. He pulled off his jumper and gave it to Tim, then put an arm around his shoulders, trying to subdue the trembling.

'Poor Tim,' I said. Poor Kirsty. Poor Sarah, for finding her body. Poor Daisy. Poor panto – the show *wouldn't* go on, not without their principal boy.

'They should probably look at Alex, too,' said Jocasta, joining us.

'Who's Alex?'

'The props master.' Jocasta gestured to a pale young man sitting with a couple of people all dressed in black –

other members of her stage crew, I guessed. 'We realised the lamp was missing during that scene with Shirley and Tim, so I sent him off to get it. He was running around like a headless chicken trying to find it before Tim did the reveal. He tripped over it in the corridor—'

'Tripped over?'

'It's pitch-black backstage during a performance. I have a torch to show the cast where to go when they come off stage, but everyone else just takes up their position before the lights go down and then stays there. I did offer it to him but he took off in a panic before I could give him it.' Pitch-black? Then Daisy probably wouldn't be able to shed much light – no pun intended – on who was where before and after the interval.

'Did he not realise it was covered in blood when he picked it up?' I asked.

'No, of course not. He said it felt a bit sticky, but there was no time to wash it. He only just got it in place behind the flap in the scenery before Tim opened it.'

I looked over at the unfortunate props master again. At least we knew now how the lamp had ended up back where it was supposed to be. But it would be covered in so many fingerprints; half the cast had handled it at some point during the performance, and God knew how many of the crew had. It would be impossible to find the murderer that way.

As the audience members gave the police their details and left, Carmen and I put on the big metal water urn for tea and coffee, and offered food to the cast and crew – the remaining suspects, I reminded myself, although I knew most of these people and none of them looked like killers to me. What did a killer look like, though? If only they were physically obvious, like the baddies in the old silent movies, with their twirly moustaches and big black capes! It would make investigating crime a lot easier…

Chapter Four

I t took a few hours to get around the whole of the cast and the crew to get initial statements from them, but eventually Nathan was satisfied that he, Matt and Chrissie had got as much useful information out of everyone as he was likely to get at that time of night, and he allowed the remaining witnesses/suspects to leave. I waited for everyone else to go before I approached him.

'So, who did it?' I asked, and he gave me a rueful grin.

'If only it was that obvious,' he said. 'We've got eight million statements to go through before we can even work out when it happened.'

'Shame the ME can't narrow down the time of death to within a few seconds,' I said wistfully.

'Again, if only... Our murderer's window of opportunity is already pretty narrow,' he pointed out. 'It's just a shame it encompasses the interval, when a ton of people potentially had the opportunity to nip backstage and do the deed.'

'Not all of them, though,' I said. 'Probably not many of them, in fact. Most of the audience stayed in their seats, and those that didn't either went to the loo or to the bar to get a drink.' The theatre had a tiny bar in the foyer of the building, big enough to house a counter to sell drinks from, but too small for more than five people to loiter in. So most people buying drinks in the interval would've returned to their seats to drink them.

'No, that's true. It's among the cast and crew where the real fun takes place.' He sighed and sat down in a recently vacated seat. I sat next to him. 'Between cast members doing costume changes, or waiting in the green room because they weren't on for a few more scenes, and crew members moving props and furniture into place, not to mention just how many people seem to have weak bladders – it seems like the toilets were almost constantly in use, which is unfortunate because I noticed a sign up there earlier that says "no flushing during performances"—'

I wrinkled my nose in disgust. 'Eww. But don't worry, your secret weapon is back tomorrow, isn't he?'

Nathan laughed. 'Sunil? Yes, thank God. I'd never begrudge him his paternity leave, but that man bloody loves combing through witness statements and putting timelines together. He's only been away a couple of weeks but we've missed him.'

'Hopefully the twins have started sleeping better now,'

I said. 'When Daisy was little, I used to like going to work for a rest…'

DC Sunil Bakshi was a total sweetheart (my words rather than Nathan's), but also a complete weirdo (Matt's words rather than Nathan's) who loved nothing more than getting his teeth stuck into a big pile of paperwork. He was brilliant at analysing phone records, CCTV footage, witness statements, bank statements, you name it, and much preferred it to physically chasing after people, which I'd always found much more exciting when I was a copper in the Metropolitan Police Force. Mind you, when you're in uniform, that's more or less your whole job. It kept me fit, anyway.

Sunil's wife Eesha (also a total sweetheart) had not long ago given birth to two tiny but very loud bundles of joy, and Sunil had proudly brought his two daughters, Aadya and Aashna, into the station to show them off during his two weeks of paternity leave. I had just so happened to be lurking around the station that day, waiting for Nathan to get a lunch break, and I had felt a bit of a stirring in my ovaries when I'd seen Nathan pick one of the babies up. I was well past the stage in my life where another child would've seemed like a good idea, plus I already had my own (now seventeen-year-old) baby. But Nathan… He'd always wanted kids, and he was a brilliant stepdad; was I wrong to stop him having one of his own? And then Aashna had howled and filled her nappy with an enormous and frankly alarming poop, and that stirring had disappeared. And Nathan had laughed and happily handed her back to her father to deal with.

'Are you done for the night? Are you coming home or have you got to stick around?' I asked.

'I'll probably be another hour,' he said. 'Forensics can't have a lot more to do, and to be honest me and Matt are just getting in their way, but I have to show willing. You take Daisy and Shirley home, I'll get a lift with someone. The dog will be crossing her paws in desperation if you don't let her out soon.'

I laughed and kissed him. 'Poor Germaine. I'll see you later.'

I went out to the car, where Daisy and Mum were waiting, and drove home to rescue my poor dog. We didn't leave her at home very often, but a theatre was no place for a dog and, as most of my usual dog sitters were either involved in the panto or watching it, I'd had no choice. Even Jade, Daisy's friend a few doors down, who had been known to take the dog in a pinch, was unavailable, her family spending time in Spain with relatives. I shivered as I opened the back door and let Germaine into the garden; it would be a bit warmer in Andalusia than it was here in Cornwall, I thought, hugging myself against the cold while Germaine did her business next to a bush. She normally took her sweet time deciding which plant to water, but she was obviously feeling the cold too, because she just got on with it and then looked at me with an expression on her face that said, *'Well? We going back indoors or what?'*

We went back indoors.

Daisy and I said goodnight to Mum and then headed up to bed. Daisy was a lot calmer now, but I still offered to let her sleep with me rather than on her own, in case she needed a cuddle.

'I'm not five, Mum.' So that was me told. I kissed her goodnight and got into bed, pulling the covers up to my chin. *There's no way I'll be able to sleep*, I thought, but by the time Nathan got home I was so far into dreamland that I never even felt him get in next to me.

———

The next day was a Saturday. It was less than a week until Christmas, and normally I'd be thinking about going shopping for the final few presents, getting a few bits of food that would last until the big day (although they probably wouldn't, because we'd end up eating them and having to get more), but all I could think about was poor Kirsty. I've seen enough dead bodies to not have nightmares about them, but this one... I hadn't really known her, but Daisy had, first of all through her job at Daisy's school as a teaching assistant, and now as part of the panto team. So that was upsetting for me, knowing that my daughter was upset. But worse than that was what Nathan had said the night before: that Daisy had probably been very close to the scene when the murder had taken place, and what would've happened if she'd heard Kirsty cry out and had gone to her friend's assistance? I'd dealt with bereaved parents before, and it was always a horrible part of the job.

But not as horrible as actually *being* the bereaved parent. If anything happened to Daisy, I would – I couldn't finish that thought. I couldn't think like that. My daughter was safe and sound, and still fast asleep in bed upstairs. I felt immense relief, and then guilt, because Kirsty's family would not be able to say the same thing this morning.

'Penny for them?' said Nathan, coming into the kitchen, where I sat at the table with a cup of tea. He bent down and kissed me on the top of my head. He'd already showered and dressed, and smelt good.

'Just thinking about Kirsty's parents,' I said. 'I can't imagine what they're going through. I mean, I *can*, but my daughter's upstairs. I think my heart would just stop if—'

'I know.' Nathan pulled me in for a hug, and I burrowed my head into his chest. 'Try not to think about it. I know that's crap advice, but you can't let it get to you.'

'I know.' I pulled away and looked up at him. 'How *did* her parents take it? Devastated, obviously?'

'Parent, not parents. It's just her dad. Her mum died about a year ago.'

'Oh no, poor bloke. Losing your wife's hard enough, but to lose your daughter as well… What happened to her mum?'

'Nothing sinister. Cancer. There is another daughter, but she lives in the US. She's flying home.'

'God. It makes you realise how lucky you are, doesn't it? To have your family healthy and safe.' I shook my head. 'Poor man. You off in a bit?'

'Yes. Witness statements to go through. *Lots* of witness

statements. Even with Sunil back it's going to take all day to read through every single one properly.' He gave a thin smile. 'Davey Trelawney did well to get so many from the audience last night, but bless him, his handwriting is terrible, so we'll have to decipher that first before we can even think about what people actually told him. What are you up to today?'

'Christmas shopping,' I said, 'although I'm not really in the mood now.'

'No, I know what you mean. You can't have that much left to get, though. But you might want to keep Daisy busy.'

'Keep her mind off it, yeah. I will.'

He kissed me goodbye and headed out the door, leaving a disappointed Germaine in his wake; would no one in this godforsaken house take the poor, neglected furry creature out for a walk?

'Give me half an hour, Germaine,' I said, heading upstairs.

But the dog was destined to be disappointed, because as I passed Daisy's room I heard her talking on the phone to someone.

'What for? He can't seriously expect the show to carry on, can he?'

I quietly backtracked and stood outside her bedroom door.

'Yeah, well, you know what he's like… Okay, I'll see you at ten.' There was a pause, and then – 'I know you're there, Mum, you can come in.'

'My ninja stealth skills seem to have deserted me,' I said, opening the door. 'What was that all about?'

'Colin has called a meeting about the panto,' she said, looking grim. 'I swear, if he comes out with *"the show must go on"*, there'll be another murder.' She considered for a moment. 'Maybe not a murder, but at least assault with a deadly script.'

'It would be pretty poor taste to carry on with the run,' I said. 'Do you know how any of the others feel? Who did you just speak to?'

'Hayley. She's in the chorus. She said everyone she's spoken to is dead against it. There'd be mutiny.'

'Well, maybe that's not what he wants to say to everybody. You should hear him out before you lead everyone out on strike. Are you going to go? Do you need a lift?'

'You mean, can you come and eavesdrop?'

I grinned, unfazed. My daughter knows me so well. 'Of course.'

'If I didn't let you come you'd only grill me about it afterwards, wouldn't you?'

'Yep.'

'Now I know how Nathan feels...'

After giving Mum a knock and seeing if she wanted to come with us, and letting Germaine out for a brief run around the garden (she gave me a right look when I called her back indoors), the three of us (and the dog) jumped in the car and headed into town. We drove along Fore Street, which was criss-crossed with strings of fairy lights. The

Penstowan Business Association had pulled out all the stops this year, with every single shop window beautifully (or in a few cases, gaudily) decorated with tinsel, pine cones, Christmas trees and fake snow. It felt cold enough this morning for *real* snow, but we rarely got it in Penstowan, being on the coast. The town would look beautiful once it started to get dark, which at this time of year was about three o'clock in the afternoon.

Once through the town, we followed the road as it climbed over the clifftop and began to wind down towards the harbour. This was the less picturesque part of Penstowan, the part few tourists bothered with, as it was mostly tiny stone fishermen's cottages, the rundown quayside, and what was left of the local fishing fleet. In the summer it smelt strongly of fish, and seaweed, and, underneath it all, decay. It always made me feel a bit sad, coming here, because I remembered what it had been like when I was little; full of well-maintained boats, with seals playing around in the harbour at high tide, hoping to share the catch.

I parked the car at the quayside car park – the roads here were narrow, and it would be difficult to park outside our destination – and we got out. I took a deep breath in; the air was only slightly fishy, and I could smell the ozone and dried-on sea salt on the nearby boats. Mum smiled.

'I remember your dad bringing you here when you were about seven, to see the fish market,' she said. I shuddered. The sightless, staring eyes of the fish laid out on beds of ice had freaked me out a bit. 'Put you off fish and chips for months, it did.'

'I don't know why we're having this meeting here,' said Daisy, wrinkling her nose, not as immune to the smell as I was.

'You could hardly go back to the theatre,' I said. 'Even if Forensics have finished, it's still a crime scene.'

Germaine had been sniffing around – it was probably a very exciting place to be, if you were a dog's nose – and her tail had been wagging furiously. But a loud shriek from a noisy seagull had her flattening herself against my leg. I reached down to pat her. 'Don't worry,' I told her, 'it's just a silly old bird.'

'That's not a nice way to talk about Nana,' said Daisy, and Mum pretended to swing for her.

Even without the nervous dog shivering next to me, it was too cold to be standing around outside, so we made our way to the address Daisy's friend Hayley had texted her.

Colin Sweeney lived in the old harbour master's cottage. Built on the edge of the hillside that swept around and hugged the quay, the house overlooked the bay full of softly bobbing fishing boats. In front of the pretty stone cottage was a tiny garden with a wrought-iron bench which, in the summer, would've been a beautiful place to sit and look at the sea. But not in mid-December, with a cold wind coming off it. A festive wreath had been hung on the front door, the red berries and glossy green leaves of the holly contrasting with the chipped and faded blue of the painted wood, and fairy lights festooned the branches of a couple of gnarled old apple trees either side of the garden gate.

'I remember when Wild Bill Hallett lived here, when he was the harbour master,' said Mum, as we walked up the hill.

'Wild Bill?' asked Daisy. 'He sounds like fun.'

I laughed. 'Don't you believe it. The "wild" was ironic, as I remember.'

Mum nodded. 'Probably the most boring man I've ever met. And I've met John Major.'

'Who?' Daisy looked bewildered.

'Ex-Prime Minister. Famously quite nice but incredibly boring,' I said, 'but then that's probably what you want from a prime minister, rather than someone who makes a tit of themselves getting stuck halfway down a zip line, waving Union Jack flags. Hang on,' I said, stopping in front of Colin's gate and looking at Mum. 'When did you meet John Major?'

'1998,' said Mum, promptly. So promptly I was certain she was making it up. 'He was down here on holiday. I was still working in the Co-op at the time. He asked me where the baked beans were, and we had a long conversation about Heinz versus Co-op own brand.'

'That sounds legit,' murmured Daisy, and I laughed.

'Exactly what I was thinking.'

Before Mum could refute our scepticism the door of the cottage opened, revealing Colin, clad in a chunky fisherman's jumper and brown corduroy trousers. He was certainly dressed for his surroundings, I thought sardonically, like those women of a certain age who dress in nautically themed navy and white stripes when they go on a cruise. Just in case the captain needs a hand splicing the main brace or something.

'Ladies, I'm so glad you could join us,' said Colin, smiling but also managing to exude a respectfully mournful air, which was fair enough in the circumstances. He stood back to let us in, glancing down at the dog for a moment.

'Do you mind me and Germaine being here?' I asked. 'Only I'm the designated driver. I can wait in the car if you'd prefer?' I smiled at him, showing just how willing I was to wait outside with the dog whilst also being so polite that he couldn't possibly take me up on the offer. I hoped.

'She's housetrained,' said Mum. 'And Germaine went before we got here, so she'll be all right for a bit too.'

Colin smiled. 'In that case, come on in, all four of you.'

Even from the front door I could see that the house was rather more flamboyantly decorated than it had been in boring Wild Bill's time. The thick stone walls had been whitewashed to make the space feel lighter, and the whole hallway was lined with pictures and brightly coloured posters advertising theatre productions. As Colin led us into the kitchen diner, I stopped to study a large framed photograph. In it, five young men posed in front of a pub on the corner of what looked like a very familiar London street. I recognised the pub, but it wasn't one that I'd ever been in.

'That's from *Mile End Days*, isn't it?' I said. The London-set soap opera had been going for a good thirty years now, and the photo looked like it had been taken on day one of filming. Colin stopped and smiled.

'Ah, yes. My glory days,' he said.

'Wait – that's you?' I said, pointing at one of the young men. 'You were one of the McCafferty brothers?'

'Ewan McCafferty,' he said. 'The middle brother and a real terror.'

'*That's* why your name sounded familiar,' I said. 'Nathan – that's DCI Withers, who you met last night, obviously – he recognised your name but he couldn't think why. He thought he might've nicked you.'

'Oh my God, Mum!' hissed Daisy, but Colin, after looking mildly affronted for a few seconds, just laughed.

'I've only ever been arrested on TV,' he said. 'Come through.'

Several other members of the panto cast and crew had already arrived, and were sitting around the kitchen table. A few of them wore Christmas jumpers and solemn expressions, which felt a bit incongruous, but then I supposed Christmas didn't stop for everyone else because someone had died. At least they'd stopped short of wearing Santa hats and elf ears. It was a bit of a squash in the kitchen and there were no seats left, so I just sort of loitered at the back while Daisy squished onto a seat with Hayley, who had waved her over, and Mum glared at one of the younger members of the crew until they got up and offered her their seat.

'Oh, thank you love, that's very nice of you,' she said.

The crew member gave her a thin and somewhat defeated smile.

'Thank you all for coming,' said Colin, looking around at us. 'I think this is everyone who could make it today. I will try to contact whoever's left, and if of course you see anyone please pass on what we discuss today.'

I looked around again, wondering if Tony was there, but it was the Saturday before Christmas and his family's department store, Penhaligon's, would be very busy. Jocasta was absent too, but Tim and Maurice had made it, Tim still looking shocked, Maurice clutching his hand tightly.

'First of all,' continued Colin, 'I want to say that I am so proud of all of you. You've all worked so incredibly hard on this show. There were times when I did think we'd never make it to opening night—' I saw Daisy's head swivel towards my mum, and I knew she was thinking about her grandmother's inability to learn her lines until the last minute '—but make it we did. Last night was magnificent, right up until – well, you all know what happened.' He took a deep breath. 'Kirsty Dunwoody was a wonderful actress, and a beautiful person. She had a great future ahead of her. She was taken from us, from her family, her friends and her cast mates, far too soon.' He stopped to clear his throat, visibly upset. There was a lot of sniffing from the assembled pantomimers, several of them wiping at their eyes, and I felt my own eyes beginning to water. I hadn't known Kirsty very well, but she was one of ours. I looked over at Daisy, who was crying softly, and I swore that if Nathan didn't find out who had killed her, I would.

An older woman who I hadn't seen before, who had been sitting at the head of the table, stood up and reached for the box of tissues that sat on the kitchen counter. She handed the box to Daisy, who took a tissue and then passed the box on. The woman was in her late fifties, early sixties – she was very well maintained so it was hard to tell – and very composed. She also gave off a kind of proprietorial air, as if she lived there, although as far as I knew (in other words, as far as Mum had told me), Colin was single. And to be honest he was a bit camp, which didn't necessarily mean anything – I mean, he *was* an actor, and they do like to show off, but… I got the impression she wouldn't have been his type.

Colin cleared his throat again. 'There's an old saying in showbiz circles, that the show must go on—' And now the atmosphere in the room changed quite noticeably, from sorrow to hostility. 'I've used it myself, when things have gone wrong, when costumes have ripped, props have gone missing, fire alarms have gone off mid-performance. I was in the cast of *Seven Brides for Seven Brothers* on that fateful day when one of the brothers fell off the stage and broke his leg, and we carried on with him doing an entire song and dance number from a chair with his leg up. But this…' He shook his head sadly. 'This is not an occasion where I feel the show must go on. The show *can't* go on without Kirsty.'

And just like that, the atmosphere changed again, into one of relief. Everyone was nodding or murmuring in agreement, even the Christmas jumper wearers, apart from one man who said, 'But Ellie's the understudy, she knows the part.' But the glares, scowls and muttered insults he received from everyone else made him sink lower into his chair. Colin didn't even appear to notice him.

'Are we all agreed? As sad as it is to just stop after all our hard work, it feels like it would be disrespectful to Kirsty to carry on. So I propose we cancel the remaining run of the panto. Agreed?'

Everyone answered in the affirmative, although there were a few murmurs, and one of the younger cast members grumbled quietly, 'This meeting could've been an email.'

Colin obviously heard her, but he just smiled. 'I expect you're wondering why I insisted on having this meeting, rather than just having a Zoom or, yes—' and here he smiled at the girl, who blushed '—sending an email. But I wanted to feel the emotional energy in the room before I made a final decision. I am only too aware that a big part of me – the part of me that will always be a performer – is absolutely *desperate* to carry on with the show, and if I'd felt that from all of you then we might have come to a different decision.' Everyone nodded and 'fair enough'ed. 'Also, I think by gathering together, we have an opportunity to start to rid ourselves of any sadness and negative energy from last night.' Now everyone started to get a bit shifty, not meeting each other's eyes. 'We have an opportunity for a spiritual cleanse, which I really think will help many of us here.'

There were a few mutterings of 'Is that the time?' and 'I really should be pushing off now…', but Colin looked so disappointed that everyone shut up and remained in their seats. I could probably have just about sneaked away, but Germaine chose that moment to investigate the contents of someone's bag – that dog could sniff out a packet of Extra Strong Mints from a mile away – and all eyes turned to me. Plus, to be honest, I was interested to see exactly what form this 'spiritual detox' would take, even if I wasn't that keen in taking part in it myself.

Colin smiled at everyone again. 'No need to look so nervous,' he said, and everyone chuckled, albeit a bit self-consciously. 'If you pray, please feel free to use the prayer of your choice. If you'd prefer to meditate, I'm happy to guide you. And if neither of those appeal to you, please just take five minutes to sit here and think about Kirsty, about what she meant to you, and about the last time she smiled at you. Because Kirsty smiled a lot, didn't she?'

'Yes,' said someone hoarsely, and I thought, *There might just be something in this 'spiritual cleanse' after all.* How often do we let ourselves just sit there and think? Whenever I've been sad, or even grieving, I've always done everything I can to distract myself from it. And it's never really worked.

'Should we close our eyes?' someone else asked.

'If you want to,' said Colin. 'Whatever you feel comfortable with. This is a safe space.' Those words – *this is a safe space* – would normally be the cue for eye rolling from Mum, but to my surprise she just sat there quietly, staring at a spot on the wall behind Colin. Of course – she would've got to know Kirsty quite well doing the panto. Whenever Mum heard about someone in her friend group, or friend-of-a-friend group, dying, she would always say, 'Well, they had a good innings.' But Kirsty hadn't, and I knew that would upset her a lot more than she'd let on.

I stood there, wrestling with my mint-obsessed dog, and tried to assume a spiritually and emotionally open state of mind. But it wasn't easy. To be fair, I hadn't really known Kirsty that well, and I was angry with the murderer rather than grieving for the young woman herself. And of course I was used to murders, and as corpses go I'd seen far worse. But this was still a tragedy. I shut my eyes and willed Germaine to stop wriggling in my arms, telepathically telling her that if she behaved herself now I'd take her for a long walk later. It was bloody cold outside though, so I was half-relieved when she carried on squirming.

It was no good. I opened my eyes again and discreetly looked at my fellow spiritual detoxers, although as they all seemed to have their eyes shut or at least their heads bowed, I didn't really need to be that discreet about it. I turned my head to Colin, expecting to see him levitating or ascending to a higher spiritual plane where all his chakras would be aligned or something – whatever *that* would look like – but to my surprise he was doing exactly the same as me; peering around at everyone, studying them carefully. He looked over at me and his eyes widened as he realised I'd rumbled him. He carefully made his expression calm and neutral again, before resuming his sweep of the assembled pantomimers.

Although he'd only said five minutes, most of them seemed to be enjoying the calm, or maybe they were starting to nod off; it had been a late night for most of them.

Eventually though people began to surface from wherever they'd found themselves. A few of them wiped tears from their eyes and hugged their neighbour, while others gave themselves a shake. Colin smiled benevolently at them, releasing them.

'Thank you again for coming,' he said. 'I'm sure we will all work together again. We make a great team.' Everyone smiled at that and began to get to their feet, gathering coats and bags before heading for the door and causing a traffic jam in the narrow hallway. All except the unknown woman, who just sat there with her arms crossed and a slight smile on her face.

I reached for Daisy and gave her a hug, which she accepted despite her friends being there – she really was upset, I thought. Mum joined us, and we were about to leave when I felt a hand on my arm. I turned to see Colin.

'Can I have a quick word with you, Jodie?' he said, looking into my eyes in a meaningful way. Meaning what, I wasn't sure, but I guessed it was something to do with whatever had passed between us earlier. 'I just need to make sure I've paid you for the buffet last night.'

He had, but I just said, 'Of course. Daisy, can you and Nana take Germaine outside? The little madam is being a right pain. I won't be long.'

Daisy was too preoccupied to do anything but agree, but I could see Mum's eyes narrow. Thankfully she didn't say anything, and just took Daisy's arm and led her out.

Soon there were just the three of us left in the kitchen: me, Colin, and the unknown woman. His wife? Partner?

'Thank you,' said Colin, waving me towards a seat. He sat down next to the woman, and I turned to her.

'I'm sorry,' I said, 'but I don't know who you are. I know everyone else in the cast and crew, by sight at least, but I don't think you and I have had the pleasure…?'

'No, we haven't,' she said. 'Sorry, all this upset has made me forget my manners.' Although she didn't look that upset. 'I'm Hilary, I'm Colin's agent.'

So that was why she looked kind of proprietorial – of Colin, rather than his house. I was surprised that he still had an agent, though, as he'd seemed to disappear after leaving the cast of *Mile End Days*.

Colin seemed to know what I was thinking. 'Hilary has been with me through thick and thin,' he said. 'I was arrogant in my younger days, I did what so many soap stars have done before and left the show, telling everyone I didn't want to be typecast, but really it was because I thought I was better than a soap opera. And then of course I found out that I wasn't.'

'That's not entirely true, Colin—' began Hilary, but he shook his head.

'No, it is. You don't bite the hand that feeds you, do you? So anyway, after taking an unplanned career break—'

'You mean no one else would cast you?' I asked, and Hilary frowned. 'Sorry, I didn't mean that the way it came out. I just meant—'

'No, you're absolutely right. I went away and reinvented myself. Got into theatre, which I'd never even considered before, and discovered I loved it. Acting and directing.'

Colin shook his head, musing. 'I didn't go to drama school, you know, so I never had that grounding in live performance. Never did Shakespeare, not even at school – it wasn't that sort of school. And all through it, Hilary never lost faith in me.'

'Of course I didn't, you're a fabulous actor,' said Hilary brusquely. 'Sometimes it's the film and TV landscape that changes, not the talent.' She looked at me mulishly, and I made a mental note not to get on the wrong side of her. I could just imagine her on the phone, doing deals with producers and earning her fifteen percent. She'd be a difficult woman to say no to. I kind of admired her, whilst also being a tiny bit terrified.

'Anyway, all this is to say that anything we discuss now can be said in front of Hilary,' said Colin.

'Okay,' I said. 'What did you want to discuss?'

'You're married to DCI Withers, aren't you?'

'I am, yes. But that doesn't mean I know anything about the case, or that I can keep you up to date on the investigation.'

'No, I suspected as much.' Colin drummed his fingers on the kitchen table, a rare sign of nervous energy from a man who always seemed so calm to the point of being really irritating to everyone else.

'My turn now,' I said. 'When everyone had their eyes closed, you were looking around very closely at everyone. Why?'

'Why were you?'

'I asked first.'

Colin sighed. 'I don't know… One of the roles I did get a chance to play after *Mile End* was a private investigator. Short-lived TV murder mystery thing. And I thought, what would he do?'

'Invite all the suspects to a meeting, discuss the murder with them and see who reacts,' I said. Colin looked surprised but nodded. 'Yes, nice try in theory, but in reality it doesn't work. For starters, not everyone turned up, did they?'

'No, but they always say that the murderer returns to the scene of the crime,' said Colin. Hilary patted his hand, still tapping, and held it still.

'But this *isn't* the scene of the crime, is it, darling? The theatre is. The only crime that's been committed here is when you tried to cook coq au vin in the air fryer.' She wrinkled her nose.

'I don't know about your coq au vin, but she's right,' I said. 'And anyway, that's another thing that's not true in real life. *Sometimes* the killer will return to the scene, maybe to check that the body hasn't been discovered, or the murder weapon or something, or if it would look odd if they weren't there, but other than that most murderers are probably more likely to put some distance between themselves and the crime.'

'I suppose you're right…' said Colin. He sighed again. 'I just hate the thought that someone in the cast or the crew might have murdered her. They can't have done, can they? It could've been someone from outside, couldn't it?'

I couldn't say for certain that it had been a panto person,

although it looked the most likely explanation to me, but I just nodded. 'Yes, it could've been,' I said carefully. 'At this stage no one really knows anything, do they? But the police will get to the bottom of it. And I'm not just saying that because I'm married to the senior investigating officer.'

'I know you can't promise, but... at least promise me they'll do everything they can. That poor girl...'

'I promise,' I said, standing up. 'I'd better go before Mum starts wondering what we're doing. But please, you need to promise *me* that you won't do anything like this again, will you? No more amateur sleuthing. Just leave it to the police to do their job.' And then I fled before he could see how much of a hypocrite I was.

Chapter Five

Mum and Daisy (and the dog) were waiting semi-patiently by the car, stamping their feet in an attempt to keep warm in the cold air.

'Finally,' said Mum. 'Can you drop me off at Rowe's? I'm meeting the girls for a cuppa.'

'A gossip, more like,' said Daisy. 'Can you drop me off at Hayley's? It's on the way.'

'Hayley who just drove off in her own car?' I asked. 'Why didn't you go with her?'

'There wasn't enough room, and I knew you wouldn't mind.'

'What am I, a taxi? When are you starting driving lessons?'

'When you give me the money for them,' she said. 'It was you who wanted me to stay on in the sixth form. Not my fault I'm not earning anything...'

'Cheeky,' I said, but I didn't really mind because Nathan

and I had already decided to pay for her driving lessons for Christmas.

I dropped both of them off – and of course Hayley's house *wasn't* on the way because the one-way system around town meant I had to do almost a complete circuit and start heading back towards the harbour before I could turn off – and then started for home. But all that awaited me there was housework. I needed to at least have a stab at Christmas shopping, and Germaine would need a walk, so instead of driving home I parked up in the beachside car park which *just happened* to be over the road from the police station.

'Might as well pop in and say hello to everyone, eh Germaine?' I said, strapping on her lead and attempting a cheery, nonchalant I-was-just-passing air.

I reached the door into the station just as PCs Chrissie and Brett were walking out of it. Brett rolled his eyes before he could stop himself – he really didn't like me poking my nose into things – but Chrissie just grinned.

'Wondered how long it would be until you showed up,' she said.

'Well, you know, the dog needs a walk…'

'There's a massive beach over there,' said Brett, pointing across the road.

'Is there?' I asked innocently. 'How very remiss of me not to notice it, specially when I'm parked right in front of it and all.' Brett very nearly scowled, but then I was married to the local DCI and was (if I say so myself) popular with every member of the local constabulary, apart from him, so he could suck it, frankly. I turned to Chrissie. 'Is Nathan about?'

'Yeah, Matt reckons they'll be there all day going through all the witness statements.' She grinned again. 'I would've helped, of course, but the local community need to see the comforting presence of uniformed officers on the beat, don't they?'

'Indeed they do. Although don't assume you've had a lucky escape. My mum and her gang are meeting up for coffee in Rowe's, and if the mince pies run out there could be a riot.'

She laughed. 'Thanks for the tip-off, we'll keep an eye on them.'

Brett reluctantly stood aside to let me in. Inside, the desk sergeant, Sally, looked at me and shook her head.

'I dunno, always turning up like a bad penny,' she said. 'And is that Germaine with you? Is she a good girl?' Germaine gave an excited bark and stood on her hind legs, front paws against the desk trying to see Sally, but she was too short (the dog, not Sally – she was average height). Sally was in her late forties, slim build with a kind face and soft eyes. Out of uniform she looked more like a Sunday school teacher than a copper, but I'd seen her in action on a Saturday night, in charge of the cells: banging up drunks, never breaking eye contact with scumbags who were right in her face, trying to intimidate her, and taking no shit from aggressive blokes twice her size.

She laughed and rummaged in her desk before coming out into the foyer. 'Here you go,' she said, squatting down to give Germaine a dog biscuit and make a fuss of her. 'I can honestly say this is the only station I've ever worked at where I've had to keep doggy treats in my desk drawer.'

I laughed. 'Your predecessor, Harry Adams, used to have a drawer full of jelly babies. He always pretended they were for me when I used to come in and see my dad, but there's a reason he hasn't got that many teeth left...'

'Ah, yes. Old Harry was what they call "a bit of a character", wasn't he? One of Eddie Parker's boys.' She smiled. 'I never met your dad, of course, but I feel like I know him, because people still talk about him.'

'He'd have had a thing or two to say about letting a dog into the station,' I said. 'And then he'd have let her in anyway, because he was a right softy.'

Sally ruffled Germaine's hair and then straightened up. 'Of course he would have. How could you say no to that little face? Let me give DCI Withers a call and tell him you're here.'

'I know where to go,' I said, and she laughed.

'I know you do. But this bit of the station is my domain. Wait there.' She nipped back behind the security door and appeared behind the desk again, phone in hand. I wandered off and read some of the posters on the community notice board, which someone had attempted to festive-ise by pinning tinsel around the edge. They'd also stuck some mistletoe up as well, which I thought was possibly ill-advised, bearing in mind this was a police station, but maybe that was one of their new, seasonal weapons in the constant fight against crime; get yourself on the naughty list, and stroppy PC Brett would give you a smacker on the lips and send you away with a warning not to do it again. It would certainly put me off doing anything illegal, anyway. At this time of year most of the notices were exhorting people to lock their doors and windows to guard against Christmas present thieves. Every Christmas Penstowan saw a sharp increase in burglaries, or attempted ones anyway. Seaside towns can be difficult places to live in the winter; a lot of local jobs are seasonal, connected to the tourist trade, which means that while a lot of people manage to get some work from April to September or maybe even October, over the winter many of them find themselves unemployed again, through no fault of their own. Add to that the rising price of housing and rents, made worse by all the holiday lets – half of which, certainly in Penstowan, would be empty for most of November, December and January – and it left a fair number of local people struggling to survive on benefits. Christmas just made everything worse, and some found it hard to resist the temptation to steal from those they perceived to be better off.

'Babe.' I turned to see Nathan standing behind me. He leaned in to give me a kiss on the cheek. 'I've been expecting you.'

'So has everyone else, apparently,' I said, and he laughed.

'Well you have got form. Do you want to go for a coffee? I need to get away from all those statements.' He looked at me more closely. 'Have you found something already?'

'Not really. But maybe…'

'It was a sad day when you left the force. Again. Come on.'

We left the station, Germaine giving Sally a little wave goodbye (okay, I picked her up – Germaine, not Sally – and waggled a paw in her direction, which earned me a broad smile from the desk sergeant and an 'Oh my God, what are you two like?' from Nathan). We headed over to Wave View, a small but busy café that had opened in the summer and had (so far) managed to stay open. We squeezed into a table in the window, next to a lavishly decorated Christmas tree, so we could admire the view of the beach. Nathan ordered a coffee while I plumped for a cup of tea and a mince pie, because talk of them earlier had made me fancy one. Germaine settled herself under the table with a bowl of water, no doubt waiting to pounce on any crumbs.

'Okay, spill,' said Nathan, expectantly.

'It's nothing much, really. I just took Mum and Daisy to a meeting at Colin Sweeney's house – oh yes, I found out why his name sounded familiar!'

'Why?'

'He was in *Mile End Days*, years ago when it first started. He was one of the McCafferty brothers. Ewan.'

Nathan slapped his hand on the table, making all the baubles on the Christmas tree rock. 'Of course! I remember him now. He's changed a bit, hasn't he? Wasn't he a real hard man?'

'His character was,' I said, reaching out to steady a furiously swinging dangly Santa before taking a bite of my mince pie. The buttery shortcrust pastry was lush.

'No, not his character, *him*. Or am I thinking of someone else?'

'You must be,' I said, thinking of Colin leading everyone in a spot of meditation and quiet contemplation. Although of course he hadn't been participating in that himself, he'd been too busy watching everyone for signs of guilt or suspicious behaviour. 'He's into all that airy-fairy New Age stuff Jocasta's always going on about. He's worse than she is.'

'Yeah...' said Nathan, stirring his coffee thoughtfully. 'I must be thinking of someone else.'

'Loads of actors had dodgy pasts before they got famous,' I said, 'or went that way after their fame died down. The bloke who played Dirty Den in *Eastenders* killed someone when he was younger, didn't he? And then there was another bloke in Corrie who played a drug dealer, who turned out to actually be one—'

'Not that you watch a lot of soaps or anything,' said Nathan with a grin.

'I don't!' I protested. 'Mum does, and I kind of get sucked in... There's always a few ex-cons in Guy Ritchie movies as well, aren't there? I suppose it helps them play the role, if they can draw on their own experience of being a criminal toe rag in real life.'

'Criminal toe rag? Spoken like a true ex-cop.' Nathan reached over to nick a piece of crumbly pastry off my plate. I thought, *Oi! Get your own!* But I let him have it because I loved him. 'But that's not what you were going to tell me, is it? Or are you losing your ability to sniff stuff out?'

'How dare you!' I said, pretending to be outraged and clutching at an invisible string of pearls around my neck. 'Nah, there is more, but I don't really know if it's relevant.'

'Doesn't normally stop you…'

'I can't deny that. Anyway, after everyone agreed that the panto will have to be cancelled, Colin suggested that we all have a five-minute spiritual detox.' Nathan groaned. 'Yeah, see? He's definitely not a hard man anymore, if he ever really was. It wasn't actually as bad as it sounds. He just wanted us all to sit there and spend a few minutes thinking about Kirsty and what she meant to us, or meditating or praying or whatever people felt comfortable doing. He was so eager to do it that everyone did. But this is the interesting bit…' I told Nathan the interesting bit, which was Colin keeping his eyes open to study everyone.

'Hmm, that is quite interesting,' he said. 'And he saw you watching him?'

'Yes. He explained to me afterwards that he didn't want to believe that someone involved in the panto could possibly be guilty of the murder, because they were like a family.'

'Lots of murders involve family members,' pointed out Nathan, and I nodded.

'Yeah, I know. But the fact he was trying to catch someone out, or spot anyone that looked guilty or whatever – you know what that means?'

'Whoever did it, it wasn't Colin.'

'Exactly.'

'Or… he wanted to see if anyone was watching *him* for

signs of guilt, because he *did* do it and he wanted to make sure no one suspected him.'

'Well – yeah, I suppose that is possible…' I conceded. 'Either way, it marks him out, doesn't it? He's come to our—'

'My.'

'—okay, *your* attention now. Instead of just sitting back and hoping to blend into the background, which a murderer would do.'

'If they had any sense, which a lot of them don't.' Nathan finished his coffee. 'You know what some of them are like – they don't have the brains to just keep well away from the investigation. They always want to know what's happening, or they think they can steer us in the wrong direction or something.'

'So basically what you're saying is, I've wasted your time with this,' I snapped. He smiled gently and reached across the table for my hand, making me feel guilty for getting moody with him.

'Babe, time spent with you is never wasted, especially when you let me nick your mince pie.'

'*Part* of my mince pie…'

'I wouldn't dare take all of it. I don't have a death wish. But the stuff about Colin, that's not a waste either. It could prove to be very relevant. I just don't know what to make of it at the moment.'

'No, fair enough.' I took a sip of my tea. 'I think I just want this sorted out quickly, for Daisy's sake as much as anyone else's.'

'She still upset?'

'Yes. They didn't even know each other that well until this panto. I think working on a production like this, where they have to rehearse a lot, and of course she and Daisy went through a lot of her lines when they were rewriting bits – it just brings everyone together. It *is* like a family. And then suddenly a member of that family isn't here anymore, and what's worse is that another member is probably the reason why.'

'Yes,' said Nathan. 'That makes it all the more painful, doesn't it? Grieving but also now not knowing who to trust.' He gave my hand a little squeeze. 'Just make sure that if anything occurs to Daisy, or if she suddenly remembers something, like seeing someone backstage who shouldn't have been there, she tells us first.'

'I will,' I said. We finished our drinks and went our separate ways, Nathan back to work and me to look around the shops for Christmas present inspiration. As I stood and stared in the brightly lit window of Penhaligon's, Nathan's words came back to me, making me shiver. *'Make sure she tells us first.'* Because if she trusted the wrong panto person and told them instead, she might end up like the unfortunate principal boy.

'Excuse me, madam, I hope you weren't thinking of bringing that filthy animal in here.' I jumped as a snooty voice spoke in my ear. I turned round, already knowing who it was.

'Tony Penhaligon, how *dare* you call my Germaine a filthy animal—' I started.

'I was talking to the dog, not you.' Tony ducked as I pretended to aim a punch at him. 'You coming in or what? It's bloody freezing out here.'

'I'm not leaving her tied up out here,' I said, and Tony laughed.

'That was clever, Germaine, I didn't even see your lips move,' he said, preemptively ducking again. 'No, bring her in. Come into the office and we can catch up.' He stepped aside and held open the big glass door of the shop. The sound of Michael Bublé exhorting us to have ourselves a merry little Christmas drifted out into the street.

'In other words, you heard about this morning's meeting and you want the goss,' I said.

'Busted.'

We walked through the homewares department and through a door marked 'private' into the back offices, but not before Tony had stopped to have a word with a member of staff who was standing around in the toasters and kettles section looking bored, although it might just have been the incessant Christmas music driving her insane. We reached the manager's office, and he again opened the door and waited for me to go through. He shut the door behind us, cutting Bublé off in his prime.

I sat on one of the seats in front of his desk, letting Germaine sniff around. 'Ooh, I haven't had this sort of special treatment since that time your dad caught us shoplifting.'

He laughed. 'Oh my God, I'd forgotten about that! We

were, what, ten? Eleven? I can't even remember what we nicked.'

'It was Easter, remember? You said, "My family owns this shop, I can help myself to whatever I want" – you were going through a particularly irritating phase, if I remember rightly. Still waiting for you to grow out of it…'

'That's right! We took a couple of Easter eggs each, didn't we? And that old bag who worked on the shop floor, what was her name…'

'Dilys! Dilys whatsherface.'

'Dilys Riley, that was it. Now *she* were a miserable old baggage and no mistaking. She grassed us up to my dad and he went ballistic.'

'As ballistic as your dad ever got, anyway,' I said, because Malcolm Penhaligon was one of the softest, quietest and nicest men you could hope to meet.

'Yeah,' said Tony, settling back into his chair with a smile on his face. 'My old man never liked telling me off.'

'It shows,' I said sniffily. 'Totally spoilt.'

There was a knock on the door. Tony leapt up and opened the door to the bored-looking staff member, who was carrying a tray with two mugs of tea and a plate of mince pies on it.

'Thanks, Pauline,' said Tony. 'And remember what I said: toasters are exciting!'

'If you say so,' she said, and left.

'Poor Pauline,' said Tony. 'She used to work for an accountancy firm in Launceston, but she got made redundant. She's not really cut out for retail work.'

'Why not?'

'She hates people.'

'Ah, right.' That probably *would* make you unsuited for customer service. Tony handed me a mug of tea and offered me a mince pie, which I took after a moment's hesitation. Yes, I'd already had one, but calories don't count in the run-up to Christmas, do they? And you could argue that I was in training for the slap-up meal we'd be having on Christmas Day. It doesn't do to come at these things unprepared.

'So come on, then,' said Tony, through a mouthful of his own mince pie. 'Spill the tea, like the kids say.'

'Oh my *God*, you're so *cringe*,' I said, in a stroppy teenage voice. '*No one* says that anymore. But I'll tell you what went down at the meeting. Everyone was waiting for him to say, "The show must go on", but he didn't.'

'Really?' Tony looked relieved. 'He cancelled the run?'

'Did you think he would want to carry on?'

'No, not really... Don't get me wrong, I think it will have been a struggle for him, and I think anything less than a murder and he'd have had us back on stage tonight, but with it being Kirsty... No, I'm not surprised he cancelled it. I'm relieved.'

'What do you mean, with it being Kirsty?' I asked. 'Were they particularly close?'

'Not inappropriately so, if that's what you mean.' He grinned. 'They weren't shagging.'

'Eww. That's not what I meant at all, actually. I just didn't know they were friends.'

'Yeah, it surprised me an' all, to be fair,' he admitted. 'But Kirsty was proper good, weren't she? Not only that, she learnt her lines and did everything Colin asked her to do. He was well impressed with her, said she had real talent and professionalism.'

'She was good,' I said, and then added loyally, 'you were too, though.'

'Thank you very much,' he said, in the worst *Elvis Presley live in Vegas* voice I'd ever heard, and then in his normal voice he said, 'I think it was mutual, like. She was very interested in his career, and you know what actors are like. They do like to talk about themselves.'

'He was flattered.'

'Exactly. She was too young to have seen him on the telly, of course, so she was very keen to find out how he got the part in *Mile End Days*, where he studied acting, all that stuff.'

'He told me he didn't go to drama school,' I said, remembering the conversation I'd had with him. 'How did he get the part?'

'I dunno,' said Tony. 'Went to an audition, I suppose. There was a big thing at the time about casting "real" people, weren't there? They wanted to give locals the chance to be on screen. I remember wishing they'd do a show set down here, so I could be in it.'

'Can you imagine that? *Penstowan Days*?' I laughed. 'How boring would that be?'

Chapter Six

I managed to buy a few daft stocking fillers for Mum and Daisy (*everyone* in our house gets a stocking full of silly presents and chocolate on Christmas morning, regardless of age) before heading back to the car. On the way to the car park I passed the florists and decided to pop in; I fancied getting a wreath like Colin's to hang on our front door, and they had some lovely ones full of holly and pine cones and what not. The fact that the flower shop was run by Emma, the mother of one of Daisy's schoolfriends, who was on the school's board of governors and head of the PTA, had absolutely nothing to do with it. Honest. Because while Nathan and his crew were having fun sorting through all those witness statements (most of which would be no help at all), I thought I might just find out a little bit more about the victim.

'I won't be long, I promise,' I said to Germaine, as I tied her lead to the lamp post outside. I had taken her into a florists once. *Once.* I still occasionally had nightmares about the experience, although it hadn't been me clearing up the mess. Germaine really does not like yellow flowers for some reason, and there had been a large display of daffodils…

I went inside and browsed the wreaths and Christmas table displays while Emma finished serving another customer. And I wasn't *intentionally* eavesdropping, but I heard their conversation anyway. Just about. I moved a bit closer so I could (intentionally) hear better.

'So sad,' the customer was saying. 'She had her whole life ahead of her. Although I was surprised she stayed in Penstowan after all that business.'

'Yes, that was a right mess,' said Emma, wrapping a bunch of white lilies. 'It all came out all right in the end, though. Her heart was in the right place.'

'And he definitely never…?'

'Not as far as we know,' said Emma. 'Although they do say there's no smoke without fire, don't they?'

'Terrible business. And now this. It seems worse happening at Christmas, don't it?' The customer paid for her flowers. 'I shall leave these outside the hall. I wonder if they'll carry on with the panto?'

'No, they've cancelled it,' I said. They both looked over at me. 'Sorry, I couldn't help hearing. I saw Colin Sweeney this morning and he said they're not going to carry on without Kirsty.'

'Quite right too,' said the customer. She took her bunch of flowers and left.

'Such a sad business,' said Emma. 'Are you looking for anything in particular?'

'A wreath,' I said. 'For my front door, I mean, not a funeral wreath…'

'No…' We were both quiet for a moment, thinking about Kirsty. I picked up a wreath and studied it, waiting for the right moment, but as it turned out Emma beat me to it. 'So does that husband of yours have any idea who did it?'

'Not yet,' I said. 'I don't know why anyone would want to kill her, do you?'

'No, no, lovely girl…' *Although…*, I thought. Wait for it. 'Although there was that business at the school…'

'I heard about that,' I said. 'I heard she left under a bit of a cloud. What was that all about?'

Emma looked around to make sure no one else would hear, in the time-honoured tradition of all good gossips. But there were only the two of us in the shop.

'She accused one of the male teachers of having an inappropriate relationship with one of the students.'

'Really?'

'Yeah. Said he was texting the girl, only fifteen she was, and saying all sorts. Suggesting stuff, you know.'

'What sort of stuff?' I asked, but the look Emma gave me told me exactly what sort of stuff. 'What, sexual stuff? That's awful. What happened?'

'As you know, I'm on the board of governors, so I heard all about it, but I shouldn't really talk about it…' She was clearly dying to tell me about it, though. I mimed zipping my lips shut and locking them with a key, then throwing the key away.

'I can keep a secret,' I said.

'Kirsty reckoned she'd seen text messages between them. You know she was a teaching assistant? Well it was one of the pupils she was helping with English and Maths. Constantly on her phone, that girl. Kirsty confiscated it to try and help her concentrate, and told her she could have it back at break time. When she went to hand it back to her, she saw a message flash up from someone called Mark. Proper smutty, it was. She asked her who this Mark was, thinking it was one of the boys in her year or something, although there aren't many Marks about these days, are there? Name's gone out of fashion a bit.'

'How did she work out it was a teacher?'

'Well, first she had a good chat with the girl. Told her you couldn't always trust boys, specially not when they were asking you to send them dirty pictures. Told her sometimes people say that they love you to get you to do things.'

'I bet that went down well,' I said. 'Teenagers always think they know better, don't they? Even from people who have literally been through all that before them.'

'Yeah. Well, apparently the girl told Kirsty that she didn't know what she was talking about, and that she knew she could trust Mark, because he wasn't a boy, he was an adult who wanted an adult relationship.'

'An adult who wanted an adult relationship with a fifteen-year-old girl,' I said, shuddering. 'Bloody hell, that's a massive red flag, innit? But it still didn't necessarily mean it was a teacher…'

'Except it was break time,' said Emma. 'Bit of a coincidence that an adult outside of school would be messaging her at the exact time she should've been free. Plus how many adult males do most teenage girls know, outside of school teachers and family?'

Hmm. Nathan would've called that 'reaching'; it was circumstantial evidence at best. But then, how many adults had I known as a fifteen-year-old? Actually, quite a few, because I'd been a regular at the station and I knew a lot of the police officers there. But most teenagers probably wouldn't be that familiar with their parents' workmates. 'But she did find out who it was?'

'She went along to the staff room, still with the girl's phone, and one of the science teachers was in there, apparently texting someone.'

'And his name was Mark…?' I let my voice trail off, hoping she would jump in with his surname, but she didn't. She just nodded.

'And *then* the girl's phone went off again, with another message, just as the teacher finished typing.'

'Right… But that could all still have been a coincidence,' I said. 'Did she confront him about it? Or show anyone else the text messages? Any of the other teachers?'

'No, there was no one else in the room so she didn't feel safe asking him about it. She did keep hold of the phone so she could show it to someone else later, but all hell broke loose when the girl rang her mum from a friend's phone and complained that Kirsty had stolen her phone.' Emma rolled her eyes. 'Her mum was one of *those* parents. You know the sort. They tell their kids not to let the teachers tell them what to do, and that if they don't agree with the school rules they don't have to follow them.'

I knew exactly the type of parent she was talking about, because Daisy's useless dad Richard had been a bit like that himself. Luckily Daisy had been too smart from a very early age to take any notice of her father.

'So what happened?'

'The girl's mum rang up and caused a huge fuss, demanding Kirsty give the girl's phone back immediately, as she had health issues and she needed her daughter to be contactable at all times. She threw a fit when Kirsty mentioned the text messages – which she hadn't been able to read all of, just the preview that came up on screen, because the phone was locked – she started going on about invasion of privacy and all that rubbish. And of course the girl denied that the messages were inappropriate and said she'd never said Mark was an adult, he was a boy she'd met at some sports club.'

'But surely the headmaster would've been involved? Surely he would've said something?' But I knew the headmaster of Daisy's school. He was a timid and perpetually nervous man, usually to be found hiding in his office. The deputy head, who admittedly could be quite scarily efficient and capable at times, was the real power at the school. 'Or the deputy head? She doesn't strike me as the sort of person who would put up with nonsense from the parents.'

'No, absolutely not, but she was away on some "skills exchange" thing with another school,' said Emma. 'She was away for a whole month. Kirsty had no one to back her up.' The bell above the door of the shop tinkled, and she looked startled. 'It all got sorted out, though. Kirsty found another job and the teacher moved away, so all's well that ends well.'

'But how did it get sorted out?' I asked. Emma shook her head.

'Sorry, I shouldn't have let my mouth run away with me like that! The main thing to remember is, he was cleared of any wrongdoing and everything went back to normal. Is that the wreath you're going with? Good choice. I'll stick it in a bag for you.'

It was clear I was getting nothing more from Emma – apart from a wreath – so I thanked her and, after rescuing Germaine from the sheer indignity of being tied to a lamp post, headed home to hang it up. I'd had the presence of mind to also buy a wreath hanger – a hook that went over the front door – so I didn't have to bang a nail into it or anything. I was just standing back to admire my handiwork when Nathan came home.

'That looks nice,' he said, kissing me. 'Very festive.'

'You're home early,' I said. 'I thought you'd be working late, this early on in the investigation.'

He sighed. 'We would be if we had anything to go on.' I followed as he walked through to the kitchen and dumped his messenger bag on the table. 'I brought some statements home to look through after dinner. I was starting to go cross-eyed, reading all these.'

'Don't tell me Sunil has lost his touch? I thought this sort of thing was right up his street.' I flicked the kettle on and got out two mugs. 'Tea, or something stronger?'

'Tea. I need to stay awake… Which is more than Sunil was capable of. The twins have been keeping him and Eesha up all night.'

'The early days can be exhausting,' I said.

'How long do the "early days" last? Because we need him back at full capacity.'

'Only about eighteen years.'

'Right.' Nathan chuckled. 'I feel like I lucked out, inheriting a daughter who was well out of nappies.'

'But full of teenage sass,' I said. 'At least she's not texting nude photos of herself to adult men.'

'What the hell?' Nathan looked surprised. 'That got dark very quickly. Where did that come from?'

'An interesting conversation I had at the florist today…' I handed Nathan a mug of tea, only to see him looking at me, amused. 'What?'

'I *knew* you would find a way to get involved in this,' he said. 'It *is* linked to the murder, I take it?'

'Take a seat, my lover, and I will reveal all…' I said, and he laughed again.

We went through to the living room and sat down on the sofa, where I told Nathan all about the mysterious Mark, and the situation which had been 'very messy' and only solved by Kirsty quitting her job and the teacher leaving.

'Hmm…' said Nathan, which meant he was cogitating.

'I mean, I know Emma reckoned it was all sorted out, but the guy had to move away! And she lost her job. It doesn't sound very "sorted out" to me, not if those were the lengths they had to go to.'

'No, I see what you mean. But we don't know that this Mark bloke *had* to move away, do we? He might've been offered a better job in a school somewhere else.'

'Or he might've found it impossible to stay in the area, because as everyone says, there's no smoke without fire. Although there is. There are plenty of people who've been found guilty by social media or popular opinion, without ever having actually done anything. Either way, he might've moved because he *was* guilty, or because everyone thought he was.'

'And that would be Kirsty's fault, because she's the one who accused him?' Nathan looked thoughtful. 'On the face of it, that *could* be a motive. It wouldn't stop everyone thinking he was guilty, but it would be revenge on the person who ruined his life.' He paused. 'If she did ruin his life. He might be having a whale of a time somewhere else. And of course, if he'd left under those circumstances, would he have come back to watch a pantomime? Would he even know about it?'

'Depends on who he is,' I said. 'He might still have family here. You can find out his name, can't you? You can ask the school about it.'

'Can I? Okay.' Nathan looked bemused. 'I'm glad one of us has a plan. Pity it's not the one with the warrant card. You sure you don't want to join up again?'

'If they'd let me sign up just for the odd interesting murder, that would be cool,' I said, 'but I don't think it works that way.'

'If Kirsty accused this Mark of having an inappropriate relationship with a pupil, she must've had more proof that it was him,' said Nathan. 'Just seeing someone called Mark typing into his phone at the same time as another message turned up is, well, it's a pretty big coincidence and it might make you suspect them, but it's not conclusive, is it? Yes, he was typing a message out at the same time, but he's a teacher – if he needed to contact someone, when else would he do it? He'd have to wait until break time. He could've been texting someone else.'

'I know,' I said. 'I did get all this third or even fourth hand, remember. Emma wasn't there, and although as a governor she would've heard about any investigation the school did, she wouldn't have been part of it, would she? Or would she? I have no idea what school governors do, other than argue with the PTA over ridiculous things like school uniforms.'

Nathan smiled. 'I bet you were one of the rebellious ones at school, who never wore the right uniform. I bet you turned up every day in trainers and took up the hem of your skirt so it was above the knee.'

I laughed. 'You're right about the trainers, but I never

shortened my skirt. I always wore trousers so I could kick boys' butts in the playground.'

'Really? I like women with a bit of spirit...' said Nathan, moving closer. 'How long did you say Daisy and Shirley would be out?'

I laughed and pushed him away. 'I didn't, so you can get *that* idea out of your head right now. Especially not on the sofa! We nearly got caught by my mum last time. Concentrate on the investigation, please!'

'All right, spoilsport. So yes, I think this Mark geezer is a line of enquiry we need to look into.' Nathan took out his phone and tapped some notes into it. 'I'll get Matt to contact the school on Monday. Did you sniff out anything else?'

'Only that Kirsty and Colin were close.' Nathan raised an eyebrow. 'No, not *that* type of close. He really rated her acting skills. He said as much to me earlier, and then I bumped into Tony—'

'And had a good gossip, no doubt...'

'Just keeping my ear to the ground. Tony said the same thing, that Colin thought she was very talented and professional. It sounds like he took her under his wing a bit. And it sounds like it was mutual. She was very interested in his career and his days on TV, and she asked him all about it. He would have been very flattered.'

'That's all it was, though? There wasn't anything else going on between them?'

'I doubt it. Isn't Colin gay?'

'No. He's just well spoken.' Nathan grimaced. 'Oh God, I sounded like your mother there.' We both laughed. 'No, he was married, but she passed away a few years ago. That seems to be why he moved down here, to start afresh.'

'I think if he *was* going to be in a relationship with anyone, it would have to be Hilary, his agent,' I said, remembering her proprietorial air as she bustled around Colin's kitchen, dispensing tissues to people. 'I don't think he'd dare get involved with anyone else while she's on the scene.'

'Scary, is she?'

'Yes, she is a bit. They're obviously close, too – she's been his agent for a long time.'

'Now that's interesting, as well,' said Nathan. 'If she suspected that Kirsty was out to seduce Colin—'

'No, I can't see that at all,' I said. 'Kirsty was young and attractive, and Colin – well, he's a nice enough bloke, but… No, I can't see either of them being interested in each other in that respect.'

'Maybe not, but you said she was always asking him about his career and stuff like that, she was impressed by him being on the telly. Maybe Hilary thought she was making a play for him, trying to use him as a springboard for her own career? Or she was blinded by jealousy from years of unrequited love, and genuinely thought they were attracted to each other, and decided to remove her rival?'

'A woman scorned, you mean?' I said, shaking my head. 'Nah. Hilary strikes me as being far too level-headed and businesslike to let her feelings take over. I can't see her losing it over a man. You'll be telling me she did away with the late Mrs Sweeney as well in a minute.'

'She might've done,' said Nathan stubbornly.

'You sound like me now,' I said. 'I'm the one with the melodramatic theories, remember?'

'Yeah, but your melodramatic theories seem to quite often have a grain of truth in them.' Nathan took a swig of his tea and sat back, defeated. 'I don't know, I'm seeing revenge and petty jealousy and conspiracy theories all over the place now. I need something tangible to go on.'

'You need dinner,' I said, patting him on the arm. 'Leave it to me.'

'You need a hand? Put me to work so I stop thinking.'

'You can chop an onion.'

So I put four panko breadcrumbed chicken breasts into the oven while Nathan chopped an onion. He put on a pan of rice to cook while I sweated off the onion in a pan with some vegetable oil, a squeeze of garlic paste and some freshly grated ginger. I added two big heaped tablespoonfuls of curry powder and a couple of teaspoons of turmeric, and immediately the kitchen was filled with a wonderful, spicy aroma. I added two tablespoons of flour to thicken the sauce and cooked it out, then poured in some vegetable stock, simmering and stirring until all the flour had melted into it. A tin of coconut milk, a dash of soy sauce and a pinch of sugar, and my sauce was done.

'Are we having katsu curry for dinner?' called Daisy, coming in through the front door.

'Yes,' I said, and I heard her go, 'yay!' in the other room – it was one of her favourite dinners. 'Five minutes. I don't suppose you saw Nana on your way back, did you?'

'I'm here,' said Mum, appearing beside me and making me jump.

'Bloody hell woman, you can move quietly when you want to. How long you been in?'

'I got back hours ago. I didn't want to disturb you two on the sofa just in case you were, you know…'

'Eww, Nana!' said Daisy, entering the kitchen. 'Like they're going to get up to anything down here.'

'No, exactly,' I said, not daring to meet Nathan's eye. Or Mum's. I cleared my throat. 'Right, one of you can set the table, the other one can get the plates out.'

We managed to get through dinner without any more references to the sofa – chicken katsu has that effect on my family, all of them too busy eating to talk – and then while Daisy and Mum cleared everything away (without being asked! It truly was a Christmas miracle!) Nathan took his bag full of witness statements into the living room.

'Oh dear God, there's one or two statements there, isn't there?' I said in horror, looking at the mahoosive pile of paper on the coffee table. 'Are those all of them, or just the ones you haven't gone through yet?'

'No, thankfully that's all of them,' said Nathan. 'Sunil and Matt have already read most of them, but we're still trying to build up a clear picture of where everyone was at the time of the murder, and so many of them have said things that contradict each other.'

'Like what?'

'Like saying someone was in one place, while someone else says they saw them somewhere else,' said Nathan vaguely. He flicked through the pile and pulled out a statement. 'Here. Tim says he was in the green room during most of the murder window, and there are a couple of other people who corroborate that, albeit vaguely. But there were others in the green room who don't remember *anyone* else being in there because they were going through their lines for Act Two or redoing make up or whatever. So who's to say Tim really *was* in there?'

'You don't suspect Tim though, do you?'

'No, no more than I suspect anyone else at this point. I'm just using him as an example.' He shook his head. 'There seems to have been a pervading atmosphere of panic and confusion behind the scenes, which makes them all bloody unreliable witnesses.'

'Ah, you've never been involved in amateur dramatics, have you? That panic and confusion is pretty much par for the course during a performance,' I said.

'How do you know? Don't tell me you've trodden the boards?' Nathan perked up, obviously waiting to hear about my exploits on stage. I shrugged coyly.

'Might've done…'

'You know I'll only ask Shirley if you don't tell me, and she'll give me all the gory details. Better for me to hear it from you.'

'Oh all right. I never did any acting as an adult, but I was in all the school plays and I was actually very good.'

'And modest too, I see.'

'I was! My English teacher tried to persuade me to go to drama school, but I was already set on being a copper.'

'The world missed out on a great talent the day you joined the Met,' said Nathan pompously, and I swatted his arm.

'Cheeky bugger! My Mr Toad was a sight to behold.'

'Your *what*?'

I immediately regretted mentioning Mr Toad, but it was too late. 'We did *Toad of Toad Hall* and I had the lead role.'

'Oh *wow*.' Nathan had a big grin on his face. 'Did you have to wear toad makeup?'

'I had to wear green face paint if that's what you mean, yes.'

'Oh *wow*.'

'Yes, you already said that.'

'Have you still got the costume?' He raised an eyebrow in a suggestive fashion. If you don't believe a raised eyebrow can be suggestive, then you just haven't met the right person yet.

'Oh stop it! I was thirteen years old in green face paint and tweed plus fours, okay? Yes, it's hilarious. And no, there aren't any photos of me in it. Can we get on?'

'If we have to.' Nathan grinned at me and shook his head. 'Honestly, you think you know someone…' He cleared his throat. 'Sorry, just got a frog in my throat.'

'Oh you're *so* funny. It was a toad. Now focus on the witness statements, not on my past life as an amphibian…'

Nathan reluctantly let it go and settled in to read through the statements one more time. Mum brought us both a cup of tea (would wonders never cease?) and then made herself comfy in an armchair, ready to watch

Gladiators on the telly with Germaine stretched out across her lap. Every time the referee said 'Gladiators – ready!' before an event, her ears would prick up and her tail would wag ten to the dozen. And so would the dog's.

Daisy wandered through the living room on her way upstairs, talking to her boyfriend Joe on the phone. He was away in London on music business, but from what I could hear of her side of the conversation, he'd just heard about the murder and was ready to jump in his car and hot foot it back down to Cornwall to be by her side.

'No, babe, there's no need. You'll be back on Tuesday anyway,' she said. Mum and I exchanged looks and, once she'd left the room, smiled at each other.

'That Joe's a lovely boy,' said Mum. 'Grandson-in-law material.'

I snorted. 'Don't let Daisy hear you say that, she'll never marry him,' I said. 'But you're right, he is.'

'Oh God,' groaned Nathan.

'What? Don't tell me you don't like him?' I asked, surprised. 'I mean, I know Daisy's far too young for us to be talking about her wedding, but—'

'What? No, this statement. Tim was apparently in two places at once. One of the stage crew says they saw him near the storage area around the time of death. But like I told you, we've got two other people who reckon he was in the green room.'

'Whose statement is that?' I said, leaning over. Nathan bent the page over so I couldn't see. 'Oh, come on, I'm not going to say anything, am I? But if you want to know if they're a reliable witness or not…'

'You know I can't tell you who said it,' said Nathan, but I'd spotted something that meant I didn't care anymore.

'Hang on,' I said. 'Read out exactly what they said.' Nathan looked over at Mum and then back at me, meaningfully, but I shook my head. 'She's not listening, she's too busy drooling over Bradley Walsh.' Nathan rolled his eyes.

'You are such a bad influence… Okay, 'I saw Widow Twankey heading down the corridor towards the storage area—'

I interrupted him triumphantly. 'There you go! They saw the Widow Twankey, not Tim.'

'Tim *is* Widow Twankey—'

'No, he's only Widow Twankey when he's wearing the outfit. And he had at least three costume changes, because he kept changing his bust.' Nathan looked bewildered. 'Forget about the bust. He had at least three costume changes, maybe more. So who's to say this wasn't someone else wearing one of those costumes? That means Tim could well have been in the green room, and this was someone else disguising themselves as Widow Twankey while they nipped off to bash Aladdin in the head with his lamp.'

Nathan reread the statement, then looked at me. 'You might just be right. What better way to disguise yourself backstage at a panto than in a ridiculous costume, complete with wig?'

'A ridiculous costume that has a lot of padding, too,

which would completely hide their shape.' I stared at the TV, not really seeing the equally ridiculous costumes of the on-screen gladiators, although they were so muscular they didn't need padding. I was imagining the murderer, dressed as a pantomime dame, moving silently but not inconspicuously through the backstage areas. As well as looking like a member of the cast and therefore entitled to be there, it had the added bonus of throwing suspicion on Tim if anyone did spot them and connect them to Kirsty's murder. 'You know what this means?' I said, adopting my best (but still terrible) Sam Spade hard-bitten gumshoe voice. 'This dame ain't no lady, she's a cold-blooded killer!'

Chapter Seven

'Thank you for coming,' said Nathan. It was Sunday morning, bitterly cold, with a fog that had rolled in off the sea and looked to be making itself comfy; I got the feeling it would be sticking around for at least the next couple of days.

'No problem,' said Li. Li Zhāng was the Penstowan Players' wardrobe mistress, for this production anyway; normally, she was to be found studying Fashion and Textile Design at Central Saint Martins college in London. Her grandparents had escaped Communist China back in the 1960s, and had somehow found themselves in Cornwall with their baby son. That baby son, Bill (although I suspected that wasn't his actual Chinese name), now ran the Golden Dragon restaurant in town. Apparently Bill had harboured dreams of his daughter being a doctor or a lawyer, or at least taking over the restaurant when he retired (not that he had any intention of ever doing that), but dammit, if she was determined to be a fashion designer then she would at least take the most prestigious course available. I knew all of this because one of Mum's friends had a grandson who washed dishes at the Golden Dragon, and he'd overheard them talking. None of which had any bearing at all on the case. Sometimes I really wished I didn't know so much gossip.

'No problem,' said Li. 'If we're not carrying on with the run then I might as well take back the costumes we've hired and see if we can get some money back.'

'You didn't make them all, then?' I asked, and she laughed.

'Has my dad been bigging me up again? I'm only back for the holidays, I'm not spending all my time sewing. I only got guilted into doing this because my mum's in the chorus.' She turned to Nathan. 'What do you need me to do?'

'Just make sure all the costumes are accounted for,' he said, careful not to explain too much; it's always best not to suggest things to people, not that she was a suspect exactly, but anyone who had been backstage at the time of the murder couldn't be completely ruled out.

'Did you know Kirsty?' I asked, ignoring the slight, involuntarily shake of his head. If he hadn't wanted me asking questions he shouldn't have let me come. 'You must've been at school together?'

'I knew *of* her,' said Li, 'but she was in the year above me, so we weren't really friends. She seemed nice, though.

I can't believe what's happened.' She looked at me. 'Are you in the police, then? I thought you were a caterer?'

'I am, I'm just here to pick up some stuff I left behind on Friday night,' I said. 'I did a load of food for after the performance, but obviously no one was very hungry.'

'Of course, yes. I had some of your sausage rolls.' She didn't say if they were nice or not, and what with her family's background in running a restaurant I decided not to ask.

'I'll take you through into the backstage area now,' said Nathan. 'If I could ask you not to touch anything, other than the costumes? And I'm afraid I can't let you take them just yet, but I will make a note to get them back to you as soon as we can.'

Li nodded, and we followed Nathan through the double doors into the building. Inside, the Forensics team had done their job and it was deserted. All the lights were off and it felt somehow eerie, as buildings that are normally bright and full of people bustling around inside often do. Nathan reached out and flicked on the lights, then led us through the auditorium, which still bore traces of Friday night's unexpected end to proceedings. Mugs of tea had been handed round to the panto cast and crew while they were waiting to give their statements, and now those mugs were scattered around the room, some empty, some with dregs of cold tea still in them. The room felt abandoned.

'I should probably get those mugs cleaned up while I'm here,' I said, and Nathan nodded.

'Yes, you're okay to move them,' he said.

We walked through the door at the side of the stage which led to the rooms beyond, Nathan turning on more lights as we went. It really *did* feel spooky back here, a kind of ghostly aura of performances past lingering in the air. Forensics had finished with the crime scene, and we could see ahead of us the entrance to the storage area and cupboard where Kirsty had been found, crisscrossed with incident tape. Li stared at it as Nathan stopped in front.

'Where are the costumes kept?' he asked. 'Is there a separate room for them?'

'Yeah, over there,' she said, nodding to the corridor in front of us. 'Next to the green room.'

Nathan and I shared a look. If someone *had* taken a costume to disguise themselves and then headed to the storage room, then this must be the bit of corridor that they'd been seen in. Although it was hard to know for sure, such was the labyrinthine layout of the building and all its later additions.

'Okay, if you want to lead the way...' Nathan stood aside so Li could lead us.

The wardrobe department was an Aladdin's cave, aptly enough. A rail of brightly coloured costumes on hangers stood along the back wall, although they were from wildly different time periods and locations. Sequins sparkled in the dim light from the overhead bulb – there were no windows in here – and feathers shivered in the slight breeze our bodies created as we entered. A pile of top hats, bowlers and assorted other headgear sat in one corner, topped by an Egyptian-looking crown.

'Those are the company's own costumes,' said Li, noticing me looking. 'Most of them weren't really suitable for the panto, so we hired the main ones in. We did a few alterations on the less important costumes and just hoped no one would notice that a thirteenth-century serving woman was wearing a Regency outfit.'

'I don't think anyone would've minded, even if they had noticed,' I said. 'So this lot are the panto costumes?' I indicated another, larger rail along one side of the room. Where the costumes on the other rail had been neatly hung up to avoid creasing, the ones here looked like they'd been flung onto hangers, the rail itself, and in some cases the floor, in a complete panic. Li pursed her lips.

'Yes. Honestly, the state of these…' She reached out to pick a dress off the floor and then stopped. 'Am I all right to hang these up properly? Everyone's just yanked their costumes off and dumped them in their hurry to get away. It's painful to look at.'

'In a minute,' said Nathan. 'Can you just have a look and tell me first if they're all here? There's no costumes missing?'

'I don't think so…' Li walked along the rail, inspecting the costumes. They were tightly packed in places, obscured by hastily abandoned clothing in others, and she had to tug at a couple to see what they were. I looked at Nathan; his witness had said someone in a Widow Twankey costume had been spotted backstage, but when Nathan had rung them and asked if they could describe the costume in more detail they'd been pretty vague, only able to tell us it had been yellow. Possibly. Or orange. Or was it more of a gold colour? It had been quite dark, so it was difficult to tell.

'Hmm,' said Li, and we both looked at her. 'I think one of Tim's is missing. Which is surprising, because he's normally very good at hanging his frocks up properly. All of his others are.'

'Which one's missing? Can you describe it?' asked Nathan.

'Yeah, it's the bright yellow one with purple polka dots.' She frowned. 'Actually that *is* weird. If it had been one of the others that would've made more sense.'

'Why?' I asked.

'Because at the point the panto stopped, he hadn't worn it. If it had been one of the earlier costumes, or more likely the one he was wearing when they found Kirsty, I could understand it better, although it still wouldn't be like Tim to not put it back properly. But he shouldn't even have had that one off the hanger. He wasn't meant to be wearing it until the finale.'

'You're right, that is weird,' I said. 'And no one else would've moved it?'

'Why would they move it?'

'Maybe they were getting it ready for him to change into later,' suggested Nathan. 'Where did the costume changes take place?'

'The chorus had a couple of minor changes, so they usually just went into the green room, but the principal characters always came in here. Especially Tim, because the

Twankey costumes take up so much space and he needed a hand getting into some of them.'

'Right… And it's definitely not in here?' asked Nathan. 'It's not been hung up on the wrong rail?'

'I wouldn't have thought so, everyone knows that's the wrong rail…' Li walked over and examined the other rail. 'Oh!'

'What is it?' Nathan followed her.

'I was about to say, no one should have even been near this rail since we first started thinking about costumes, but it has been disturbed. Look.' She pointed. The costumes on this rail had also been packed in tightly, apart from a spot near the end, where it looked like some of them had been shoved out of the way. A few had got tangled around the upright post at the end of the rail, and some were even on the floor. She bent down to pick one of them up, but Nathan stopped her.

'No, don't touch anything,' he said. 'I think we need to get the Forensics mob back…'

Li had a photo of the cast from the dress rehearsal, with Tim in the yellow and purple costume. After sending that to Nathan's phone, she left us, looking a bit shocked and confused.

'What are you thinking?' I asked him. He clicked on his phone torch and squatted down next to the clothes railing, where the clothes had been disturbed.

'I'm thinking maybe Kirsty was attacked here,' he said, shining the torch around. 'Although Forensics seem pretty certain she died in the storage room and was dragged into the cupboard. There, look. Is that blood?' There was a reddish-brown smear on the upright pole of the clothes rail, and another small spot of it on a skirt that had fallen to the floor.

'Yeah, I think it might be… So maybe it kicked off in here,' I said. 'Maybe they were in here, arguing, and the killer pushed her over and knocked her out, or incapacitated her in some other way. They realised that if they left her in here, she'd probably be discovered quite quickly, certainly the next time Twankey or Princess Jasmine had a costume change, so they decided to drag her into the storage room, first disguising themselves in a handy costume in case anyone spotted them.'

'And then she came round, so they knocked her out again and killed her?' Nathan mused. 'They might not even have intended to kill her, just keep her out of the way until the end of the panto. Or at least long enough for them to get away.'

'Could be a ruthlessly ambitious understudy, desperate for their big break,' I said, waving my arms about dramatically, then shook my head. 'If this was the London Palladium, maybe.'

'Yeah, I don't think that would be motive enough. Or would it? You know what actors are like,' he said, and we both thought back to the case that had ended up bringing us together, where someone – or more accurately, *someones* – had sabotaged a film set, until one of the actors had ended up dead. 'Who knows? But what I do know is, we need to find that costume.'

Nathan called Matt, who was back at the station with Sunil putting together a timeline and map of where everyone had been during the murder window. Matt was always glad of an excuse to avoid paperwork, so he called the Forensics team back to the scene and then came to join us, bringing a couple of uniformed officers with him.

'They can help us search for the missing costume,' he said, and Nathan nodded.

'Good thinking. This needs to be a priority. With any luck we might be able to get some DNA evidence off it, although I'm not banking on it.'

I left the official investigators to it, both Nathan and Matt giving me a sympathetic smile as I trudged away, and went to collect dirty mugs and pick up what was left of my buffet. I might be able to save some of it – some things were still sealed up in Tupperware, or had been left in a cool box, and they would possibly be okay – but most of it was sadly destined for the bin. I hate throwing food away, but I hate giving people food poisoning even more.

I stuffed all the food waste into a bin bag and staggered around the back of the building, to where a couple of industrial-size wheelie bins were kept, one for rubbish and one for recycling. I lobbed the bag into a bin and then groaned when I realised I'd put it in the recycling by mistake. If there's one thing I hate almost as much as throwing food away, it's throwing it in the wrong bin and potentially ruining people's recycling efforts.

I groped around blindly over the side of the bin, but there'd been a collection on Friday morning and it was almost empty, so I couldn't even feel where the bag had gone. I gritted my teeth and dragged over a plastic crate, the sort that beer bottles come in and which had obviously come from the theatre bar, and used it to climb into the bin. It was only after I'd got into the bin that it occurred to me that I might not be able to climb out again... But anyway. The bag was at my feet, so I threw it out and then stopped in amazement.

A very flouncy bright yellow dress, with purple polka dots and white feathers around the neckline, lay in the bottom of the bin. Even without touching it I could see blood stains on the bodice, and along the hem of the skirt. I stepped back in revulsion – it was a hideous dress – and almost slipped on a banana skin, swearing as I reached out to steady myself on the side of the bin and muttering, 'Well, *that's* not recycling!' I realised there was indeed no way I was going to get out of the bin on my own, so I was forced to take out my phone and call for help, although I avoided mentioning exactly what help I needed, only that I'd found the dress and I needed assistance with it right now.

'You do get yourself in some scrapes,' grinned Matt, pulling me out. Nathan had been busy talking to the Forensics lads, so he'd sent his right-hand man instead.

'Yeah, but good thing I do, isn't it? You could've wasted hours looking for that dress.'

'Not really. I was on me way out here to look in the bins anyway. Obvious place to get rid of it, innit?'

'Whatever. Just do not tell Nathan I was stuck in a bin.'

Matt shook his head, still grinning. 'I can't promise that,

he's the SIO...' He vaulted into the bin like a flipping gazelle or something. He snapped a couple of photos of the dress in situ on his phone and then leapt out again (making a total a mockery of my pathetic climbing skills) clutching the frock, now clad in a bin bag, because none of the evidence bags were big enough. 'That's nasty.'

'I know. Whoever put yellow and purple together had a serious lack of taste.'

'I meant the blood. And the *smell*! What the hell are these people recycling?'

'Jokes,' I said, thinking of Friday night's performance. 'Anyway, no need to thank me—' I waited, pointedly.

'What? Oh yeah, *thank you*, Jodie, saving the day again, what would the Devon and Cornwall Constabulary do without you?'

'No need to take the piss, either,' I said, but I wasn't really grumpy. I was thinking, *How did they get the dress out here without anyone noticing?*

'So how did they get the dress out to the bins without anyone noticing?' asked Nathan, when he joined us.

'Exactly what I was wondering,' I said. 'Is there a back door? Because I ended up coming out the front entrance and walking around the side of the building. But they couldn't have done that on Friday, because they would've walked through the audience.'

'Could they have stuffed the dress in a bag and taken it with them?' asked Matt.

'No, look at it, it's all big and flouncy. You only just got it in the bin bag. If it was someone from the audience – say they'd sneaked backstage during the interval and done the deed, then come back to their seat for Act Two, people would've spotted the massive bin bag at their feet. And we would've spotted whoever had it while they were waiting to give their statement. *And* it wasn't in a bag when I found it. Why would they bother taking it out?'

'There's a fire exit round the other side of the building,' said Nathan. 'They must've nipped through that, dumped the dress and then gone back inside.'

'They would've had to prop the door open with something, though, because otherwise it would shut behind them, and there's no way to open a fire exit from outside,' I said.

'Or they could've strolled in through the front door,' said Nathan. 'There were quite a few people in the bar during the interval, and it's only small, so they could've slipped in and mingled with the drinkers, and then gone back to their seat.'

'Or gone backstage again,' said Matt. 'Although no one in the audience witness statements remembers seeing anyone going in or out from backstage during the interval. But if people were taking their seats again for Act Two, or coming back in from the bar, it would be easy for someone to slip in unnoticed.'

'Maybe,' said Nathan. He sighed heavily. 'I'm afraid the witness statements are not going to solve this for us. We need to find out more about our victim. Who would want to kill her, and why?'

Chapter Eight

'Hello? Who's in charge here?'

A woman's voice reached us from around the front of the building. We exchanged glances and headed towards it.

'Why won't you let me in? I demand to see whoever's in charge!' The woman, who looked to be in her late twenties, early thirties, stood toe-to-toe with one of the uniformed PCs who had come along with Matt.

'Step back please, madam,' said the PC, calmly but firmly, but the woman was too wound up to take any notice.

'Not until you tell your superior officer that I want to see him!'

'That would be me, Miss...?' said Nathan, quickly stepping forward. She stepped back in surprise but recovered quickly.

'Lesley Kendall. I want to know what you're doing to find my sister's killer.'

'We are doing everything in our power, Ms Kendall,' said Nathan. 'Am I right in thinking you've just arrived from the US?'

'Yes. I dropped everything and got on the next available flight, and came straight here.'

'Where will you be staying?'

'With my father. But you haven't answered my question. What are you doing to find my sister's killer?'

'We are doing everything—'

'Don't fob me off with platitudes!' Her voice was brittle and shrill. It looked to me like she was struggling to contain herself, but was rapidly approaching breaking point. 'I want to know what's happening. My father has suffered too much to be left needing answers.'

'And I will be happy to give you and your father answers, when I have them,' said Nathan. 'But the investigation is still in the very early stages, and we owe it to Kirsty to follow the proper procedures.'

'You say you came straight here?' I asked. 'Have you spoken to your dad yet?'

'No. How can I, when I don't know what to say to him?' And just like that the facade of control was shattered. Her face crumpled, the anger replaced by utter bewilderment and grief. I approached her and put my hand on her arm.

'I know your family have been through a lot already,' I said softly. 'I can only imagine how you must feel. Angry, heartbroken, and impotent, knowing that there's nothing you can do to make it better—'

'I wasn't even in the country!' she said, sobbing. 'I left my little sister…'

'There's nothing you could've done, even if you had been here.' I fumbled in my coat pocket and found a tissue, which I handed to her. 'Look, my name's Jodie. I'm done here,' I said, although I wasn't really, but tidying up could wait. 'Why don't we go for a coffee and you can get yourself together before you see your dad.' I glanced at Nathan to make sure he approved, and he gave me a slight nod. 'You don't want to turn up on his doorstep like this.'

'Okay,' she sniffed.

It being a cold December Sunday in Cornwall, there wasn't a lot open in town, but there was a branch of one of the big coffee shop chains which seemed to be serving 24/7. Inside it was warm, and the air was scented with coffee, cinnamon and gingerbread. I sat Lesley down and went to order a latte for her, and a hot chocolate for me, from the young woman behind the counter wearing a green and red elf costume, complete with a red hat topped with a jingly gold bell. I couldn't resist making a crack about helping my elf to sugar and, to her credit, she managed not to groan or roll her eyes at me for saying it. Top class customer service.

'Are you with the police?' asked Lesley, as I sat down opposite her.

'I'm more… *police-adjacent*,' I said. 'I was with the Met for twenty years, and I'm married to DCI Withers, who you just met. He's the senior investigating officer, and I might be biased but he's a good copper.'

'I just can't believe anyone would want to kill her,' said Lesley, fighting to keep her voice under control.

'I know. I didn't really know Kirsty, but everyone involved in the panto loved her, and she was well thought of.' I sat back as the waitress brought our drinks over. 'Thank you…' I waited for her to leave, and then turned back to Lesley. 'So, you're living in the States?'

'Yes. I'm married to an American. I met Pete in Thailand, when we were both doing a gap year. Ended up going back to California with him and the rest is history.' She sighed. 'I work for a talent agency in LA. When Kirsty told me about being in the panto she was so excited, I told her she should come out and visit us, and I'd see if I could get her an audition with one of the agents.'

'She was very good,' I said. She raised an eyebrow. 'I was at the panto when she… when it happened. She was really good in Act One. Everyone rated her.'

'The last time I saw her act was in a school play,' said Lesley. 'I couldn't believe it when she ended up working there.'

'Why's that?'

'Just that we both went there ourselves. When she got that teaching assistant job I teased her a bit. But she enjoyed school, so I can understand why it appealed to her.' She grimaced. 'I hated it. Glad to leave and in no hurry to go back.'

'Do you know what happened there? I heard she left

under a cloud. Obviously she accused a teacher of being inappropriate with one of the students, but...'

Lesley shook her head angrily. 'Her leaving had nothing to do with that horrible man,' she said. 'My mum was ill, and Dad couldn't afford to give up work to look after her, so Kirsty did.'

'She quit to care for your mum? Nothing to do with the accusations?'

'I'm sure it made it easier for her to leave, but it wasn't the reason. They treated her really badly, though. They made it look like she was a stalker or something.'

'Really? That's terrible.'

'Yeah. That bloke – Mark Matheson – there was definitely something going on there, but she couldn't prove it.'

'How did she know, if there was no proof?'

'There *was* proof. She saw those text messages he'd sent that silly girl – the girl even admitted it to her – but then her parents, or her mum anyway, didn't want anyone to know about it, so they got her to deny it and delete all the text messages. And of course he deleted them from his end, too.'

'But the police would've been able to trace them—'

'The police never got a look in. I don't know what hold he had over the headmaster, but the school refused to report it because the girl and her parents asked them not to.'

'That's frustrating. You said she looked like a stalker, though?'

'Yeah.' Lesley hesitated for a moment, taking a sip of her coffee. 'Kirsty got a bit obsessed by it. She didn't like to be wrong, but mainly she didn't like the thought of a grown man having *that* kind of relationship with a teenage girl. So she started… This sounds bad, but it wasn't really like that. I was in the States while all this was happening, but Mum and Dad were both right behind her, so I can't imagine it was as bad as Matheson made out.'

'What happened?'

'He caught her spying on him. She'd been following his car for a couple of weeks, wanting to see if he was meeting up with the girl, but he was too crafty. Anyway, he spotted her lurking outside the pub and instead of just being a man and confronting her about it, he called the police.'

'Oh no…' I said, but I was thinking, Oh Kirsty, it shouldn't have been up to you to investigate! The school should've reported it.

'Yeah. He got a restraining order against her.'

'Bloody hell, he sounds like a right piece of work. But then he moved away, didn't he?'

'Yes, but by then she'd already left her job and was looking after Mum. After the way the school treated her, I don't think she'd have stayed there anyway.'

'No, I don't blame her,' I said. 'It sounds like she had a strong moral compass, a strong sense of what's right and wrong.'

'Yes, she did,' said Lesley, wiping her eyes.

'What about happier times? Did she have a boyfriend? Or girlfriend?'

'I don't think so. She was going out with someone but they split up in the summer.'

'Who was that?'

'Jamie someone. I don't know, I never met him. They were together less than a year, I think. Dad didn't like him.'

'No? Any reason why?'

She laughed softly. 'No one's good enough for his girls. He's only just warmed to Pete, and we've been married for six years and have two kids.'

'Do you know why they split up? Was it acrimonious?'

'I don't really know. I think it was her idea to break up, though, and he was pretty upset.'

'What about any other close friends?'

Lesley narrowed her eyes. 'I thought you said you weren't with the police?'

I gave a self-deprecating smile. 'I'm not, but I kind of forget sometimes... But this is all stuff the police will ask you and your dad, so it's a good idea to start thinking about it.'

'Yes, I suppose you're right. She still had loads of friends from school – from when she was a pupil, I mean. I don't know if she was still friends with anyone she'd worked with there.'

'What about family? Will your dad have anyone around to help him when you go home?'

'Yes,' she said. 'There's a lot of family on Dad's side. He grew up in Launceston and most of his family still live in the area. There's an aunty and uncle, and a couple of cousins, although they're upcountry somewhere I think – I've not kept in touch with them, and I don't think Kirsty did either. And his parents are both still alive. Kirsty did see them, but they're retired and they're always off on cruises and that. On Mum's side there's only Nana.' She gulped as a sob threatened to break free. 'Oh God, what's Nana going to say?'

'They were close?'

'Yes. Nana's been on her own a long time. She moved down here when Mum was about fifteen, after Grandad died. When we were kids we went round there every week for Sunday lunch, and when Mum was working we'd go round to Nana's after school. After I moved away, and then Mum died, Kirsty made sure she still visited Nana at least once a week. Dad does too, but her and Kirsty... they were as thick as thieves. Same sense of humour. She's going to be devastated, especially after losing Mum as well.' Lesley wiped away the tears that were silently streaming down her face. 'I'm sorry, I can't do this now.'

'No, I'm sorry, I shouldn't have asked you.' I reached out and held her hand. 'I am so sorry about Kirsty. Everyone is shocked, including the police, and I promise you they will do everything they can.'

'Don't promise me that. Promise me they'll find her killer.'

But that was the one thing no one could promise her.

We walked back to the theatre together – Lesley had parked her hire car there – and I watched as she drove away before

I went inside, the PC on the door letting me in with a brief nod.

Nathan was inside, talking to Robbo from the Forensics team, who had been taking swabs from the bloodstains inside the wardrobe room.

'Might've known you'd be involved,' grinned Robbo. I held up my hands in defence.

'I was only here to do the catering, honest, guv,' I said, and he laughed.

'Yeah, and that's why I didn't hire you to do my wedding,' he said. 'No offence.'

'Absolutely none taken. So that is blood, then?' I asked, nodding at the bloodstains.

'Some of it…'

'Some of it?' I turned to Nathan. 'What does that mean?'

'The substance on the clothes rail is blood,' said Nathan, 'although of course we don't know yet if it's Kirsty's—'

'Give us a chance!' said Robbo.

'—but most of the stains on the clothing are lipstick.' Nathan picked up the skirt that had fallen onto the floor, which was now in a plastic evidence bag. He turned it over so I could see. 'That spot is blood, but see this smear? That's lipstick.'

'Red lipstick? Who was wearing red lipstick? Kirsty wasn't, she was meant to look like a boy,' I pointed out.

'No,' said Nathan carefully. 'I rang Li to ask her, and according to her there's only one character who would've worn bright red lipstick.'

'Who?' I asked, but I had a sinking feeling I already

knew, because I could see their fully made up face in my mind.

'I'll be off,' said Robbo, awkwardly, because he obviously knew who it was too. 'Need to get these swabs analysed...'

Nathan waited until we were alone, and then opened his mouth to speak.

'If you're going to say Widow Twankey, you're wrong,' I said.

'Why am I wrong?' asked Nathan. 'You must remember what he looked like. There's nothing subtle about the costume or the makeup.'

'But why would Tim kill Kirsty?'

'Why would *anyone* kill Kirsty? We don't know, do we?' He pulled me into his arms and hugged me. 'I know you like Tim. So do I, as it goes. And no, he's not someone I would ordinarily suspect of being capable of murder. But you know as well as I do, in the right circumstances most people *are* capable of it. Certainly of losing their temper, anyway.'

'But where's the motive? And – I know this probably sounds stupid, but I think it's true – Tim was having a whale of a time performing. If he was going to bump off a fellow actor, I reckon he would at least have waited until the end of the show.'

'Not if he lost control of himself,' Nathan insisted. I sighed and he pulled me close again. 'I'm sorry, he's a friend, I get it. But you know how this goes. We have to look for who had motive; well, at this point we don't have a motive. We have to look at who had opportunity; most of the cast and crew had the opportunity to sneak around back there in the dark, either just before the interval or during it, although that's less likely. And then we have to look at the physical evidence, and at the moment the only physical evidence we have is red lipstick and, of course, one of the Widow Twankey costumes. And we have someone who saw a person in that costume sneaking around. You can see why Tim is now a person of interest, can't you?'

'Yes, I suppose so,' I said reluctantly. 'But I'm still convinced it's not him.'

'Believe me, I hope it isn't,' said Nathan, 'but I need to find her killer, and I can't let the fact that I know and like a suspect stop me following any legitimate leads.'

'I know,' I said. 'But I might have some more leads for you. Mark Matheson, the teacher Kirsty accused? He had a restraining order taken out against her, because he said she was stalking him, but she wasn't, she was following him to see if he met up with the girl so she could prove they were having a relationship.'

'Okay, but that sounds more like a motive for her to kill him, not the other way around,' said Nathan, quite reasonably, but I didn't want to hear it and he could tell by my face that I didn't. 'But I will look into it. He's already on the list of people to check up on. You got this out of the grieving sister, I take it?'

'Don't say it like that, I handled her very sensitively! There's also an ex-boyfriend, Jamie somebody, who was cut up when she broke off their relationship. That was back in the summer, but he could've been harbouring a grudge. If he couldn't have her, nobody could, that sort of thing.'

'Was he in the panto?'

'I don't think so…'

'So how would he have got backstage?'

'I don't know the logistics, but that's definitely a motive, isn't it?'

'It could be, yes. He could just've been upset at the time and then got over it.' Nathan's tone held the tiniest hint of exasperation. I felt myself getting riled up, but forced myself to take a breath and calm down.

'You don't really think Tim could've…?' I said, because while of course I *knew* he wasn't a murderer, a quiet, timid little voice at the back of my head had started to whisper that Nathan was right, the evidence (what little we had) did look bad for him.

'If he did, we'll prove it,' said Nathan firmly. 'And if he didn't, we'll prove that instead. Deal?'

'Deal.'

———

I left Nathan to it and headed home. Germaine was very happy to see me; she'd given me and Nathan a reproachful look when we'd gone out without her earlier which would've broken the heart of a lesser dog owner. I made a fuss of her, hoping she'd at least let me take my coat off and put the kettle on for a quick cuppa, but no, the poor neglected creature needed a walk and she needed it

RIGHT NOW. I was just getting her lead when Daisy came into the kitchen.

'Oh, you *are* here,' I said. 'From the fuss Germaine was making I assumed she'd been left home alone.'

'No,' said Daisy, looking puzzled and reaching for the biscuit tin.

'Do you remember when we first got her? And how you promised to take her for walks so I'd let you keep her?'

Daisy snorted. 'Yeah, like you ever believed that. And there was no way you were ever going to give her to anyone else.'

'Not the point I was making, but true. Give us a biscuit.'

She held the tin out. 'There's only frowsy bourbons left.'

'Bourbons? Frowsy? How dare you. Those were considered posh biscuits when I was your age. Nana always insisted on buying boring Rich Tea biscuits because they lasted longer.'

'Only because no one ever eats Rich Tea biscuits, except as a last resort.'

'Exactly. We only got bourbons on special occasions. You've been spoilt by me buying chocolate digestives, you have.' I grabbed a couple of bourbons, shoved one in my mouth, and then bent down to clip the lead on Germaine, who was practically pogoing up and down in excitement. 'Bloody hell, dog,' I said, through a mouthful of biscuit, 'calm down, we're only going up the cliffs.'

'I'll come for a walk,' said Daisy, and I rolled my eyes.

'You could've done that while I was out, and I could've

come home and had a sit down. She'll not go without me now.'

Daisy got her coat on and we headed out. It was still freezing cold, but the fog looked like it was actually starting to thin a little. We walked down the end of our road – we were the last but one house – and took the footpath that led across the sheep field behind our house.

'We doing the long route, all the way to Elephant Rock?' asked Daisy.

'I wasn't planning to go that far, but we can head in that direction,' I said.

We walked in silence for a while, Germaine bounding ahead as her lead spooled out behind her. Normally I would've let her off the lead up here, but with the fog still lingering in patches I didn't dare, in case she ended up going over the cliff edge.

Daisy was quiet, and I had the feeling something was on her mind; it had been a while since she'd volunteered to come for a walk with me, especially on a day as cold as this one. But eventually—

'You like Joe, don't you?' she asked. Oh no, was it boyfriend trouble of some sort? Was she going to dump him? Were they planning to elope? Was she pregnant?

'Yes, I do,' I said. 'But to be honest I'd like anyone who made you happy and who treated you properly.'

'Which he does,' she said quickly.

'Glad to hear it.' So not dumping him, then… *Please don't be pregnant,* I thought. 'You've been together a long time now, haven't you?'

'Almost a year and a half,' she said. 'Most of my friends have had at least three boyfriends in that time.'

'Always better to go for quality rather than quantity, when it comes to men,' I said, and she laughed.

'God, yeah. Did I tell you about that moron Jade started going out with?'

'I thought she was asexual?'

'She is, but she's not aromantic – she still wants to fall in love. Of course he said he was asexual too, but he dumped her after a couple of weeks because she wouldn't sleep with him.'

'What did he think "asexual" meant?' I asked. 'Honestly, some blokes will say anything to get you into bed with them. You're very lucky with Joe.'

'Yes...' Her voice trailed off and she looked very awkward. I stopped to let Germaine sniff at some gorse bushes and turned to her.

'I don't mean you're lucky because he doesn't want to get you into bed—'

'Oh my God, Mum!'

'I'm not daft, I was your age once. Teenagers are a seething mass of hormones, not just teenage boys but girls too. And you love each other, don't you?'

'Yeah, but...'

'Is that what all this is about? Are you in trouble?'

'Trouble?' She looked puzzled at that, and then as my meaning dawned on her she looked mortified. '*Oh my God,* Mum! I'm not up the duff!'

'Phew, thank God for that, although of course if that

ever *did* happen you could tell me and we'd sort it out, no judgement—'

'Mother, please, I am not pregnant and I don't intend to be pregnant, not until I'm at least thirty-five. I've got stuff to do.'

'Well, good, that's good… So what's going on?'

'Well, like you said… teenagers are a seething mass of hormones, and we… you're not going to make me say it, are you?'

'You and Joe are having sex,' I said, and she looked like she would've welcomed a sinkhole opening up beneath her feet and swallowing her. 'Not right at this moment, obviously, because that would be inappropriate in front of your mother.' It was a stupid comment, but it worked, because she laughed and looked a tiny bit less embarrassed. 'Honestly, you know Nana, do you think I got away without having this conversation at your age? It was worse for me, because I didn't even have a steady boyfriend. She just gave me that look, you know the one—'

'The I-know-what-you've-been-up-to look?'

'Yeah, that one, crossed with a little bit of a *way-hey!* Look. So embarrassing. So what do you want to ask me? Or tell me?'

'We've been using condoms, and I was a bit worried because one time it split and I thought I might get pregnant, but obviously I didn't.' The words all came out in a rush, and I put my arm round her shoulder, sad to think of my little girl – my not so little girl – worrying about something like that on her own. Not on her *own* own, obviously, because she would've told Joe, but without me to reassure her. 'So I was wondering about going on the pill…?'

'I think that's probably a very good idea,' I said, and she looked relieved. 'Very sensible. It's much more reliable, as long as you remember to take it. You do know that at your age, you could've just gone to the doctor and asked for it, and she wouldn't have told me?'

'I know, but I wanted to talk to you about it. I didn't want to hide it from you.'

'Oh, baby,' I said, my voice going husky. Daisy rolled her eyes.

'I knew you'd go all mushy,' she said, but she looked happy. I pulled her in for a hug and we stood there for a while. Germaine rushed over and sat at our feet, looking up, clearly thinking, *Oh dear Lord, they're being soppy again*, but she didn't bark or anything.

Finally Daisy pulled away. 'You're vibrating,' she said.

'I am?' I patted myself down, and then stopped when I felt my phone in my jeans pocket. 'Oh, I am. Don't usually get a signal up here.' I pulled the phone out and looked at the caller ID, suddenly wishing I hadn't got a signal after all. It was Maurice. I grimaced and answered it. 'Maurice, hi! How are you?'

'Don't you *how are you* me, Jodie!' Maurice sounded furious, and I thought I could guess why. 'What the bloody hell is your husband playing at, arresting Tim?' *Bingo*.

'Ah,' I said, and I heard him scoff down the end of the phone.

'Ah is about right,' he said. 'What's going on?'

'Now don't go panicking about it,' I said. 'No one thinks Tim is a murderer—'

'He is *NOT* a murderer!'

'No, I know he isn't, and so does Nathan,' I said, thankful that Maurice couldn't see my face. 'When we eventually charge someone with Kirsty's murder, the Crown Prosecution Service will have to review all the evidence before deciding whether we – I mean, the police – have got a case.'

'So?'

'So at the moment, there is some evidence that could possibly make it look like Tim did it – I know, I know, he didn't – just a couple of small things, but if Nathan ignores it and the CPS see it, they could say he didn't follow the proper process and that could make Tim look guilty in itself. Nathan has to talk to Tim and look into this evidence now to prove that he didn't do it, so that there are no accusations or recriminations against either of them later on. And I doubt very much that he's actually been arrested, just taken in for questioning.'

'Hmm,' said Maurice. I wasn't sure if that meant he bought what I was saying or not.

'Trust me, going through this now is actually a good thing for Tim, because he'll be ruled out and then the police won't have to bother him again.'

'Are you sure?'

'Absolutely,' I said, gritting my teeth. Daisy was watching me, her eyes wide. 'This just clears the way for the police to find the real killer.'

'And they know Tim's innocent?'

'Of course Tim's innocent. Everyone knows that.' I certainly *hoped* that.

'Well… okay. I'm sorry to have a go at you, only I was worried.'

'That's understandable. The whole thing has been horrible, hasn't it? But don't worry. Tim will be back in your loving arms before you even have a chance to miss him.'

'You promise?'

'I promise.' Daisy shook her head as I disconnected the call. 'What?'

'I hope for your sake Nathan does let Tim go, otherwise you won't be doing any more catering jobs for Penstowan District Council…'

Chapter Nine

I vowed to carefully screen any incoming calls after that, but Nathan obviously hadn't arrested any more of our friends because I didn't get any other irate partners ringing me up to give me an ear bashing. As I stood in the kitchen making dinner (pork chops with sage and caramelised apples, served with mashed potatoes – real winter comfort food) I went over the evidence against Tim.

There wasn't a lot of it, but… Someone had claimed to have seen him in the corridor near the storage area during the murder window. Correction: they had seen someone dressed as Widow Twankey, but in a costume that Tim wasn't due to wear until the final scene of the show. Why would he change out of one costume into another to kill Kirsty? It made sense if the murderer was dressing up to avoid being recognised, or to throw suspicion on someone else, but in this case Tim would be dressing up *as himself*; the only person Tim was making look guilty was Tim. It didn't make sense. To me, that was enough to cast doubt on everything else. But then other people who had been in the green room when Tim had claimed to be in there didn't remember seeing him – although one or two others thought they did. *Bloody actors*, I thought, probably uncharitably. *They're all completely self-obsessed, even the amateur ones. They wouldn't notice a murderer right in front of them, even if he was jumping up and down waving an axe.* There were people backstage who would've been more reliable witnesses, I thought, not least of all Daisy and Tony, but neither of them had been anywhere near the crime scene or the green room. (Tony had apparently been going over a stunt that was set up for the finale, involving a trap door in the stage, with Jocasta. He'd told me privately that he was absolutely terrified of it going wrong, and so of course I was bitterly disappointed that he'd got out of doing it.)

And then there was the lipstick. No one else's costume involved wearing bright red lipstick. None of the crew had been wearing lipstick, not noticeably, anyway. Had any audience members been wearing it? Possibly, but then Penstowan wasn't the sort of place most of us dressed up like that, not even for a night at the theatre.

'Wow, that smells good,' said Nathan, coming in. He came up behind me and put his arms round me, kissing me on the cheek. 'I'm knackered. It's been a long day.'

'It must be tiring, arresting our friends,' I said, and he let go of me.

'What are you talking about?'

'Maurice rang me up to berate me about you hauling Tim off to the station in handcuffs,' I said. Nathan scoffed.

'Handcuffs? I know Tim's the actor, but you've got to admit Maurice does a good line in theatrics as well.' He shook his head. 'You know I never use handcuffs unless someone's actually waving their arms about trying to lamp someone. And Tim's not under arrest.'

'No?'

'No. We asked him to come down to the station to answer some questions, which, yes, now I say it out loud does sound like you're being arrested, but that's not true.' He sneaked a slither of apple off the chopping board and ate it.

'Couldn't you have just talked to him at home?'

'With Maurice hanging around and butting in every five seconds? No, not really. And we needed a DNA sample from him and that's just easier at the station.' He looked at me. 'Are you really upset with me? Maurice shouldn't have rung you and had a go, but I can't ignore the evidence. God knows we've got precious little of it.'

'I know.' I sighed. 'It's just difficult when there's loads of our friends involved in a case, isn't it? I mean, I know Tony didn't do it – don't look at me like that, *you* know Tony didn't do it as well – but half of Penstowan are in the cast and the crew, and I hate the fact that it could be one of them.'

'Yeah,' he said. 'I do know how you feel. I've grown to love all these Cornish weirdos...'

'Oi!' I said.

'Oh come on, it's an amateur dramatics society, none of them are normal, and that's saying something for down here…'

'Just you keep talking that way, mister, and there'll be no pork chops for you!' I said, waving the potato masher at him.

Nathan laughed and caught my arm, pulling me towards him. 'I'm winding you up. I hate the thought that someone we know could be a killer, too. But all we can do is follow the evidence until it proves or disproves something.'

'I suppose so,' I said.

We'd just sat down to dinner – Mum had graciously agreed to eat with us when I told her what was on the menu – when the doorbell rang.

'I'll get it,' said Daisy, leaping up and following Germaine, who had very kindly got there first but who lacked the opposable thumbs required to open the door.

We heard voices, and then she came back in followed by Sunil, who looked very embarrassed to have caught us eating.

'Oh, I'm so sorry to interrupt your meal – I can come back—' he said.

'Nonsense, come in,' I said. 'Please take a seat. There's more food in the kitchen if you'd like some?'

'What are you doing?' hissed Mum in a very loud stage whisper as Sunil sat down at the table. 'It's pork! They can't eat pork.'

'Sunil's Hindu, aren't you?' said Daisy. 'Hindus can eat pork.'

'No they can't! Or beef!' insisted Mum, again in the weird stage whisper that everyone, including Sunil, could hear. I glared at her, trying to send her *Be quiet, woman, you're actually making it worse* vibes, but Sunil saved us.

'No, Mrs Parker, I can eat pork if I want to, but thank you for being concerned,' said Sunil politely. 'Thank you for the offer, Jodie, but I'm fine. I have some news on the case.' He looked at Nathan. 'Normally I'd ask to talk to you in private, but…'

Nathan gave a resigned sigh. 'No, it's okay, unless you're going to tell me who did it?' He looked at his DS, who shook his head. 'No, I thought not. Go on.'

'I talked to Li Zhāng about the lipstick,' said Sunil, pulling out his notebook. 'She said the actors mostly did their own makeup, including Tim, and that they left all the makeup behind in the dressing rooms. So I went back to the theatre and took all the red lipsticks I could find. There were several different shades in amongst it all, but the one Tim's been using was set aside so he could find it. That one's called "Sundown Seduction".' He blushed a little as he read out the name.

'Okay,' said Nathan, waiting for him to continue.

'Well, I went into the wardrobe and I found another costume made in the same fabric and in the same colour as the skirt with the blood and lipstick on, and I smeared some Sundown Seduction on it, and look…' From his bag he took an evidence bag, and a piece of fabric, and placed them both on the table. We all craned over our dinner plates to look.

'They're not the same,' I said, and everyone else nodded.

'I also tested the other lipsticks, Velvet Vixen—' he pointed to another smear of lipstick '—Scarlet Siren, here, and Crimson Crush, here, and none of them match the original piece of fabric.' He sat back, looking pleased with himself.

'You're right, they're completely different shades of red,' said Nathan.

'Hmm,' I said, 'but maybe the way they got onto the fabric makes a difference.'

'What do you mean?' asked Daisy.

'If you're just drawing or dabbing it on the fabric straight from the lipstick, then it's going to go on thicker, isn't it? Which could be why the colours look darker or deeper in tone. Whereas the smear came from lipstick in situ – actually on someone's lips.'

'I already thought of that,' said Sunil, blushing again and self-consciously wiping his lips with his hand. Nathan laughed.

'Sunil, that is excellent detective work. Trying out four different lippies in pursuit of the law. Well done.'

'Thanks, Guv.' He looked even more pleased with himself. 'None of them were really my shade.'

'So does this mean Tim's in the clear?' I asked. 'Because it was already pretty tenuous, so without the lipstick it looks even less likely.'

'Well, Forensics have sent off a swab from the lipstick for testing, so we can't officially rule him out until that comes back,' said Nathan, 'but unless it does come back with his DNA on it, I think we can safely say we're still looking for our murderer.'

'I was thinking about that,' said Daisy, pushing her dinner plate away. 'You need to find other people who might have had a reason to kill Kirsty, yeah?'

'Yes,' said Nathan.

'Well, I did catch the end of her and Ellie having a big row, like really going at each other, but that was ages ago when rehearsals first started,' said Daisy. 'I hadn't really thought about it again until just now, because they seemed to have made it up. I didn't see them arguing again, anyway. I don't think you could call them mates, though.'

'Did you hear what it was about?' Nathan asked, but Daisy shook her head.

'No, but whatever it was, they were both proper furious with each other.'

'Ellie, Ellie... why does that name ring a bell? Where have I heard it?' I pondered.

'She was Kirsty's understudy,' said Mum. 'Someone brought her name up at the meeting yesterday morning.'

'Oh yeah.' I turned to Nathan. 'See? I told you it was a ruthlessly ambitious understudy, bumping off the talent to get their own shot at the big time.'

'The Penstowan Players' annual Christmas panto being the big time?' asked Nathan. 'In what universe?'

'Actors are all mad,' I said, and then turned to Mum. 'Present company included. No offence.'

'None taken.'

'What's Ellie's surname?' asked Sunil, turning over a leaf in his note pad. 'I'll go back to the office and have a look at her statement again—'

'No you won't,' said Nathan firmly. 'It's Sunday night. You've got a wife and two beautiful babies waiting at home for you.'

'Yeah… Eesha's fine, she knows work's important—'

'Sunil Bakshi,' I said sternly, 'do *not* tell me you're putting work before your family? Are you using this as an excuse not to go home?'

'No, of course not,' he started, but then he looked at my face and collapsed in his chair in self-loathing. 'No, you're right, I am. It's a madhouse. The babies won't sleep and Eesha can't cope and we're both so tired…'

'I thought your mum-in-law was staying with you?' asked Nathan.

'She was with us for two months,' said Sunil, with a shudder that spoke volumes. 'That's why I didn't take my paternity leave until a couple of weeks ago. She drove us both mad, but at least the house was tidy and we had food cooked for us. But finally Eesha had had enough and sent her home, so I had the fortnight off to help her. But now…'

Mum got up and went over to Sunil, patting him on the shoulder.

'I know having little ones is tough, especially having two little ones at the same time,' she said, 'but hiding out here isn't the answer. Go home, order a takeaway so neither of you has to cook, and just enjoy being with your family. Ignore the mess, it ain't going to kill you to have washing all over the house and dirty dishes in the sink for a few days. No sleep is hard, but it'll pass. And tell Eesha I'll pop round in the morning to give her a hand.'

'*That'll* make her tidy up,' I murmured under my breath. Nathan snorted.

'Thank you, Mrs Parker,' said Sunil. 'That's very kind of you. And you're right, I should go home.'

'Come on, I'll walk you out,' said Nathan, standing up and leading his exhausted detective sergeant out of the room.

'And *that*,' muttered Daisy under her breath, 'is why I'm going on the pill.'

Chapter Ten

Nathan got up early the next day and went for a run before work, leaving me drowsing in bed. I considered getting up, throwing my tracksuit on and going with him for all of about three seconds, but I've never enjoyed running, not even when I was in the police force and had to stay fit. As a civilian, I can't see the point of running unless someone's chasing you, and my days of being the one chasing had long gone. Plus it was dark and cold outside, and the dog had sneaked in at some point during the night and she was far too cosy on my feet for me to disturb her, and—

'All right, lazy bones, I don't need your excuses,' said Nathan. 'Stay here and keep the bed warm.'

'Are you getting back in after your run, then?' I said, attempting to strike a seductive pose without dislodging the dog.

'I'll be all sweaty and out of breath,' he said.

'You think that would put me off? It's like you don't even know me.'

Nathan laughed and lent down to kiss me. 'You say that now, but when I come back all smelly you'll go—' he put on a high-pitched voice that was nothing like mine '—eww, Nath!'

'Go on then, go, reject me…'

'Okay then,' he said, and he left. I looked at the dog.

'Looks like it's just you and me, Germaine,' I said. 'At least you still love me.' She raised her head and looked at me, then got up and padded out of the room. 'Traitor,' I muttered.

I could hear her downstairs, pawing at the back door, so I dragged myself out of bed, pulled on an old hoody and my fluffy slipper boots, and headed down to the kitchen. I let her out into the garden to 'do her business', as Mum euphemistically called it, and put the kettle on.

'Ooh, you making tea?' I jumped out of my skin as Mum spoke behind me.

'Bloody hell, woman, stop doing that! I'm going to replace your slippers with tap shoes, so I can hear you coming. What's wrong with your own kettle?'

'I can't help it if I fancied having my morning cuppa in the company of my beautiful daughter, can I?' She gave me an ingratiating smile, but I refused to be gratiated.

'Okay, I'll make you a cup of tea and then you can tell me what you're after…'

Mum sat at the kitchen table with a glass of water and her daily tablets (one for angina, one for high blood pressure and one for her cholesterol), while I made the tea and took my own daily tablet. I'd just started HRT because, as well as getting a bit moody (who, me?!), I'd been having hot flushes since just after our wedding, and Nathan had finally convinced me that I was probably overheating due to the onset of perimenopause, and not just because I was now married to a sexy younger man – his words. I also had some supplements that my friend Debbie had suggested. Debbie was a nurse and had retrained recently as a menopause champion at our local GP surgery, so I was constantly getting messages from her saying stuff like 'start taking collagen NOW!!' and 'change to soy milk'. Bless her, it was handy to have a friend like that, but if I'd taken all the supplements and health foods she'd suggested, I'd have had no room to eat *proper* food like chocolate and crisps.

'State of us,' said Mum, indicating all the pill bottles.

'Breakfast of champions,' I said, chewing a magnesium gummy bear. 'Now, what are you after?'

'I'm not—' she started, and then stopped. 'Okay, I said I'd pop round to see Eesha and help her with the housework, didn't I? But it's been a long time since I changed a nappy—'

'Or did any housework,' I said. 'Despite living in a house…'

'Exactly.' Mum sat back with a satisfied smile, like she'd made her case. I sighed.

'You want me to come and give you a hand?'

She attempted to look surprised. 'Oh, would you? What a lovely, unexpected offer.'

'Yeah, right,' I said, trying to sound grumpy, but I wasn't really. 'No, it's fine, I've not got anything else to do today, and I do feel for poor Eesha. But it's been a long time since I changed a nappy, too.'

'Oh my God, you're not pregnant, are you?' Daisy stood in the doorway, still looking half asleep. 'Is that why you asked me if I was, yesterday?'

'Of course I'm not pregnant,' I said. 'That ship has long sailed. We're talking about Eesha.'

'Oh yeah, of course.' Daisy yawned and sat down.

'You up to anything today?' asked Mum.

'No, why?'

Oh you poor misguided fool, I thought, you have just sailed straight into your grandmother's trap...

'We're going to give her a hand today, you can come and help.'

Daisy sat up straight, suddenly a lot more awake. 'No, no, actually, I'm meeting Jade—'

'Jade's away,' said Mum calmly.

'Not Jade, I mean some of the others from sixth form. We're going to make a start on some of the coursework that's due in when we go back in January.'

'Doing homework on the first day of the Christmas holidays? You're dedicated,' I said, grinning at her.

'Well, you know, grades are important...'

Mum cackled. 'Relax, sweetheart, I'm only kidding. Eesha won't want a house full of people fussing around her.'

'Oh good,' I said. 'Does that mean I don't have to go?'

'No.'

So that's how I found myself in Sunil and Eesha's pretty little cottage on the edge of town. Pretty, but cramped, and overflowing with baby stuff.

'Thank you so much,' said Eesha, looking overwhelmed and a bit tearful. 'It's all starting to get on top of me, and I don't know where to start…'

If this was the result of her and Sunil being left on their own for a fortnight, I thought, then our intervention was just in time.

'The first thing you need to do,' said Mum, putting the kettle on – tea is a big part of any intervention in the UK, especially one where exhausted mothers are involved, 'the first thing you need to do is give yourself permission to live in a bit of a mess.'

Eesha looked even more tearful, but also relieved. 'My mother is so organised, she would be ashamed if she saw this.'

'I say this from a place of love, and as a grandmother myself,' said Mum, 'but blow your mum and her standards. This is *your* house, and *your* family. I bet your mum irons socks, doesn't she?'

'She does,' said Eesha. 'Don't you?'

Mum and I looked at each other and laughed.

'You've got to prioritise,' said Mum. 'Sunil's a grown man, he can make sure he's got clean pants and a shirt for work. All you need to think about is keeping them beautiful girls of yours fed and watered.'

'I'd just like a shower where I don't have to listen out for them, or have them in the bathroom with me,' Eesha sighed.

'Well that's easily arranged,' I said. 'Drink your tea, then go and have a nice relaxing bath or shower and leave the babies to us. We'll have a bit of a tidy round too. You go and make yourself feel human again.'

Eesha immediately downed her tea and headed upstairs before we could change our minds. One of the twins – I wasn't sure who was who, as at that age babies all basically look like each other – started to grizzle, so I picked her up and snuggled her before she could start the other one off. I nestled her into my chest and sniffed at her head, which might sound weird but honestly, have you ever smelt a baby's head? It's adorable. If you don't know what I'm talking about, don't go and sniff a random baby on the street or anything as you will (rightly) get arrested, just trust me.

'Suits you,' said Mum, and I felt my own eyes get a bit watery.

'Don't,' I warned her. 'My breeding days are over, aren't they, what with my wizened old ovaries. But I do feel bad that I've stopped Nathan from ever having kids of his own.'

'Don't be daft,' said Mum, peering over the top of a pile of stuffed toys that she'd picked off the floor. 'He knew that was the case when you first got together. He wouldn't have married you if it was an issue. He loves being Daisy's stepdad, and that's enough for him.'

'I hope so,' I said, sniffing, but Mum was right; Nathan and I had had this conversation before, and he'd assured me he didn't mind, which was just as well because I really did not want another baby. I wasn't broody – not really – just hormonal. Bloody perimenopause! I never knew if I was going to jump down someone's throat or burst into tears these days.

Mum dumped the toys into a plastic crate and started tidying through the piles of paper and random junk on the dining table. 'This is all junk mail, why haven't they just chucked it away?' She made one pile of advertising leaflets and takeaway menus, and another, much smaller pile of letters and bills. 'Oh dear, goes to show how tired Sunil is,' she said, holding something up. It was the evidence bag containing the lipstick-stained dress, and on the table beside it was the other piece of fabric Sunil had smeared the other lipsticks on.

'Poor Sunil,' I said, 'he's normally so well organised, I'm surprised he left that behind.'

We managed to clear enough stuff away that the floor of the living/dining room was actually visible again, before Eesha came back downstairs. She looked much refreshed, wearing a nice dress (she'd been in a baggy old tracksuit when we'd arrived, which wasn't unusual for me when I wasn't working, but I knew it was out of character for her), and she'd done her hair and makeup.

'You look lovely, dear,' said Mum, and I nodded, but my eyes were drawn to her lips.

'I love that lipstick,' I said. 'I could never pull off a bright red, but it looks great on you.'

'Do you like it? I bought it when I was eight months pregnant and felt huge,' she said, flattered. 'I felt like I needed pampering, so I treated myself. The shade is "Sunset Boulevard", I got it from that organic beauty shop next to Penhaligon's.'

'It's lovely,' I said. 'Have you worn it in front of Sunil before?'

'Only once,' she said, looking puzzled. 'We haven't really gone out since the girls were born, and it feels a bit decadent wearing it around the house.'

'Hmm,' I said, and Mum looked at me.

'Are you thinking what I'm thinking?' she asked me.

'Rarely, but I might be in this case,' I said. Eesha looked even more puzzled. I picked up the piece of fabric Mum had found on the table and held it out to her. 'Do you mind smearing your lips against this?'

'I hope you're not suggesting my wife murdered a woman she didn't even know,' said Sunil. He was staring at the piece of fabric Nathan was holding. I'd brought it straight round to the station, leaving Mum and Eesha chatting over more tea.

'We're not even sure it's the same lipstick yet,' said Nathan. 'Although it does look like the same colour. We'll send the lipstick swab Jodie took off to the lab so they can compare it to the one on the dress.'

'But there's probably loads of women with that lipstick,' said Matt. 'It doesn't really narrow it down, does it?'

I shook my head. 'No, actually, it does. This isn't a brand you can just buy in Boots or wherever, it's an organic brand that's made here in Cornwall. I checked at the shop where Eesha bought it. They're one of only three stores that stock it, as the woman who makes it can only do small batches at a time. I don't even know how you *make* makeup, but apparently she does it in her kitchen at home.'

'So the chances are, if someone in Penstowan was wearing it, they got it from the same shop as Eesha,' said Nathan. 'I wonder if we can track down everyone who's bought it?'

'We – you – might be able to trace a few of them, but the owner tries to get people to pay in cash rather than by card, so she can avoid transaction fees,' I told him. 'If they paid by cash, there's no easy way of tracing them.'

'But you think there might be a hard way of doing it?' Nathan pounced on my wording. I nodded.

'That shop hasn't been going that long, and it's expensive,' I said. 'She has a small core of regular shoppers. She wouldn't give me any names, obviously, but she should do for you. Of course, if it was bought by someone who was just visiting the area she won't know their name.'

'But they're unlikely to have been at the panto,' said Matt. 'And if we're thinking the killer is someone actually involved in the panto, that makes it even less unlikely.'

'Yes,' I said. 'So it might all come to nothing, but what else have you got?'

'Not a lot,' said Nathan. 'But it's a lead. Nice work, babe.'

'That's *Detective* Babe to you,' I said.

'Really?'

'Well, no, not really. That sounded much cooler and far less cheesy when I said it in my head. Have you had any luck tracking down the dodgy teacher? Or Kirsty's ex? And then there was the girl Daisy saw her arguing with—'

'It's all in hand,' said Nathan. 'Now, haven't you got Christmas shopping to do? It's only a few days away.'

'I've got everything apart from the veg for Christmas dinner,' I said, 'so you can't get rid of me that easily.'

Matt coughed into his hand, but it sounded suspiciously like 'not a copper'. Sunil grinned and then hurriedly wiped the smile off his face. I sighed.

'Oh all right, I know it's got nothing to do with me. I just feel a bit useless and unneeded.' I picked up my bag. 'I'll leave you to it.'

I turned and left, but Nathan caught up with me by the door. He took my arm and led me out into the corridor, and then pulled me into a quiet corner.

'Are you okay, babe?' he asked, looking concerned, and all of a sudden I wanted to cry.

'I just feel old and washed up today,' I said, sniffing furiously. 'I've got no work booked in for the whole of December and January, Daisy doesn't need me anymore, you're busy with work – I know it's not your fault, I'm not complaining – and I can't do the one thing I was really good at, because I'm not a copper. I feel like I don't have a purpose anymore.'

He pulled me into a big hug. 'Of course you have a

purpose. Me and Daisy and your mum will always need you, not to mention the dog—' I laughed and sniffed at the same time. 'I know officially you're not a copper, but you always help me, don't you?'

'Your arrest rates would be way down without me,' I said, and he laughed.

'That's more like the Jodie I know and love,' he said. He smiled at me gently. 'Is this – is this anything to do with seeing Eesha and the twins?'

'No,' I said, 'not really. It's just my hormones.' I sighed, burrowing my head into his shoulder. He stroked my hair for a moment until I felt better. I pulled myself together and smiled up at him bravely. 'I'm all right now,' I said.

'You sure?'

'Yes.'

'Good. If Daisy's around, why don't you take her out for some cake or something?' suggested Nathan. 'Take your mind off us looking for Jamie Westall and Ellie Huggins.'

It was only after I left that I realised Nathan had (deliberately, I suspected) just given me the full names of two of our suspects...

Chapter Eleven

'I know Ellie from the panto, of course,' said Daisy, 'but I don't think I've met Jamie. He's Ellie's boyfriend.'

We were sitting in a corner booth in Rowe's, eating chocolate cake and drinking hot chocolate topped with whipped cream and marshmallows while Germaine tucked herself under the table and waited for crumbs to be forthcoming. What I'd intended to be a devil may care, sod-it-who-counts-calories-these-days-anyway afternoon treat had actually made me feel a bit sick. Maybe there *was* such a thing as too much chocolate after all, even at Christmas. Who'd have thunk it?

I toyed with the chunk of cake left on my plate. I was defeated, by the cake if not the case, but I wasn't ready to admit it yet. 'No, he was *Kirsty's* ex.'

'Maybe he was, but now he's going out with Ellie.' Daisy pushed her plate away, grimacing at the leftover cake. 'She's always going on about him. She even said something about

Westall being a better surname than Huggins.' She stuck her finger in some cake frosting and sucked it thoughtfully. 'She's not wrong there.'

'Maybe that's what she and Kirsty were arguing about?' I said. 'Did you hear anything that might suggest that?'

'Yeah…' Daisy looked thoughtful. 'I thought Ellie was telling her to stay out of it, or stay away from her or something, but maybe she was warning her to stay away from Jamie? Maybe she thought Kirsty wanted to get back with him.'

'Were there any young men hanging around after rehearsals or during the panto that could be him?'

'I don't know, you know how many people were in the cast and crew, I didn't know all of them. Hang on.' She got out her phone and typed something in. 'Here we go. Jamie Westall. There's a few…' She showed me her phone screen. 'It's obviously not him – he's bald and he looks about seventy.'

'He's fifty-three!' I said, reading the caption under the photo. According to Google there were quite a few Jamie or James Westalls out there. 'What about that one? He's nice-looking.'

'Who said he's nice-looking?' Daisy rolled her eyes. 'He might be pig ugly.'

'One, not a nice thing to say about that one—' I pointed to one of the less attractive Jamies '—and two, Kirsty was pretty, and she was a nice person, and I think she would've gone out with someone more in her league. Like him.'

'Except he lives in Edinburgh…' Daisy and I studied the

screen again, then we both pointed to the same young man and said, 'Him!'

'James Westall. Twenty-nine. A vet in Hatherleigh,' said Daisy. At the word 'vet' Germaine, under the table, gave a little whine.

'Lot of farms round there,' I said, reaching down and patting her head. 'If Nana was here she'd make some joke about him spending half his time with his arm up a cow's backside—'

'—and then going to work. Thank God she's not here, then.' Daisy sat back, studying the screen again, lips pursed. 'This must be him,' she said, 'there aren't any others who live anywhere near here.'

'You don't look convinced,' I said. She was getting into the investigating, I could tell; she was a chip off the old block. If she ever changed her mind about getting into political photojournalism (which was her current career plan), she would make a brilliant detective.

'I can see him and Kirsty together,' she said, 'but him and Ellie? Nah. Ellie's a bit… immature? Kirsty was really bright and intelligent, you could have a good conversation with her. Ellie just wants to be Cornwall's answer to a Kardashian or something.' To prove her point, she pulled up an Instagram picture of a young woman, heavily made up and pouting at the camera.

'To be fair, the Kardashians have made a ton of money and been very successful, just for wearing stuff and posing,' I said. 'That might not be the kind of look I'd go for, but some men like that sort of thing.'

'Well, I suppose he's used to dealing with dumb animals…'

'Oh, meow! That's really not a nice thing to say. Remember the sisterhood. Be the woman who straightens another woman's crown, not tries to throttle her with it.'

'I know, but *Ellie*? I don't see it.'

'Anyway, whether they were actually Love's Young Dream or not makes no difference. It sounds like Ellie thought they were, and she didn't want Kirsty getting in the way. Does she wear organic lipstick?'

'Does who wear organic lipstick?' Debbie sat down beside me with a mince pie and a coffee. She eyed the remains of my chocolate cake and the smear of whipped cream that ran around the edge of my mug. 'The healthy eating plan's going well, I see.' She moved her own plate further into the centre of the table as Germaine, the scent of pastry reaching her nostrils, popped up and lay her head on Debbie's lap, looking up at her beseechingly.

'Hate to tell you this, it might have sultanas in it but your mince pie doesn't count as one of your five a day,' I said. 'Germaine, stop begging, it's unbecoming.'

'No, but I did order a soy milk latte. Phytoestrogens, innit? Good for ladies of our age.' Debbie took a sip of her coffee and tried not to grimace.

'Is it nice, that soy milk?' I asked, grinning.

'It takes a bit of getting used to,' she admitted. 'Callum keeps giving me stick about it, but I'm just trying to look after myself. He's taken the kids Christmas shopping in

Exeter. It'll be mad, this close to Christmas. I did all my shopping in October.'

'Freak,' muttered Daisy, but not maliciously. Debbie laughed.

'That's what Callum said. How are you? Did you know Kirsty when she worked at the school? She used to help Tilly with her maths, she's really upset about it.'

'Poor Tilly,' I said. 'Daisy only really got to know her through the panto, didn't you, sweetheart? It's all very upsetting.'

'Given you something to do, though,' said Debbie, her eyes gleaming. 'Come on, spill. You were talking about the investigation, weren't you?'

'Might've been,' I said, but there was no point trying to hide anything from Debbie, she was too good at winkling things out of me.

'Okay, so what about the lipstick? Fill me in.'

I filled her in.

'Ooh, from that shop in Fore Street? They've got some nice stuff in there but it's bloody expensive. I really liked some of the lipstick but it were nearly thirty quid a pop, and I don't even wear it that often. When I were Ellie's age I'd have been buying my makeup in Superdrug or somewhere like that, not some overpriced organic place.'

'That's probably a fair point,' I conceded. 'I don't know what Ellie does for a living, but there are very few jobs round here where you'd earn enough to drop a load of money on makeup.' I thought for a moment. 'I mean, *I* wouldn't drop that much money, but then I'm not really into it. If Ellie really wants to be some fashion influencer or something, then it would probably be more important to her.'

'But then she'd be buying stuff from Sephora or MAC or whatever, not some little shop in Penstowan,' said Debbie. 'Tilly's always on at me to take her to Sephora when we go and see my mum and dad in Manchester.'

'Yeah, *Manchester*,' said Daisy. 'There's nothing like that down here, is there?'

'Anyway,' I said, attempting to get the conversation back on track, 'the whole business with the lipstick could turn out to be nothing. It was on a piece of clothing in a costume department. Someone could've tried it on ages ago and got lippy on it by accident. We don't even know if it's Kirsty's blood on it yet.'

'So why's Nathan focusing on it?' asked Debbie.

'He's not really, he just has to look at every lead that comes his way. And so far, there aren't many of them.' I shook my head. 'I dunno, I think we need to be finding a motive. What about this Jamie?' I tapped the screen of Daisy's phone. Debbie looked at the photo we'd found of the vet.

'I don't think "Sunset Boulevard" would suit him, do you?' asked Debbie. 'Not with that skin tone. Too ruddy-cheeked and outdoorsy.'

'Can we forget about the lipstick?'

'You brought it up,' said Daisy.

'I know, and now I'm dropping it,' I said firmly.

'Let's think motives. Ellie wanted Kirsty out of the way because she thought she would steal Jamie from her.'

Daisy nodded. 'She definitely wanted her away from Jamie.'

'Cool. On the other hand, if Jamie's the killer, he wanted her back but she wasn't interested—'

'If I can't have you, no one can,' said Debbie, and I nodded.

'Yes. Or, she knew something about him and was threatening to tell Ellie about it, which would make her dump him, so he needed Kirsty to be silenced before she ruined that relationship.'

'Hmmm…' said Daisy doubtfully.

'I know, it doesn't seem as likely, but at the moment we're just theorising, aren't we?'

'That means "making stuff up", doesn't it?' asked Debbie. 'Because we're good at that.'

'Yes, we are. So that's two people who had a, let's call it "intense" relationship with Kirsty, and their possible motives.'

'Okay,' said Debbie, rubbing her hands together. 'Who else have we got?'

'We can't ignore the teacher she had the run-in with at the school,' I said. 'He sounds like a right piece of work. Not only was he having a relationship with a student – we think – but he then tried to turn it around and make Kirsty look like a stalker.'

'I heard about that!' said Debbie. 'Taking out a

restraining order, honestly! She was lovely. If I ever meet that nasty little pervert I'll give him a piece of my mind.'

'Go on, then,' said Daisy. 'He's just over there.'

'Where?' Debbie and I cried, both twisting around in our seats to see where Daisy was pointing, Debbie inadvertently dumping the dog on the floor in the process. Daisy rolled her eyes.

'You'd be *really good* at undercover work, wouldn't you? Don't let him see you, he'll be taking out another restraining order in a minute.'

'Yeah, but I've got a special relationship with the police in this town, he'd have no chance…' Nevertheless I grabbed Debbie's arm to stop her standing up and full on staring at the man. We both peered a little more discreetly in the direction Daisy had indicated. 'Why didn't you tell me he was in here?'

'Well, one, he only came in here about five minutes ago, and two, he doesn't look like the sort of person who'd be wearing lipstick either.'

'Can we forget about the lipstick? Please?'

'You started it,' muttered Debbie.

Mark Matheson sat on his own at a table near the counter, sipping his drink. He looked to be in his early thirties, well dressed and surprisingly attractive. He certainly didn't fit the mental image I'd conjured up of a creepy older bloke perving over a much younger student. His phone was on the table and every now and then he'd look at it and type something, obviously replying to a text message.

'I wonder who he's texting,' sniffed Debbie. 'I wonder whether they're actually old enough to have taken their GCSEs this time.'

'So he's here now,' I said. 'I wonder if he was here in Penstowan on Friday night? And if he was at the panto?'

'Only one way to find out,' said Daisy, standing up. I put my hand out to stop her.

'Oh no you don't! What do you think you're doing?'

'Mum, look at me. I'm the right age group for him not to suspect me.'

Debbie shuddered. 'You mean you're young enough for him to fancy you?'

'What? No, bloody hell! I mean I was at that school while he was teaching. Jade was in his class. I can go over and pretend that I was one of his students and that I'm surprised to see him.'

'I don't know…' I said, doubtfully, but she was my daughter and Mum's granddaughter, and if she'd made her mind up there would be no way to stop her.

'Mum, I can do this. If one of you goes blundering over there it'll be obvious you're questioning him about the murder. Let me do it.'

I stared into her eyes for a second, and then let go of her hand. 'Okay. But don't ask him about Kirsty. At this point we just want to know if he was here on Friday.'

We watched as Daisy wandered over to the sandwich chiller and picked up a sausage bap, then as she turned she gave a start of recognition. I leapt to my feet and headed for the counter as discreetly as I could, pretending to browse the cakes while I eavesdropped, while Debbie kept hold of Germaine to stop her following.

'Oh my God, Mr Matheson? Is that you?'

Mark Matheson looked up from his phone in surprise, and then smiled. 'Yes, er…?'

'Rochelle Lowe,' said Daisy, twisting a strand of hair in her fingers. Flirting, the little minx. 'I was in your class at Penstowan Comp. Not for very long, though. I couldn't get my head around Physics, I ended up doing Biology instead.' She smiled at him and, disarmed, he smiled back.

'Rochelle? Oh yes, I remember you,' said Matheson, a little awkwardly. He obviously had no recollection of either Daisy or whoever Rochelle was (if she was a real person), but was trying to be polite.

'Are you back, then? I *told* Jade it was you I saw, getting fish and chips from the Captain's Table on Thursday.'

'Oh, you're Jade's friend? Of course…' Matheson relaxed a little; he clearly remembered Jade. 'That wasn't me, though. I didn't get here until Friday.'

'Really? He looked just like you. Are you coming back to school? Jade will be pleased, she's doing A level Physics.'

'Oh no, I'm just here visiting family for Christmas. I'm teaching at a school in Bristol these days.' His phone beeped and he looked relieved. He picked it up. 'That's my mum now, actually. I was waiting for her to finish at the hairdressers.' He drained his coffee and stood up. 'Nice to see you again, Rochelle. Merry Christmas to you.'

'And to you, sir.' Daisy gave him a big smile and watched him leave, then put the sausage bap back in the chiller, ignoring the stern look the barista behind the counter gave her. The two of us rejoined Debbie, who had given up trying to look discreet and had been trying to lipread the conversation, without success. Daisy repeated everything for her benefit.

'So he *was* here on Friday,' I said.

'Could he have been at the pantomime?' asked Debbie.

'No, because if he was, Nathan or one of the others would've taken his statement and they'd be interviewing him.' I thought for a moment. 'But interesting that he was in the area. I wonder if there was any way he could've got backstage?'

'Yeah…' said Daisy. 'I don't know, I don't think he had anything to do with it.'

'How'd you work that out?' said Debbie.

'Mum, you saw him. I knew you were watching from beside the gingerbread… He looked dead awkward, but that's because he had no idea who Rochelle was.'

'Is there a real Rochelle?'

'Nah, I made her up. But he didn't look awkward or shifty or anything like that when he mentioned he got here on Friday. Surely if he'd dropped his stuff off at his mum's, popped over to the panto, murdered Kirsty and then gone home, he wouldn't have said he got here that day? He'd have lied, or just said he wasn't here on Thursday.'

'Hmm,' I said. 'You might have a point there. But just because he didn't look guilty, it doesn't mean he isn't.'

'He probably didn't look guilty when he was lying

about sexting with a fifteen-year-old, either,' pointed out Debbie.

'True…' Daisy shook her head. 'Honestly, what was she thinking? He's an old bloke.' Debbie and I exchanged looks. Matheson looked considerably younger than either of us. 'I mean, he's not ancient, but he was old enough to be her dad.'

'I'd like to know what *he* was thinking, for exactly the same reason,' I said. 'But the main thing I'd like to know is, where was he on Friday night?'

Chapter Twelve

Daisy and I took the dog for a brisk walk before we headed home. A bitterly cold wind had picked up and the air felt gritty with sand, so we avoided the beach and marched along Fore Street instead, up the hill and then round the one-way system, past the post office and the council offices, before heading for the car.

As we passed the library we almost literally ran into Maggie Tiddy, who was just coming through the big glass doors clutching a couple of books to her chest. She had a woolly hat rammed down over her ears and a big scarf wrapped around her neck, over her mouth and almost up to her eyes – it was a wonder she could breathe.

'Look out, Maggie!' I said cheerfully, sidestepping to get out of her way and almost tripping over Germaine's lead in the process. She tugged the scarf down and looked at us sheepishly.

'Sorry, I didn't see you there,' she said. 'The weather's turned proper nasty, hasn't it?'

'Those'll keep you warm, though,' I said, indicating her library books which were of the, shall we say, rather spicy variety. She giggled.

'They are a bit naughty,' she said. 'What's a girl to do when her husband works away from home a few nights a week? Without my books and *Bridgerton* on the telly, I don't know what I'd do.'

Daisy wrinkled her nose in disgust – no doubt at the idea of someone over the age of thirty feeling fruity – but didn't say anything.

'I prefer a good murder mystery myself,' I said, and Maggie rolled her eyes.

'I'd never have guessed that,' she said. 'Ooh, talking of which, you were there on Friday, weren't you? I saw you and Nathan right down the front. What do you think? Who done it?'

'It's a tricky one,' I said carefully. 'Kirsty was well loved, wasn't she? I don't know why anyone would want to kill her.'

Maggie scoffed. 'You must be losing your touch. I can think of someone right now. That teacher. Mr Matheson.'

'Do you know him?'

'Our Ryan had him for Physics in his last year of school. Arrogant, he was. I met him at Parents' Evening, never liked him or the way he went on.' She scoffed again. 'Although I was obviously completely safe, as I was far too old for him.'

'You might be right,' I said. 'He's back and all, we just saw him in Rowe's.'

'I know he's back,' she said. 'I sat next to him at the panto.'

Daisy and I exchanged surprised looks. 'He was there? But he's not down on the list Nathan's got. He didn't give a statement.'

'No, I don't suppose he did – he left at the interval.' She smiled grimly. 'Nothing to do with me constantly mentioning how good Kirsty was and what a lovely person she was or anything.' She looked suddenly disturbed. 'Oh no, you don't think I wound him up too much and he…?'

'No, of course not,' I said. 'If he did do anything, it's because he's not a nice person, not because you were talking to him.'

'Brian's always telling me to think before I speak,' she said. 'Maybe he's right.'

'No, of course he isn't,' I said. I could feel Daisy stiffening beside me, clamping her own mouth shut, because while Maggie was a lovely person she could talk for Great Britain in the Olympics. Germaine thought Maggie was a lovely person too, and chose this moment to lie on the ground in front of her, begging for attention.

'Oh Germaine, look at you!' Maggie bent down and made a fuss of her, then straightened up again with a groan. 'Right, I'd better get going. No B&B guests this week, thank goodness, but plenty of un-paying family ones are coming down for Christmas. I won't have much time for reading these!'

We said our goodbyes and watched Maggie scuttle down the road, heading for the B&B she ran, which overlooked the beach.

'So, what now?' asked Daisy.

'Home.'

'Really?' She looked at me in amazement. 'But the police station's right there. You not going in and telling Nathan what we've found out?'

I thought of Matt saying, 'not a copper', and Sunil smiling, and felt heat rising in my cheeks. It was daft – they were both friends, and I knew deep down that they were only messing about – but I didn't feel like I could face them.

'No, it can wait until he gets home,' I said. Daisy looked at me, concerned.

'Who are you and what have you done with my mother?'

I was desperate to tell Nathan what we'd learnt about Mark Matheson though, so I was relieved when he came through the door at five o'clock on the dot.

'Blimey, you're early again,' I said. 'Have you solved the murder already? Or are you keeping office hours now?'

'Not a lot we can do until we get the forensic results back on everything,' he said, putting his bag on the table. 'Still waiting for the full DNA report on the murder weapon – there's too many fingerprints on the handle to be useful, but the killer might've left something else on it.

I'm not holding out a lot of hope on that, though. Analysis of the blood and lipstick on the fabric will take another few days yet.' He sat down heavily on a kitchen stool. 'What else is there? Oh yeah, we've got Kirsty's laptop, once we get into that we'll be able to see if there's anything useful on there. Haven't been able to get into her phone yet, but the tech guys are working on it. And we tracked down the teacher she had a problem with, Mark Matheson. He moved to Bristol, got a job as head of science at some fancy school, so it looks like he's gone up in the world. I can't see him thinking she ruined his life and wanting revenge.'

'Maybe not. But we tracked Mark Matheson down too. To Rowe's.'

'He's in Penstowan?' Nathan looked surprised. 'What's he doing here?'

'He was waiting for his mum to have her hair done when we spoke to him.' Nathan raised an eyebrow. 'Well, not we – Daisy. She managed to get out of him when he arrived.'

'When?'

'Friday.'

'Interesting…'

'Not as interesting as the fact that he was at the panto on Friday night.'

'Bloody hell!' Nathan looked even more surprised. 'How did that get past us? His name's not on the list of audience members.'

'No, because he left during the interval. During the murder window…'

'Right… Well that puts a bit of a different spin on things, doesn't it? Why was he there, and why did he leave early?'

'Maggie Tiddy reckons he left because she kept going on about how good Kirsty was,' I said, and he laughed.

'He might've just left because Maggie Tiddy gave him earache.' He gazed at me thoughtfully. 'Is he staying with his mum, do you think?'

'I don't know, but it sounded like he was. Why?'

'Well, I know where she lives, and you know I'm not very good with little old ladies. I'll need someone to keep her out of the way while I question her son.'

'You could take Matt with you, or Sunil.'

'Matt's gone to pick up his sister from the train station at Exeter, and I don't want to disturb Sunil, you know how he and Eesha have been struggling…' He grinned. 'Come on. Don't tell me you aren't desperate to get involved in the investigation? I can bring you in as a consultant again. I need someone with your particular skills on this one.'

'*What* particular skills?' I asked, but I couldn't deny I wanted to go.

'Dealing with difficult elderly women. God knows you've had enough practice. But don't tell your mother I said that. Plus you know the school, and some of the people involved. Sort of…'

And that was how I found myself sitting on the Matheson family's very large sofa, trapped under a large ginger cat, while Mrs Matheson bustled around in the kitchen, making dinner and occasionally sighing loudly and exclaiming about rude people who turned up uninvited at this time of the evening. I didn't need to keep her out of the way at all, but I was at least able to stop the cat climbing all over Nathan's dark grey suit. The room felt overly warm and claustrophobic, with Christmas decorations covering every spare inch. The mantlepiece was covered in greetings cards, and one of those battery-powered musical Santas stood in front of the fire.

'I can guess why you're here,' said Mark Matheson, perching opposite us on the edge of an armchair. Nathan didn't say anything, just did that eyebrow rise thing that was *sooo* annoying when you were on the receiving end of it but so cool when you weren't. 'Someone killed Kirsty Dunwoody and you think it was me.'

'Why would we think that?' asked Nathan. 'We're just getting statements from everybody who was at the pantomime on Friday. We missed you on the night as you'd left early. Right around the time of the murder, in fact.'

'Really?' Matheson now looked somewhat alarmed. 'Well it wasn't me. That was all water under the bridge as far as I was concerned.'

'Can you tell us about your relationship with Kirsty?' asked Nathan.

'Relationship? We didn't have one.'

'I mean the situation at Penstowan Comprehensive,' said Nathan. 'The string of events that led to both of you leaving.'

'She left long before I did,' he said. 'I don't know what you've been told, but I left because I was offered a better job somewhere else—'

'As head of the science department at St Anthony's private school in Bristol,' said Nathan. 'Yes, we know about that. But I'm referring to the allegations that were made against you by Kirsty.'

'Allegations that culminated with you getting a restraining order against her,' I said. Matheson glared at me.

'Surely that just goes to show that she had more reason to have a grudge against me than I did against her?'

'Well, that depends really, doesn't it?' I said calmly. 'On whether her allegations were true or not.'

'The police weren't involved at the time,' said Matheson. 'I don't see why you should be interested now.'

'No? I would've thought it was perfectly obvious why we'd be asking about it now,' said Nathan.

'The only reason there wasn't a police investigation is because the girl's family wanted it kept quiet,' I said, although I'd only got this information second-, or even third-hand from Emma the florist. 'And that suited the school, of course, especially when you agreed to look for a job somewhere else.' I was guessing that bit, but I could see from his face I wasn't too far off target. 'What did they do in the meantime? Put you on "gardening leave"? Or maybe they made sure you had a student teacher or someone shadowing you, supposedly for their benefit but more as a chaperone?'

'I don't have to talk about this,' said Matheson, standing up and squaring his shoulders as if he was dismissing us. His foot nudged the musical Santa next to him and immediately we got a tinny blast of 'Rocking Around the

Christmas Tree', which I thought rather spoilt the effect he was going for. Nathan and I remained seated; to be fair, I was still trapped under the enormous ginger cat, so I didn't have much option.

'Sit down, Mr Matheson,' said Nathan politely. 'I'm sure it's more comfortable here than at the station, but if you'd prefer to do this there—' Matheson sat down again, an expression of angry resignation on his face. Even Santa fell silent. 'Thank you. Now the main thing we need to establish is why you were at the panto in the first place, and why you left early.'

'I went because my niece was in the chorus,' said Matheson. 'Ellie.'

I felt my expression turn to surprise, but Nathan had a great poker face. 'Ellie Huggins?'

'Yes. She was in the chorus, and she was Kirsty's understudy. And no, I didn't kill Kirsty just so my niece would get a chance to play the lead.' Matheson sat back, amused at his own wit.

'And why did you leave early?' I asked. 'I was there, and it wasn't *that* bad…'

'My mum warned me there were still people in this town who blamed me for Kirsty losing her job, and who still thought she was right about me—'

'Well, she was, wasn't she?' I muttered, but Nathan nudged me.

'She warned me there would be people gossiping, but I thought, it was three years ago, they'll have found something else to talk about by now.'

'But they hadn't,' said Nathan.

'You know where we are, yeah?' I said. 'Small town, long memories. They'll still be talking about it in thirty years' time, never mind three.'

'Yeah, I realise that now. I left at the interval because I got sick of people nudging each other and staring at me. I knew what they were saying.'

Mrs Matheson came into the living room, holding a tea towel in her hands. I wondered for a moment if she was going to flick it at me and Nathan to try and shoo us away, but thankfully she didn't. She definitely wasn't a soft and cuddly little old lady, more like Boudicca's granny, a fierce warrior prepared to go into battle for her precious son.

'That girl!' she spat. 'Silly little tart. It's all her fault this happened.'

'Kirsty?' I asked, shocked.

'What? No, the other one. Shona—'

Matheson looked alarmed. 'Mum, stop—'

'Sending him flirty text messages and acting like a strumpet in front of him!' Matheson glared at his mother, and I could almost hear his thoughts: *Shut up! Shut up! You're making it worse!* But Mrs Matheson was in full flow, in passionate defence of her boy, and there was no stopping her. 'Have you seen the way some of them dress? Hitching up her skirt until you could see everything, and the makeup! She didn't look or act like a schoolgirl, believe me. How's any red-blooded young man supposed to resist that? What did the silly girl think would happen?'

Nathan and I exchanged glances. Mrs Matheson's blood

was up and she clearly wasn't thinking before speaking, because everything that came out of her mouth was just making her son look more and more guilty.

'Mum, for God's sake, will you just bloody shut up!' yelled Matheson, leaping to his feet and setting the Santa off again. Nathan jumped up too, putting himself between Matheson and his mother, who finally realised that perhaps she'd said too much and stopped talking.

'I'd better go and check on the spuds,' she said, fleeing back to the kitchen. Matheson sank back onto his chair, head in his hands.

'Do you want to tell us what really happened back then?' asked Nathan, in a far gentler tone than I would've used.

'I was a bloody idiot,' said Matheson, his voice muffled. He looked up. 'If I tell you what happened, you can't prosecute me now, can you? I can't lose my job, I'm engaged, we're getting married next year…'

'Tell us.' Nathan sounded sympathetic, but he stopped short of agreeing not to take it further. 'Her name was Shona?'

'Yes. Shona Bell. I was her form tutor. I didn't have her for any lessons, but when we had registration in the morning and after lunch she was in my class.' Matheson sighed. 'I was an idiot. She was a good-looking girl – I know that sounds wrong, because she was thirteen years younger than me, but she looked a lot older than fifteen. You know what it's like, girls wear all this makeup now and—' He must've caught my disgusted expression because he quickly backtracked. 'Yeah, I know it sounds like I'm victim blaming, but I'm just trying to explain how it happened.'

'Go on,' I said, wrangling one of the ginger cat's claws from my jumper, where it had got caught.

'She was a nice enough girl but I didn't really get to know her until we went on a class trip to London. It was meant to be a fun trip before all the serious work of the mocks started, visiting the museums and that. We stayed overnight in this hostel, and I drew the short straw and got the room on the same floor as the students. It was a single room, though, while the other staff had to share, so I didn't complain too much.'

'What happened?' asked Nathan. The cat was now trying to climb all over him, and I had to keep tight hold of its squirming body to stop it.

'Shona knocked on my door at two o'clock in the morning, crying.' He looked at us, almost pleading. 'I didn't want to let her in – I knew what it would look like – but she was distraught. Her mum had sent her a horrible text message and she was really upset.'

'What text message?'

'It was horrible, calling her a useless slut. Her mum was an alcoholic – still is, probably – and she was always getting drunk and saying horrible things to Shona. But she'd promised her she wouldn't drink while she was away, because she had to look after Shona's little brother.'

'Oh God,' I said, imagining it. If it was true, no wonder the poor girl had been so upset.

'I couldn't turn her away, could I? I did try to call one of the female teachers to deal with her, but she didn't hear her phone. So Shona came in and sat on my bed and we just talked. Honestly, that's all we did.'

'But it became more than that,' said Nathan, stating a fact rather than asking a question. Matheson nodded, reluctantly.

'Yeah, it did... Shona was sweet and funny, never mind what my mum says. I really felt bad about her home life, but when I said about calling social services she begged me not to, because she'd end up in care, away from her brother. So I said nothing. I know it was wrong. I told her she could always talk to me if she was in trouble or upset, and it just spiralled from there.'

'Did you and Shona have a sexual relationship?' asked Nathan. I knew he had to ask, but I wasn't sure if I wanted to know.

'No, we didn't... not really...'

'Not really? What the hell does that mean?' I asked. Nathan gently squeezed my knee, warning me to keep it together.

'We didn't have sex. We used to go for a drive in my car, and we'd talk, and then we'd kiss, but... we never actually did *that*. She really wanted to – I really wanted to as well, but I knew we shouldn't – so I told her we'd have to wait until she was sixteen, but even then I knew it would be wrong, because I was still her teacher.'

'But you sent each other text messages,' I said. 'Explicit text messages, which is what Kirsty saw.'

'Yes.' Matheson hung his head in shame. 'I got careless.

I was flattered that this beautiful young girl wanted me. I'd just come out of a four-year relationship, and I was back here living with my mum, and everything was just really shit. And then she found me.' He looked up at me, that pleading expression back on his face, and I got the impression that he wasn't pleading for forgiveness, just to be understood. 'I look back on it now as temporary insanity. I never fancied young girls before, and I never have since then. It was just Shona. I honestly thought I had feelings for her. If we'd met ten years later, we could've been together and no one would've batted an eyelid.'

'So what happened when Kirsty saw the text messages?' asked Nathan.

'I panicked. I felt sick. I knew I was in the wrong. I begged Shona to say that she'd been messing about and that the messages were from some kid she'd met, and I got her to delete them all. Her mum didn't want the police sniffing around either, because she was still drinking and she didn't want her kids being taken from her, so she backed us up and said it was just Shona trying to wind up a nosy teaching assistant. I thought the school would still look into it, but I was lucky. That headmaster just wanted a quiet life and he was quite happy not to rock the boat, as long as Shona or I left the school. Shona's mum moved the whole family away from Penstowan, I never found out where, because I knew I had to get my head together and forget about her.'

'But Kirsty wouldn't let it lie,' I said. He shook his head.

'No, she wouldn't. I suppose I don't blame her, really –

she was absolutely right about what was happening. I felt like a massive shit, constantly telling everyone that she was wrong when she wasn't, but I wasn't going to admit to it and lose my job. When I noticed her following me – I suppose she was trying to catch me and Shona meeting up, but I'd stopped by then – I completely lost it and decided to turn the tables on her. I said she was harassing me, stalking me, and I somehow managed to get a restraining order.'

'Work must've been fun at that point,' I said.

'She'd already left. I thought it was because of me, of course, and the way the headmaster failed to back her up probably didn't help, but I heard later about her mum having cancer, and I felt awful. But what could I do? It was done.' He sat forward, his fingers interlaced as if he was praying. 'I feel terrible about the whole thing. I wasn't planning on talking to Kirsty, but if I had done I would've apologised to her, not killed her. And in the end she did me a favour. She made me see sense and turn my life round.'

Chapter Thirteen

Mrs Matheson was so keen to get rid of us that she practically pushed us out onto the footpath before slamming the front door shut behind us. Nathan grinned at me.

'I think we're off her Christmas card list,' he said.

It was really cold now, especially after the almost suffocating heat of the house, so we hurried to the car and got in. Nathan turned the engine on to get the heater working, but we sat there for a moment. It was of course properly dark outside at this time of the evening – around six-thirty – and most of the houses were lit up with Christmas lights; trees twinkled in bay windows, casting a cheerful festive glow along the street, while over the road from us a family of LED reindeer, watched over by a jolly-looking snowman, grazed in a front garden. Further down the road multicoloured lights were draped over the front of another house, flashing on and off in a way that would've done my head in and had me reporting them to the council if I'd been living next door.

'So, what did you make of that?' asked Nathan, and it took me a couple of seconds to realise he meant the conversation we'd just had with Matheson, rather than the Christmas lights.

'I don't know,' I said. 'He's finally admitted that he had an inappropriate relationship with a student, which could either be a genuine confession or an attempt to draw us away from suspecting him of murder.'

'Yes...' said Nathan.

'But?'

'Well, there's not really a 'but'. He's an adult and he was her teacher, and what he did was wrong, even if they didn't have sex.' We both grimaced at that. 'But... I think there was real remorse there, don't you?'

'I don't know,' I said again, reluctant to admit that he was right. 'Yeah, I think he does genuinely regret what happened, and not just because he got caught. "Temporary insanity", he called it, and I kind of know what he means.'

'Sounds a bit like falling in love,' said Nathan, smiling at me. I shook my head.

'No, it sounds like infatuation or obsession, *masquerading* as love.'

'Whatever it was, we've all done stupid things when we've thought we were in love, haven't we?' said Nathan. I couldn't disagree with that. I thought back to the stupid, ill-advised and thankfully very brief fling I'd had a few years previously with the painter Duncan Stovall. Looking back, I think I'd realised that I was falling for Nathan, and it had absolutely terrified me; I'd not been ready for a long-term relationship at that point, not after the disaster of my divorce from Daisy's useless cheating father. Duncan had been trapped in a loveless marriage of convenience, and he'd seen me as a way for him to escape, though not as cynically as that might sound. He'd never been a candidate for a proper relationship, but it hadn't stopped us indulging in a spot of frantic snogging, although it hadn't gone further than that. And neither of us had been underage… Temporary insanity pretty much covered it.

'Yeah, I know I have… But I don't like the thought that he's still teaching. His new school should be told,' I said.

'Yes, I was thinking that too,' said Nathan. 'I'm not sure what to do about it. At least his new school is all boys.'

'Is it? That's some relief. I'm assuming his fiancé doesn't know about Shona…'

'She doesn't know. She's not here, is she? They're spending Christmas apart, because he wanted to test the waters first and see if people are still talking about him.'

'And they are.'

'Of course they are. They were bound to at the panto, what with Kirsty being there.' Nathan stared out of the window, thinking. 'He must've known she was in it. Why would he risk going there and stirring things up? I know he said he went to see his niece in it, but she was only in the chorus.'

'You think it was an excuse to go there, so he'd have a chance to confront Kirsty?'

'Maybe. And how is Ellie his niece? There can't be that many years between them.'

'So what? It depends on how far apart you had your kids, doesn't it? Maybe Mrs Matheson had one child really young, and then Mark years later. I know someone whose uncle is two weeks younger than they are. They went to school together.'

'Yeah, I keep forgetting we're in Cornwall and that sort of thing's normal…'

'Cheeky bugger!' I said, elbowing him. He laughed.

'I can't really say anything, I had a crush on my best mate's older sister when I was younger and she turned out to be his mum. *That* was weird.'

'Temporary insanity,' I said, smiling. He leant over and kissed me.

'I prefer our full-blown, long-term variety of madness,' he said. It would've been romantic, gazing at each other in the glow of the fairy lights, if I hadn't spotted Mrs Matheson glaring at us from her living room window.

We drove home and walked in the door to be greeted by the smell of shepherd's pie. Daisy appeared from the kitchen, clad in my pinny, with a serving spoon in her hand.

'About time,' she said. 'I'm about to dish up. Nana keeps muttering about her stomach thinking her throat's been cut.'

'I didn't expect you to make the dinner,' I said, grabbing her and pressing a kiss on her forehead.

She shrugged. 'I know, but I wanted to do something

nice for you.' She lowered her voice. 'And Nana was threatening to cook, so...'

'Say no more.'

We all tucked in to Daisy's shepherd's pie (which was delicious – all that time spent in the kitchen with me had paid off), then Nathan grabbed a tea towel, rather less menacingly than Mrs Matheson had earlier.

'You wash, I'll dry,' he said. Daisy and Mum exchanged looks and then quickly scarpered before Nathan changed his mind and roped them into clearing up.

I filled the sink with hot soapy water and started washing.

'I didn't tell you what Daisy was saying about Ellie Huggins, did I?' I said, brushing hair off my face and smearing bubbles on to my cheek. Nathan wiped them off with the tea towel. 'She said she heard Ellie and Kirsty arguing—'

'You told me that,' he said.

'Yeah, but I didn't tell you that we might've worked out what they were arguing about,' I said, but then frowned. 'Although after the events of this evening, we might be wrong.'

'Go on.'

'Well, you know Jamie Westall was Kirsty's ex-boyfriend? That's not all. He's Ellie's *current* boyfriend.'

'Really? Hmmm...'

'That's what we thought. Daisy said she thought Ellie was shouting "leave it alone" or something like that, but maybe it was "leave him alone"? Maybe she thought Kirsty wanted him back. But it's just occurred to me that maybe she was telling Kirsty to leave her uncle alone.'

'There's no sign that Kirsty had still been pursuing Matheson, though,' said Nathan.

'No, but maybe Ellie was warning her that he was coming back for Christmas, maybe even to see her in the panto, and she didn't want Kirsty dragging everything back up again. She wanted her to "leave it alone".'

'We need to talk to this Ellie, don't we?' said Nathan. 'She's already made a statement, of course, but we'll follow up on it tomorrow.'

'You should probably take Matt with you,' I said.

'Yeah…'

'Why did you take me with you today? Really?'

'Because I always appreciate your insight,' said Nathan. I turned round and took the tea towel from his hands, forcing him to look at me.

'Be honest.'

'I *am* being honest. But also… I know you've been feeling a bit…'

'Old and useless?'

'That's your words, not mine. I'm not going to say it's your hormones or menopause or anything like that, because I know how annoying that must be—'

'But it's probably true,' I said. 'Aargh! I'm only forty-five, I didn't think I was old enough to be going through this now.'

'Menopause usually affects women between the ages of forty-five and fifty-five,' said Nathan. He looked sheepish.

'I looked it up when you first started having hot flushes and getting teary.'

'I don't get teary!' I protested. 'Well yeah, I do, but I've always cried a lot, ever since Daisy was born.'

'I know,' he said, pulling me in for a hug. 'But I know you've been feeling out of sorts lately, and I just want to be able to help.'

'You are helping, right now,' I said, snuggling into him. 'Did you really look it up on the internet?'

'Of course I did.'

'Oh bless you, you're so sweet...'

'Don't you start crying, woman,' he warned me, and I laughed, whilst surreptitiously wiping my eyes on his top.

'I'm not, I just got washing-up liquid bubbles in my eyes...'

The next day Nathan went off to work and left me in bed. I hadn't slept very well – I kept waking up, feeling like my body was on fire, which I put down to those pesky hormones. Debbie had warned me that it might take a while to get my HRT right, so maybe I needed a higher dose. Or maybe it was because Nathan always felt cold and insisted on having a big duvet *and* a blanket on the bed. I'd ended up sleeping on top of both of them, and had then woken up at four in the morning absolutely freezing.

I fell asleep again and didn't wake up until Daisy and

Germaine both came bouncing into the room and leapt on the bed.

'You are *not* still asleep!' cried Daisy. 'Aren't you the one who always turfs me out of bed before eight, saying I'm wasting the whole day?'

I groaned. 'What time is it? Why are you bothering me, is the house on fire?'

'It's quarter to nine. I can't believe you were still asleep.'

'I was just resting my eyes,' I said, sitting up. 'Germaine, get off! I'm trapped!'

Daisy laughed and picked the dog up. 'Nana was wondering where you were. She said Jocasta wants to meet up in town and she wants you to go along.'

'She wants an update on the investigation, more like,' I said. I swung my legs out of the bed and stretched. 'I do need to go and pick up the last few bits of food for Christmas Day, so I suppose I can do that afterwards. You want to come?'

'Hmm, do I want to sit with some mad old biddies—'

'Oi!'

'I mean Nana and Jocasta.'

'Still rude. But accurate.'

'Do I want to sit with Nana and her mate, talking about pagan Christmas rituals and drinking tea, and then go and buy Brussels sprouts with my mum at a crowded supermarket? Let me think…'

'Cheeky mare,' I said. 'Although actually pagan Christmas rituals could be fun. If there's one that involves Nathan dancing around the tree naked but for a carefully

placed Christmas stocking and a Santa hat, I'm all for it.'
Daisy made gagging noises. 'Serves you right for being
cheeky. Joe's back today, isn't he?'

'Yeah, he should be home by lunchtime and then I think
he's coming here. I'm not waiting by the phone or anything,
but...' She grinned.

'But you are. You missed him, of course you did. He's
still welcome to come over Christmas Day, remember,
although he'll probably want to spend it with his mum and
dad. Have you got him a present? Other than you going on
the pill?'

'Oh my God, Mum, I wish I hadn't told you now...'

I laughed and gave her a kiss, then got showered and
dressed and made my way downstairs to where Mum was
waiting in the kitchen.

'We did remember to put a kitchen in your annex, didn't
we?' I said.

'Yes,' said Mum. 'But I prefer this one.'

'So I hear Jocasta wants to meet up? What's that about?'

'I don't know,' said Mum. 'But Colin's going to be there
as well.'

I put some bread in the toaster. 'Oh right, I'm going to
get a grilling about the case, then. I'm not a police officer
anymore, they do realise that?'

Mum scoffed. 'Like you don't know what's going on!
Nathan tells you everything. And anything he doesn't tell
you, you worm out of him anyway. It was the same with me
and your father.'

'Really?' I was surprised; this was the first I'd heard of

Mum getting involved in any of his investigations. 'You used to help him?'

'I dunno about helping, not the way you do, but he liked to talk things over sometimes, use me as a sounding board.' She passed me the jar of peanut butter. 'Nathan really appreciates you, you know.'

'I know.' I narrowed my eyes. 'Has he been talking to you about me going through the menopause?'

She laughed. 'Yes, bless him. He wanted to know what it's like. I told him to just be ready to give you hugs, and make sure you never run out of chocolate, so he said, "Same as usual, then."'

'Pretty much,' I said. 'I just don't want any of you tiptoeing around me.'

'Huh! As if I'd ever do that. You start any of this mood swing nonsense and I'll give you a clip round the ear.' Mum smiled and reached over to pat my arm. 'You'll be fine, sweetheart. Your toast is burning.'

After breakfast I did some housework I'd been putting off, and made a shopping list. I had the turkey and most of the trimmings, like pigs in blankets and stuffing, so I just needed to get vegetables and stock up on milk and loo roll so I didn't have to brave the festive shopping crowds any closer to the big day. I also wanted to get some chocolate (not for me and my hormones) to go in everyone's stockings; I couldn't buy it too far in advance, otherwise Nathan and I would be sitting in front of the telly in the evening, fancying something sweet, and we'd end up eating it and have to buy more. We'd already polished off a tub of Quality Street that I'd bought for Maggie Tiddy as a thank you for dog sitting Germaine several times over the past year. A replacement tub went on the list, but even as I wrote it down I was thinking, *Maggie loves having Germaine, and I do slip her a few quid for it, do I really need to give her anything else?* Just in case I bought another tub and we ate that as well.

Mum and I drove down into town – it was walkable, but it was cold and Mum struggled a bit when the weather was bad. We parked up and headed to Rowe's, where I managed to ignore the Christmas cake goodies that were waving at me from the counter and just ordered a cup of tea. To be honest I was still feeling slightly queasy after yesterday's massive lump of chocolate cake.

Jocasta and Colin were sitting at a table in the window of the café. We joined them and without much preamble, Jocasta said, 'Jodie, we need a favour.'

Here we go, I thought, bracing myself for a barrage of questions about the investigation into Kirsty's murder.

'We need you to ask Nathan if we can have access to the theatre this morning for a smudging ritual,' said Colin. So Daisy hadn't been far off with her mention of pagan Christmas rituals.

'What on earth is a smudging ritual?' asked Mum.

'It's an ancient Indigenous cleansing and protection ritual I picked up when I lived in Manitoba,' said Jocasta.

'When did you live in Manitoba?' I asked, incredulous. Jocasta had been a high-powered lawyer in her day, and had travelled and worked all around the world. I knew she'd lived in New York for a while, but Manitoba?

'I was doing some pro bono work for the local Indigenous tribe,' she said, as if that was just something most people did. 'An oil company wanted to come in and start exploratory drilling on their land, and I helped them stop it happening. Wonderful people, and Canada's such a beautiful country.'

'Okay,' I said, 'but what's any of that got to do with an amateur theatre in Cornwall?'

'Have you been back to the theatre since Friday?' asked Colin. 'I have. The police officer on the door let me pop in because I'd left my phone charger there.' He stopped. 'Oh, I don't know if they were meant to let me in? I don't want them to get into trouble. They came in with me so I didn't disturb anything.'

'No, it'll be fine,' I said, although really whoever was on duty should have turned him away or left him outside while they tried to find it for him. I wasn't about to dob them in, though.

'Anyway, the energy in that building now…' He shook his head sadly and didn't say anything more, like we were supposed to know what he meant.

'What about it?' asked Mum, impatiently.

'*Verrrrry* negative, to say the least,' said Colin. 'It always had such a lovely, calm and creative aura about it before, but now – you can tell something bad happened there, the moment you walk in.'

Mum opened her mouth to speak, but Jocasta got in first.

'We're not talking about ghosts, Shirl, because I know you don't believe in them—' Colin shook his head again, as if he couldn't believe that Mum (and I) didn't share his belief in the spirit world '—but you have to admit that places do have an atmosphere, and the atmosphere of the theatre has really changed, especially backstage.'

'Okay…' I said. The Forensics team had finished with the place and I didn't even know if there was an officer stationed on the door anymore, but it was still a crime scene, and I wasn't sure if Nathan would want a team of geriatric shamans traipsing all over it. 'What exactly does this ritual involve?'

Nathan was bemused, as I knew he would be, but as they'd finished collecting evidence and the theatre was now standing empty and unused he didn't have a problem with the smudging ceremony going ahead.

'As long,' he said, 'as you're there with them. We'll have to release it back to them in a few days anyway, but this gives you an opportunity to have a look around, see if we missed anything.'

'Oh don't you worry, babe,' I said. 'I'm not missing this for the world…'

The officer on the door had been dismissed, and the only sign now that anything untoward had happened was the crime tape across the entrance. We all ducked under it, and Colin used his keys to unlock the building.

I'd been inside since the murder, of course, but it did somehow feel different this time. It was quiet, except for the sound of Colin's breathing – he was a big bloke, and he did huff and puff a bit. It was always quite dark inside the foyer, particularly at this time of year when the sun was too low and in the wrong position to shed much light through the glass doors, but now it felt *too* dark, like all the light had been sucked out.

'We should wait here for the others,' said Jocasta.

'Others?'

Five minutes later 'the others' had all turned up; half the cast and crew of the panto seemed to be involved.

'I don't know about having all this lot in here,' I said, but Colin just smiled.

'Jodie, the more positive energy we can fill this space with, the better,' he explained. 'These people are the creative force behind the Penstowan Players—'

'*He's* our postman,' said Mum, nodding at one of the stage crew.

'Creativity drives out destruction,' continued Colin. 'Death has been here, so we need to fill it with life force.'

'And they need this, just as much as the building does,' Jocasta murmured, quietly so only I could hear. 'You're used to dealing with death by unnatural causes, but most of us aren't. Look at them.'

I glanced at the small crowd of people, all of whom looked nervous but eager.

'All right,' I said, 'but no one is to go off on their own, okay? We don't want—' I nearly said, *We don't want another*

186

murder, but I stopped myself just in time. Why on earth had I thought that? Why would there be another murder? The atmosphere was getting to me, too. 'Just stay together.'

Colin and Jocasta handed out bunches of dried herbs and twigs to the assembled smudgers. There weren't quite enough to go around, so groups formed in order to share. Colin carefully lit the bundles while Jocasta talked through the process.

'First of all, I need you to all remove anything metallic – jewellery, watches, glasses and the like – because metal can contain negative energy.' Beside her, the elderly little man who did the lighting during performances removed his glasses and stood, squinting and blinking owlishly. 'Derek, love, you can keep yours on.' He put them back on with a look of relief. 'In a minute we're going to move through the building, room by room, and waft the smoke into any dark corners or oppressive spaces. If you come across a door or window, open it, to help the negative energy and any unfriendly spirits to leave.'

Next to me, Mum started waving her bunch of sage and cedar twigs around frantically, as the flames started to get a little bit out of hand. I had visions of the whole building going up in smoke.

'Relax, Shirley love,' said Jocasta. 'You don't want an inferno, just a smoulder.' Mum calmed down and so did the flaming bundle in her hand. 'Okay, is everybody ready? First of all, draw the smoke over your head, past your eyes, ears and mouth – yes, best do it to your smudging buddy and then swap over – that's it. Now down the front of your

body and back towards your heart, to purify yourself…
Now down to your feet, so you may walk gently upon the
earth…'

I caught Mum's eye. She pulled a funny face which
almost made me laugh, but Jocasta caught us.

'You need to do this with good intentions,' she said,
gently rebuking us, and I felt bad because everyone else
was taking it so seriously. They obviously either really
believed in it, or, as Jocasta had said, they needed
something like this to make them feel better. *Sorry*, I
mouthed, and she smiled.

'Right, let's get this party started,' she said
incongruously, and led us through the double doors into the
auditorium.

Without an audience the silent auditorium felt unnatural
and oppressive. I looked at Mum, but she wasn't mucking
about now. Colin headed towards the stage and began
wafting his smoking bundle towards the closed curtains,
while Jocasta quietly began to chant and everyone else
waved their smouldering sage randomly around the room.

> *'Negativity of this sacred space, we banish*
> *you by the light of grace*
> *You have no hold or power here, we stand*
> *and face you with no fear*
> *Be gone forever, you will obey, from this*
> *sacred space you must away.'*

'Blimey,' muttered Mum, which spoilt the atmosphere

slightly. I held my breath, waiting for some sign that all this was working – a howl of pain and fury from a vengeful spirit or something – but there was nothing, except from the back of the room where someone farted. It echoed around the auditorium. Mum and I both sniggered, because we're completely immature. But hey, it *was* funny.

Colin climbed up on the stage and then disappeared behind the curtains. Everyone else seemed to be heading backstage via the door at the side, so I clambered up onto the stage and followed the director into the wings…

Chapter Fourteen

I regretted my decision almost immediately. The auditorium had a row of windows along one side, which were covered in heavy blackout curtains – no one had thought to open them since Friday night – but even so a few chinks of light managed to find their way through, penetrating the gloom here and there. But here in the wings there was nothing, no hint of illumination from anything. I stopped and took out my phone, fumbling for the torch; there was no way I was going to go stumbling around in the pitch black looking for the director who, while not someone I actively suspected of murder, was a suspect nonetheless. The atmosphere was getting to me, I thought; even in the dark, I was aware of the yawning space above my head, the 'flies', where the lights hung from rigging and bits of scenery were hoisted out of the way between scenes. I'd seen far too many murder mysteries on the telly where heavy objects suddenly dropped from the heavens, hitting unsuspecting victims on the stage below and rendering them unconscious or even dead. Heavy objects, such as corpses. Colin's corpse would be a particularly weighty one, I thought, and I had no desire to hang around in case *it* was hanging around, too. Or was he even now climbing up a ladder to the rigging, untying the rope that worked the pulley system, getting ready to drop the backdrop for the Emperor's palace on me?

I heard the creak of floorboards in front of me. I fumbled again at my phone, trying to get the torch to come on… and then I was squinting as the stage was flooded with light, and Colin was in front of me, fiddling with a row of switches. He turned around and jumped when he saw me.

'Oh, Jodie! I didn't hear you,' he said. He frowned. 'Where's everyone else?'

'They went through the side door,' I said. 'I thought I'd better follow you. Just in case.'

'Just in case? You're not expecting another murder, are you?' He smiled, but it was strained.

'No, not really. I think the building being so quiet and dark is getting to me, that's all,' I said, and he nodded.

'It feels wrong, doesn't it? Now do you get what I meant about negative energy?'

'I do.'

Colin sighed and sat down in a chair which was in the wings, probably the one Daisy had been sitting on during the performance as the line prompt. He looked absolutely shattered. Even his smudging stick was drooping.

'Don't tell Jocasta, but I'm not sure smudging is going to be strong enough to make this place feel better,' he said.

'Justice will make it feel better,' I said. 'Finding the bastard who did this.'

'Yes.' He shook his head sadly. 'I still can't believe what's happened. I thought I'd left all this behind me.'

'All what behind you? Murder?'

'Oh, no – I mean all the drama. And death. I moved here to get away from it.'

I chuckled. 'So did I. It's not worked that way for me, either.'

'Death follows you around, doesn't it? You can't escape it,' he said.

'Your wife?' I asked, gently. He nodded.

'Yes. We bought the cottage as a holiday home, but then she got ill and never had the chance to stay in it. She had a brain tumour. They operated and we thought she was getting better, but then... It all happened very quickly. I moved down here to get away from all the sadness, but it came with me.'

'How long have you lived in Penstowan?' I asked. 'You must've flown in under the radar, because my mum didn't realise we had an ex-soap star living here, and she knows everyone and everything that happens here.'

Colin laughed. 'Yes, I can imagine. It's very handy having a Shirley, though, isn't it? If you need to know anything you can just ask her, and if she doesn't know already, she'll find out.'

'Oh yes, she has her uses...'

'Let's see, it must be two years ago now that I moved down here. Although I was away touring with a production of *School for Scandal* for a few months, and then I had a cameo in *The Wheel of Time* which should've been a day's shoot and ended up two weeks.'

'That's exciting,' I said, and he nodded.

'Yes, and all very unexpected. For some reason I appear to be on the brink of a renaissance.'

'How so?'

'Well… it's not official yet, but you're looking at one of the stars of a new *Game of Thrones* spin-off that's due to start shooting next September.' He sat a little straighter, a little taller.

'Ooh, that's *really* exciting. So you've not retired and decided to limit your theatrical activities to the Penstowan Players, then? Don't blame you.'

He laughed. 'No. I only did this as a favour to Tim – he helped me furnish the cottage when I moved in, and I've been to dinner with him and Maurice a few times. But it's been fun.' His expression darkened again. 'Well, it was until Friday night.'

'What do you remember of that night?' I asked. I knew he'd made a statement and that Nathan would no doubt be following it up, if he hadn't already, but there was no harm in me asking.

'The wonderful atmosphere, pre-show,' said Colin, smiling. 'Everyone was so excited. Nervous, of course, but that's good – you want your actors to be on their toes, not too relaxed. When you get complacent as an actor, that's when things go wrong. I've always done my best work when half-crazed with fear.'

I laughed. 'Being an actor sounds stressful.'

'It can be, but it gets the adrenaline pumping like nothing else can. In my younger days I did a lot of stupid, sometimes dangerous things, just for kicks, just to make myself feel alive, but the first time I walked out on stage in front of an audience, well...' He smiled again, remembering. 'It felt like an epiphany, like everything before that moment was gone, something from someone else's life, because *this* was where I was supposed to be, and this was what I was supposed to do.'

'It's good to have a purpose in life,' I said, and felt a pang, because what was my purpose in life now? Daisy was pretty much a grown-up, and while I did have my catering business (not that I had any catering jobs lined up for the next two months) it wasn't my passion. I'd quit my real passion, after that terrorist attack in London. I knew that I didn't really regret it – I'd had to put my daughter first, and I would still put her first every day of the week – but at that moment I did miss it.

I pulled myself together. 'So... Friday night. Everyone's nervous, excited. Sometimes things can boil over when everyone's stressed out, can't they? People can get a bit snippy. Arguments can start over the smallest thing.'

'Oh God yes, I worked on a production of *Hedda Gabler* in 2003 where the entire cast were divas. There was more drama off-stage than on it. But not this cast, or crew.'

'Daisy mentioned there was a bit of tension between Kirsty and Ellie…?'

'They did have words a while back, apparently, although I wasn't there when it happened. I don't know what it was about, but it all got sorted out,' said Colin. 'I wouldn't say they were close, but they were friendly enough. Kirsty was too professional to let it affect the show.'

'What about during the performance?' I asked. 'Or during the interval?'

'You're asking where I was when the murder took place, aren't you?' said Colin, not angrily. I nodded. 'I wasn't backstage at all during the performance. By the time opening night comes around, the director's job is more or less done. I wanted to watch from the front, in case I needed to give anyone notes on their performance. I was sitting in the lighting box with Derek for most of Act One, although I did go outside about ten minutes before the interval as I was waiting for a phone call from Hilary.'

'Hilary, your agent? She wasn't at the show? I thought she was staying with you?'

'She is, but she didn't come down for that. We had a meeting about the *Game of Thrones* spin-off I was telling you about. She had a Zoom call with the production company in LA scheduled for eight-thirty, slap bang in the middle of the performance, so she took it at the cottage. I was waiting to hear the outcome.' He smiled. 'It's kind of a big deal for me. Hilary knew I'd be on tenterhooks and wouldn't be able to wait until I got home, so she promised to let me know as soon as she'd finished.'

'Where were you standing outside?' I asked. 'Out the front, or round the back?' If he'd been waiting out the back by the bins, could he have seen the murderer throw the dress into the bin? But then surely he would've said.

'I wasn't *outside* outside, I meant outside the auditorium. I stood in the bar.'

'Did you see anyone hanging around?'

'Only Gloria, the lady who runs the bar for us.' So he had a checkable alibi, I thought.

'When did you go back inside?'

'Let me think... I was out there for a good thirty minutes. Hilary thought the Zoom would be a quick one – it was basically either a "yes, we want Colin" or "no, we don't" – but it was late starting. The interval was just ending, so... quarter to nine, maybe? I didn't really look at the time. I got back to the lighting box just before Act Two started.'

'Well, at least you got a "yes, we want Colin",' I said. 'Congratulations.'

'Thank you. I've not really felt like celebrating it...'

'You should,' I said. 'It's not your fault, what happened to Kirsty. Did you know her sister works for a talent agency in LA?'

'Yes, she told me.' He gave a sad smile. 'I said to Hilary that if the producers needed me to go to LA for any reason I should take Kirsty with me. I could've introduced her to a few people, and she could've spent some time with her sister.'

I wonder how Hilary felt about THAT, I thought. Maybe

Nathan hadn't been too far off the mark with his theory about her being a woman scorned. But I still thought that was unlikely; she struck me as the sort of woman who wouldn't base her entire life around a man, someone who would always put business over relationships. And in all the murder cases I've been a part of (even when I was in uniform and just guarding crime scenes), there have always been more instances of a *man* scorned, violently taking it out on the object of his affections. Women just get drunk and scratch the other party's car, or post glitter bombs through their letter box, or leave passive aggressive comments on their latest Facebook post, and then go and get even more drunk with their friends. Not that I'd ever do that, of course. Never…

'What did Hilary say to that?' I asked.

'She told me not to be so sentimental.' He shook his head. 'Hilary is a good friend, but she's not one to let it get in the way of business. She said doing someone a favour can backfire in this industry.'

'How so?'

'If you recommend someone for a part, and they turn out not to be very good, it can make *you* look bad.'

'Which makes sense if you're an agent and your job is spotting talent, I suppose,' I said.

'Anyway…' Colin stood up and stretched, his jumper and T-shirt riding up to reveal part of a tattoo on his torso. He realised that I'd seen it and grinned, pulling his clothing up a little higher to show me. It was a shamrock. 'One of the "stupid and sometimes dangerous" things I used to do before I discovered acting,' he said. 'I got drunk one Saint Patrick's Day and my big brother persuaded me to get it.' He peered down at it and frowned. 'It looked a lot better when I had a six-pack.'

'Of course – Sweeney's an Irish name, isn't it?'

'Yes. I come from a large family of Irish immigrants, just like Ewan McCafferty in *Mile End Days*,' he said. 'I didn't have to act very much in that role.'

'Oi oi!' cried Mum, coming up behind me. 'What's going on here, then? She's married, you know.' Colin hurriedly tugged his top down. 'Oh no, don't cover yourself up on my account…'

'Honestly, Mother!' I said. 'I can't take you anywhere. At least now we know this smudging ritual doesn't purify everything. It'd take more than a bit of sage to drag your mind out of the gutter.'

We headed back out to the auditorium, where the rest of the smudgers had begun to return in a happy if rather smoky trickle. Jocasta found us and smiled.

'So, what do you think? Ridiculous nonsense, or something that's actually brought some joy back to everyone?' she asked quietly. I looked around at all the other smiling faces, hearing the cheerful voices as they talked not about Kirsty or the murder, but about Christmas and how they'd be spending it with family. There were even a few ripples of laughter.

'It's definitely helped,' I said. 'And not just them. The room feels lighter.' And it did.

'I thought it was daft, waving sage about, but then I

enjoyed it,' said Mum. 'Although halfway through I did start getting a hankering for roast chicken.'

'That's handy,' I said, 'because I need to stop at the supermarket on the way home. I'll buy you one of those Christmas chicken and stuffing baguettes they do in the café if you give me a hand.'

Mum was easily bought with the promise of lunch (as am I), so we said goodbye to Jocasta and Colin and got in the car.

'I just need to pop into the vets first,' I said, turning the engine on. Mum snorted.

'That Jamie fella works at the vets in Hatherleigh, not our local one,' she said.

'How d'you know about him?'

'I overheard Daisy telling Joe all about your investigation last night,' she said. 'She's probably got him fully briefed by now, poor lad.'

'"Poor lad" nothing,' I scoffed. 'You remember what he was like at our wedding? He was just as into it as the rest of us. We're not the only nosey people in this town, you know. Anyway, I need some of Germaine's special dog food.'

'You normally order it,' said Mum, unconvinced, although for once I wasn't motivated by the need to be nosey, I'd genuinely forgotten to order my fur baby's food. I couldn't have her eating (horror!) the ordinary stuff from the supermarket like everyone else's mutt. Nathan had accused me several times of coddling Germaine like she was an actual baby, but obviously that was nonsense.

'It's two days before Christmas, I won't get it in time now,' I said.

So imagine my surprise (and, I have to admit it, delight) when we turned into the driveway of the veterinary clinic and almost ran over Jamie Westall and Ellie Huggins having a stand-up fight next to a parked Range Rover.

Chapter Fifteen

'For God's sake, Ellie, you got what you wanted. She's out of the way now, for good!'

Mum and I had parked a couple of cars away and got out as quietly as possible, but I honestly thought we could've parked right next to the young couple and they still wouldn't have noticed us, so engrossed in their argument were they.

'Out of the way? You absolute dickhead, she's dead! I never wanted her dead!' cried Ellie. Jamie took a step towards her. He was a lot taller than she was – at least six foot three, I reckoned – and he loomed over her, threateningly. As much as I would've liked to keep on eavesdropping, I couldn't let him hurt the girl.

'Everything all right, love?' I said, inserting myself between them. Jamie looked surprised and stepped back with a scowl.

'Of course it is, why wouldn't it be?'

'Because you're at least a foot taller than she is and you were right in her face,' I said. 'I think both of you need to calm down.'

'I don't give a shit what you think,' he said, but he looked a bit shaken. I got the impression he hadn't realised just how intimidating he was being towards Ellie. 'This is none of your business.'

We all turned as another vehicle pulled up in the car park. A police car. Nathan and Matt stepped out, Nathan giving me a *might've-known-you'd-be-here* look.

'It might not be my business,' I said, 'but it's definitely theirs.'

'James Westall? We were about to drive over to Hatherleigh to talk to you,' said Nathan. 'Very handy that you and your girlfriend here decided to have a fight so close to the station. Thanks for that.' He got out his warrant card and held it up. 'DCI Nathan Withers. I'd like to have a word with you about the murder of Kirsty Dunwoody.'

'I'm working. I said I'd locum here over the Christmas holidays—' started Jamie, but Nathan shook his head.

'If it makes it easier for you to understand, I'm not asking. You too, Ms Huggins.'

Ellie looked petrified. Matt opened one of the rear doors of the police car and gestured for Jamie to get in. The young vet reluctantly complied, but when Ellie went to follow suit Nathan stopped her.

'No, I think I'd prefer you to travel separately. Er...' He looked at me.

'I can give Ellie a lift to the station,' I said.

'Thank you.' He lowered his voice. 'No detours...'

'As if I would,' I protested, but really, he knew me too well. Ellie followed me over to the car and we watched as Nathan and Matt drove off.

'Come on, Ellie,' I said.

'How do you know my name?' she asked. She still looked terrified.

'I'm Daisy's mum,' I said. 'The line prompt?'

'Oh yeah, I know Daisy,' she said. 'She did a great job on the script. I wish I was as clever as her.' I thought, *It's a good job you don't know what she thinks of you*. Just another reason why you should never judge a book by its (overly made up) cover. I made a mental note to tell my daughter. 'Oh, and Shirley! I didn't see you.'

'You were a bit preoccupied, love,' said Mum kindly.

We all got in the car, Mum and I exchanging looks. This was probably going to be the only opportunity either of us got to stick our noses in before Nathan got hold of her.

'So, Ellie,' I said, as I eased the car out of the car park and onto the road. 'We couldn't help overhearing some of that. You and Jamie are an item, are you?'

'Yeah, we are,' she said. 'Although we might not be for much longer...'

'What did Jamie mean when he said you got what you wanted?' asked Mum, and I cringed, because I'd been working up to asking that and she'd just blundered straight in. There was no way Ellie was going to answer that. Except...

Ellie sighed. 'I just wanted Kirsty to leave Jamie alone,'

she said, and I looked at Mum in amazement. Maybe sometimes you *could* just plough straight in.

'Had she been pestering him?' asked Mum. 'They used to go out together, didn't they?'

'Yeah, until she dumped him,' said Ellie, bitterly. 'He was really cut up about it for ages, and she didn't give a toss until she saw that he was happy with me. It was like she didn't want him, but no one else could have him.'

'Was she trying to get him back?' I asked. 'That's not on, is it?'

'No, it ain't. She just wouldn't leave him alone. She was always calling him, and Jamie – well, he was too soft to just block her number. He'd always answer, even if she was calling him late at night or when we was in the middle of something.'

'But if he told her he wasn't interested in getting back together with her...' Mum shook her head. 'I dunno, some girls, they got no self-respect. I never used to go round begging blokes to go out with me.' She looked quite militant about it. 'Never had to. Specially if it meant stepping on another woman's toes.'

'Yeah, I wouldn't neither,' said Ellie. 'But she was obsessed with him. You know she got the sack from her old job, right, after she was, like, stalking that teacher? Some people say that he made it all up to get rid of her, but I reckon he was right, she *is* a stalker.'

'So what did you want Jamie to do?' I asked her. 'Report her?'

'Nah, nothing like that. I just wanted him to have words

with her, make her understand that he's with me now and he don't want her. I had to keep going on and on at him to get him to do it, but—' She stopped.

'But what? Do you think he might've gone too far?' I said gently.

'No... no, Jamie's proper soft sometimes...'

'But...?'

Ellie was silent for a moment and I thought we'd probably got all we were going to get from her, but then she spoke again.

'He's proper soft and he won't do anything, but if you wind him up enough he just, like...'

'Snaps?'

'Yeah, snaps. Like today. He's never shouted at me like that before, and just before you turned up I was... I felt scared. Of him. I've never felt scared of him before. And it makes me worry, what could've happened if he did talk to her, and things got out of hand...'

'You think he could've hurt her?' asked Mum.

'No. I dunno. Maybe?' The sound of a little, frightened sob reached us from the back seat. Mum turned round and reached out a hand to her. 'Thanks, Shirley. I've been going over and over this in my head ever since that night.'

'Kirsty was killed backstage during the show, though,' I said. 'How could Jamie have done it?'

'Well, er...' There was no mistaking the embarrassment in Ellie's voice.

'Go on, love. No judgement here,' said Mum.

'He snuck backstage before the show, to, er, give me a

good luck present,' she said, and from her awkwardness I could guess what the 'present' had been.

'And where did he give you this "present"?' I asked.

'In the store cupboard. The one where they found Kirsty. It was the only place I knew that no one would need to come in, only the woman doing the catering brought all the food into the room while we were in there, and then suddenly it turned into the busiest room in the building, with Tim and Colin and some other bloke coming in and chatting. We couldn't come out of the cupboard though, cos it would've been really obvious what we'd been up to. So we had to stay in there and keep quiet. I nearly gave us away cos I was giggling.'

'You were in there before the show?' I asked, not mentioning that I'd been the one bringing the food in.

'Yeah. I weren't on until the fourth scene, so we stayed in there for a while to make sure everyone had gone, and then I had to go and get myself ready.'

'What was Jamie going to do after you left?' I asked, thinking, *Bloody hell, this could be it...*

'He said he'd wait until the coast was clear and let himself out the fire exit at the back of the building. He wasn't going to watch the show, because he didn't want Kirsty to think he'd come to see her.'

'But you don't know when he let himself out?'

'No. He told me he would leave about five minutes after I did, because everyone was busy with the show at that point and he could get out without being seen, but...'

'But now you're wondering if he actually did?' I asked,

as we arrived at the station. I parked the car and turned in my seat to look at her. 'Tell DCI Withers everything you've told me.'

'But what if Jamie *didn't* do it, and I make it look like he did?' she said, worry etched into her young face, so deep that even the makeup couldn't hide it.

'What if he *did* do it, and you say nothing?' I said. 'The police will find the truth either way, and if you help them by telling them what you know you'll also be helping Jamie. The longer the investigation drags on, the worse it will be for whoever killed Kirsty.'

'I suppose so,' she said, doubtfully.

'Come on, love,' said Mum. 'I'll walk you in so you don't have to go in alone. Do you want me to call your mum?'

We all got out of the car and headed inside. Nathan was waiting in the reception area with Sunil.

'Thanks for coming, Ellie,' said Nathan. He could obviously see that she was extremely nervous, and he set about putting her at ease. He knew when to be tough with suspects, but he also knew when to play it gentler, and that was what made him a good cop. 'DC Bakshi is going to find an interview room for you to wait in. You're not under arrest, okay? Sunil will get you a cup of tea and if there's anyone you want to contact, you can do that. I'll be with you soon.' We all stood and watched them go, before Nathan turned to me. 'Okay, I know you'll have been pumping the poor girl for information on your way here. Did you get anything useful?'

I told him what Mum and I had unearthed. 'She's scared, the poor girl. I honestly don't think she's involved, but I can't say the same for her boyfriend.'

'No, you might be right. It certainly answers the question about how someone could be backstage for the murder and then disappear afterwards.' He grinned. 'I can't believe they were at it in the cupboard while we were dropping off your sausage rolls.'

'Nor can I! And the cupboard's not the most romantic place for a rendezvous, is it?' I said. 'But what made you come looking for Jamie? Did you find something?'

'Kirsty's phone records,' he said. 'Lots of phone calls between them, not all of them coming from Kirsty.'

'He was calling her too?'

'Yes, in fact I'd say at least 75 per cent of the time it was him calling her. I think if anyone was doing any stalking, it wasn't Kirsty.'

'Poor Ellie,' said Mum. 'She's convinced he loves her, not Kirsty.'

'Hmm…' I said. 'I wonder if we've been played for fools.'

'What do you mean?' asked Nathan.

'Maybe she knew it wasn't all one-sided. Maybe she found out that Jamie was pestering Kirsty to get back together, rather than the other way round, and Ellie saw an opportunity to get rid of Kirsty and maybe even drop her cheating boyfriend in it at the same time.'

'That's pretty devious,' said Mum. 'That sounds like something I'd do, but I don't know about Ellie…'

'We'll get to the bottom of it,' said Nathan. He leant in and gave me a kiss. 'I'm just impressed you brought her straight here and not via Exeter or something so you could interrogate her for a bit longer.'

'Dammit, I missed my chance,' I said, and then we headed once more unto the breach, back to the vets to get Germaine's special food, and then to try our luck amongst the Christmas shoppers at the supermarket and buy some sprouts.

I'd promised Mum lunch – specifically something involving roast chicken, after all that sage had started her craving it – and, although she hadn't said anything, I thought she looked worn out, so I sat her down in the supermarket café and went to queue up at the counter. It had probably been a blessing in disguise that she hadn't had to perform in the panto every night leading up to Christmas Eve; she was quite fit and healthy for a woman in her mid-seventies, but her role had been fairly physical, and I thought even that one night had taken some toll on her. Not as big a toll as it had taken on poor Kirsty, of course… It was busy in the café, but nothing compared to the chaos I could see in the shop aisles, and I cursed myself for not coming earlier. I was still a customer or two away from the till when I felt a light tap on my shoulder.

'Sorry, Jodie?' Lesley, Kirsty's sister, stood behind me looking hesitant. Her face cleared as I turned around to face her. 'Oh good, it is you – I wasn't sure.'

'Lesley! How are you?' I asked, because I didn't know what else to say. 'How's your dad?'

'About as well as can be expected,' she said, which was a polite way of saying *'How the bloody hell do you THINK he feels?'* Because it was a stupid question. I waited for her to ask if there was any news, or if Nathan had any leads, but she didn't. 'My grandmother was asking about you this morning, I think she'd like to talk to you. Would you be able to come round?' I must've looked confused, because she said, 'I'm sorry, I know you're probably busy, and I don't know what she wants to see you about, but if you have time I would really appreciate it.'

'Of course,' I said hastily, because she was starting to look a bit tearful. 'I do have some shopping to do, and my mum's with me, but I could come round later? About four o'clock?'

'That would be really kind of you,' said Lesley. She grabbed a napkin and quickly wrote on it before handing it to me. 'There's the address. I'll see you later, and thank you.'

'No worries,' I said. I watched her walk away and thought, *What on earth was that all about?* But I'd have to wait until four o'clock to find out.

Chapter Sixteen

Kirsty's grandmother lived in an apartment in the new retirement complex on the edge of Penstowan. Mum had thought about buying one herself after Nathan had moved in with us, but we'd built her the granny annex instead. *Maybe we should've let her move here*, I thought, as the building manager led me through the immaculately manicured grounds to the two-storey block the apartment was in, but as much as we all appreciated the separation the annex gave us, we'd have missed having her near us. Lesley met me at the door and smiled gratefully.

'Thank you so much for coming,' she said. 'Nana's looking forward to meeting you.' She lowered her voice. 'She hasn't been very well since she heard what happened, but she insisted she had to see you.' She stepped back to let me in, and then showed me into a small but cosy living room.

'Hello, Mrs Butler,' I said, 'how are you feeling today?'

Kirsty's grandmother, Maeve, was sitting propped up in her armchair. I'd expected a frail little old lady, but she wasn't that at all. She still looked pale, no doubt from the shock, but her steel-grey hair was fashioned into a sleek bob, and her makeup was perfect. She was dressed in an emerald green jumper dress, which contrasted nicely with her hair colour, with a string of amber beads around her neck. There was a walking stick propped up next to her, though, and one of her hands looked slightly swollen and misshapen. Arthritis, I guessed.

'Call me Maeve. I'm fine, I just had a funny turn when I heard the news and everyone panicked.' She shook her head. 'Who'd have thought I'd outlive not just my daughter, but my granddaughter too? That's just not right.'

Lesley sat down next to her and took her hand. 'I'm still here, Nana.'

Maeve smiled warmly at her. 'I know, darlin', and I'm so grateful for it.' She turned to me. 'I know you, don't I? You're Eddie Parker's daughter.'

'Did you know him?' I asked, surprised, but obviously she did.

'Oh yes,' she said. 'He was ever so helpful and supportive when we moved down here. You were only little then, of course, and Tessa – my daughter – she would've been fifteen, so she would've been years ahead of you at school. Would you like some tea?'

'I never say no to a cuppa,' I said, and she smiled.

'Woman after my own heart.'

Lesley smiled fondly at her grandmother, then got up to

put the kettle on. Maeve lowered her voice, although I didn't think Lesley would be able to hear her anyway from the kitchen.

'I was a mess when we moved down here,' she said. 'We both were. Has Lesley told you about it?'

'No, only that your husband had died.'

'It was a bit worse than that. He was murdered.'

I looked at her in shock. 'Oh no, I'm so sorry to hear that. What happened? You don't have to tell me if it's too painful,' I added hastily, although to be fair it had been her who had brought it up.

'No, it's fine. It upsets Lesley when I talk about it, but Kirsty was always very interested in the story.' She took a deep breath, preparing herself. 'It was 1985. We ran a corner shop and post office in Bermondsey. You lived in London for a bit, didn't you? Do you know the area?'

'Not really, no,' I said.

'It was a nice place to live when Tessa was little. Not posh, but lots of families. But it went downhill during the Eighties. Loads of people were out of work, the housing market crashed – there was a big recession. We noticed little things at first. We had people shoplifting, which we'd never really had much of a problem with before. We knew all our customers, they were our neighbours. The thought of them stealing from us, well, it was a shock.'

'Desperate people do desperate things,' I said, and she nodded.

'They certainly do. Anyway, one day, a couple of young men came in, dressed head to toe in black, they were, balaclavas an' all. Plastic carrier bags in their hands. I knew straightaway they were trouble, of course, and I called over to Alan – my husband – to watch out, but it was too late. They pulled sawn-off shotguns out of the carrier bags and pointed one at Alan, and one at me, and shouted at Alan to open the safe.'

'Oh God,' I said, my blood running cold. All guns were scary, but if like me you grew up in the Eighties watching stuff like *The Bill* or *The Sweeney* on telly, sawn-off shotguns were even more terrifying. Because an ordinary shotgun – well, farmers had them for legitimate reasons, like shooting rabbits or keeping foxes away from their chickens or something like that, but a sawn-off shotgun had only one purpose: violence. Easily concealed, they were a lot less accurate than an unmodified gun, but the type of people who carried them didn't care about that. They worked well enough when you had them pointed in someone's face.

'The worst thing was it was after school, so Tessa was in the shop with us, helping out stocking the shelves,' said Maeve.

'Bloody hell,' I said.

'Alan and I had discussed what to do if we ever got robbed, not thinking it'd ever really happen, and we always said we would just do whatever they told us to do – give them the money and anything else they wanted. So Alan was trying to open the safe, but he was so scared he kept mucking up the combination, and the robbers were getting angrier and angrier. And that made him more scared.'

'Of course he was scared! I'd be scared too, and I've had training,' I said.

'In the end the bloke pointing the gun at Alan dragged him out from behind the counter and grabbed Tessa, and told me to go behind the counter and open it myself. The other bloke looked nervous – even with his face covered, I could see by the way he was jigging about that this wasn't going the way he'd planned it – and he told his friend to leave Tessa out of it. While they were arguing Alan threw himself at the one pointing the gun at Tessa, and then everything just happened at once.'

'Alan was shot?' I asked.

Maeve nodded. 'The one who had told his friend to leave Tessa alone, he jerked around when Alan flew at the other one and his gun went off, and it hit Alan in the head.'

'Shit,' I said. 'Oh Maeve, I'm so sorry. No wonder you were, what did you call it? – "a mess". You and Tessa must both have been completely traumatised.'

'We were. Your dad was so good, so understanding. He made sure we felt safe in our new home.'

'That sounds like my dad,' I said. 'But what happened to the armed robbers? Did they catch them?'

'No, which is one of the reasons why I felt like we had to move – I couldn't be sure they wouldn't come back.'

'I suppose there wasn't much of a description you could give the police,' I said, and she nodded.

'Young men, dressed in black,' she said. 'My only comfort is that I don't think he meant to shoot Alan, I think it was an accident. And I hope the guilt haunts him until the day he dies.'

Lesley came back in with a tray of tea and biscuits, and set it down on the coffee table with a shake of her head.

'Honestly Nana, you're not telling Jodie all about *that*, are you? That all happened years ago. You're just going to confuse the police. They need to know stuff that's relevant now.'

'That's exactly why I wanted to talk to Jodie,' said Maeve, leaning forward to look me squarely in the eye. 'I think it *is* relevant now, but I want your opinion, love, before I tell the police about it.'

'How is it relevant now?'

'Kirsty was interested in the story. Their mum never really talked about it, did she? She never really got over it, and I'm not surprised. She was so young to go through something like that, to see her dad killed in front of her. So when Kirsty heard some of the story from her, she came to me to get all the details. This was a good, ooh, five or six years ago? Before her mum got sick.'

'Okay…' I said, doubtfully. How could a deadly armed robbery from forty years ago have any bearing at all on Kirsty's murder a few days ago?

'I told her the full story, like I've just told you, and I told her that the only thing the police had to go on was something I saw as the one who shot her grandad bent over his body, to see if he was still breathing.' Maeve took a breath herself. 'He was very well built, and the black T-shirt he was wearing was tight on him. And when he bent over it rode up.'

'And?' said Lesley, exasperated, but then I supposed she'd heard this story before and couldn't understand why it would be of interest now.

'And there was a tattoo there. I couldn't look at Alan's body, so I just kept staring at it. I thought that it would help the police track him down if I could describe it to them.'

'But it didn't,' said Lesley.

'It could've helped them prove it was him,' I said, 'but they would still have to find him first. If he didn't already have previous for that sort of thing it would be pretty difficult. They couldn't go around asking every bloke in London to lift their T-shirt up and show them any tattoos they might have.' Except maybe now, here in Penstowan, the police wouldn't have to do that. Because that very morning I'd seen the exact same thing; a man with a tattoo that was only visible because his T-shirt had ridden up.

'You're right, of course,' said Maeve, 'and I wouldn't have thought any more about it, only Kirsty came to me a couple of days ago and asked me if I could describe the tattoo again.'

I looked at her, a suspicion forming in my head. One I couldn't quite believe. 'Did Kirsty think she'd seen someone with the same tattoo?'

'She did. She wouldn't tell me who, because she said she wanted to keep me safe. And of course after that business at the school, she wanted to make sure she had evidence before she went to the police this time. Can't blame her.'

'No, absolutely… Do you think it was someone connected with the panto?' I said, thinking, *Not Colin?*, and she nodded.

'That's what I assumed, because I think work and rehearsals were taking up all her time. But she didn't *say* that. It could've been a boyfriend, I suppose, except if it was the same man they would've been a lot older than her, at least early sixties.' Colin's age…

'What did this tattoo look like?' I asked, scrabbling around in my bag for a scrap of paper and a pen. 'Can you describe it for me? Maybe I can draw it.'

'I can do better than that,' said Maeve. 'I drew it for the police at the time. If your husband can get hold of the police at Bermondsey, they'll have it on file. But I can describe it to you in the meantime.' I waited for her to say it was a shamrock, but— 'It looked Celtic, like a knot drawn in thick black lines. Sort of like a triangle surrounded by a circle? It was on the small of his back.' So not the one I'd seen on Colin, then.

Lesley and I exchanged glances. She got out her phone and started typing into it, then passed it over to her grandmother. 'I just googled "Celtic knot tattoos", are any of these like it?'

'Yes, that one,' said Maeve firmly, pointing to the screen. 'Almost identical to that.'

'A triquetra,' I said, reading the screen. I turned to Lesley. 'Can you screenshot that one and send it to me? I'll pass it on to Nathan.'

'You think it's relevant, then?' asked Maeve.

'I think it's more than relevant,' I said, picking up my teacup and holding it up to toast Maeve. 'I think it'll be the final nail in the killer's coffin.' *If we can find him*, I added to myself.

I drove home, deep in thought. Colin Sweeney did of course have a tattoo, and he was the right age. But it was the wrong tattoo in the wrong place. And if, as Maeve was suggesting (and it was a good theory), the tattooed man had killed her granddaughter to keep her quiet, that ruled Colin out anyway, as he had an alibi for the time of the murder – an easily corroborated one. He'd either been in the lighting box or in the bar, and there had been at least one other person with him there the whole time.

So was there another man, in his sixties, with a tattoo, involved in the panto? Tim was the right age, but even if he did have a tattoo on his back he was black – Maeve would've spotted that… There were other older men in the cast – the Emperor was about the right age, but I was pretty certain he'd never lived in London; I doubted he'd ever got further upcountry than Dorset. Maybe amongst the crew? Mum would know. I found her in the kitchen – *our* kitchen, not hers, and I wondered again why we'd bothered to put one in her annex – putting the kettle on. She held up a mug questioningly and I nodded. 'Do you even need to ask?'

She laughed and got the teabags out. 'So where did you disappear off to?'

'I went to see Kirsty's nan,' I said. 'Maeve Butler. Do you know her?'

Mum humphed and folded her arms over her chest.

'Oh yes, I know *that* one,' she said, disapprovingly. 'Didn't realise poor Kirsty was from *that* family.' I was surprised.

'What's wrong with her? I thought she seemed nice.'

'Always trying it on with your father, she was. He soon told her where to go.'

'Really? I mean she had just lost her husband when she moved here—'

'No excuse to go fishing for someone else's,' said Mum, militantly.

'The poor woman was traumatised. Imagine seeing the love of your life gunned down in front of you...'

'She *what*?' Now Mum looked surprised, and slightly guilty. 'He was murdered?'

'Yes, that's why she moved here. That's why Dad took an interest in her, to make sure she felt safe. Her and Kirsty's mum. Didn't he tell you?'

'No... no, he didn't.' Mum looked perplexed.

'You know Dad would never cheat on you. The two of you were always like lovesick teenagers.'

'But why didn't he tell me?' She looked mortified. 'I was horrible to that poor woman. Although she *did* fancy Dad.'

'Of course she did, she had good taste and he was a bit of a catch. But you're the one who caught him.' I grinned. 'He probably didn't tell you because that would've been a proper juicy bit of gossip, wouldn't it?'

'I'm not that bad...' Mum smiled ruefully. 'Oh all right, I am. But not if he'd told me not to say anything.'

'But Dad knew it would've been absolute torture for you, not to be able to pass it on. And they probably still had hopes of catching the killer, so it was important for Maeve's whereabouts to be kept quiet, because she was a witness.'

'That's true.' Mum sighed. 'Oh dear, I think I should probably go round and apologise to her. I mean, I never said anything to her *face*—'

'Good.'

'—but I might've told everyone else she was like the Merry Widow of Penstowan, and that they needed to lock up their husbands when she was about.'

'Oh *Mother*! That's horrible.'

'What can I say? If I feel like someone's out to hurt my family, I will go full Mama Bear mode on them.' She looked so fierce that I had to laugh. 'Don't tell me you're not the same, because I remember the battles you had with Richard over Daisy while the divorce was going through.'

'No, you're right. I wouldn't have hurt him, of course, but I might've scratched "cheating wanker" on his new car and let all his tyres down...' I said. 'Just the once, though, because the bugger started parking it in his garage overnight after that.'

Mum laughed. 'That's my girl,' she said, proudly.

Chapter Seventeen

I didn't get a chance to tell Nathan about Maeve Butler's theory of the tattooed man until much later that night. I'd rung him but he'd not been able to pick up, so I assumed he was probably still questioning Jamie Westall. Despite Maeve's story, I thought Jamie was the most likely suspect; he seemed to have a motive, and he'd been backstage – indeed, he'd even been in the cupboard where Kirsty's body had been hidden, earlier in the evening with Ellie.

Mum had gone to watch telly in bed, and Daisy was still out with Joe, so I was on the sofa with Germaine watching one of those daft (but completely addictive) Hallmark-type Christmas romances when Nathan came in. He sunk onto the sofa next to me with a groan of exhaustion.

'Long day, babe?' I asked, sympathetically, and he nodded.

'Long, but I'm hoping we've got him.'

'Jamie?'

'Yes. Still waiting for the Forensics to come back on the Widow Twankey costume, and on the fabric we found in the wardrobe department, but his alibi is shaky and we know he was definitely backstage that night.' Nathan shrugged his coat off – he'd been too tired to even take that off when he'd come in – and slipped his feet out of his shoes without undoing the laces.

'You look knackered. You want a drink?' I asked, starting to rise, but he put out a hand and stopped me.

'No, I just want to lie here for a bit next to my beautiful wife…'

'Sorry, your beautiful one ain't here, so you'll have to make do with me.' He laughed and lay his head on my shoulder, yawning. 'I'm assuming Jamie's not about to confess?'

'No, of course not. He's the type who would keep denying it even if we had a hundred witnesses who saw him and video footage of him doing it. He's not going to make my job easy.' Nathan sat up again, trying to wake himself up. 'He initially said that he left right after Ellie left him, but we knew that was unlikely as backstage would have been full of cast and crew running around, getting ready. So then he admitted he'd left about ten minutes later, once the show had started, but we've got statements from a couple of crew members who were desperately trying to fix a bit of scenery that had been ripped, and the only place with enough room, far enough away from the stage that they could be sure the audience wouldn't hear them, was right outside the fire exit – they left the door propped open so they could carry it back in once it was repaired. So they would've seen him if he'd left then.'

'That doesn't look good for him, does it?' I said.

'Good for us, though. Eventually he admitted he was hanging around to see if he could get a chance to talk to Kirsty between scenes, but he realised if he waited too long it would be the interval, and Ellie would wonder why he was still there.'

'Did he say why he wanted to see Kirsty?' I asked.

'He didn't want to at first, but as I told you, we have her phone records. He rang her sixty-two times, just this month.'

'Just this *month*? Over the course of twenty-three days?'

'Less than twenty-three, because she was murdered on the nineteenth,' Nathan pointed out. 'Ellie still maintains that Kirsty was stalking him, but it was definitely the other way round. Most of the time she didn't even answer his calls. We don't know what was said when she *did*, of course, but there are text messages too, and she's telling him in no uncertain terms to get lost.'

'So what did Jamie want to see her for that night?' I asked. 'Was he going to beg her to take him back or something?'

'That's what he says.'

'But he'd just been in the cupboard engaging in you-know-what with Ellie!' I said. 'What an absolute bastard.'

'Yep. He admits he was only using Ellie to make Kirsty jealous. He'd hooked up with her on Tinder a while back and was really just in it for casual sex, but when he realised she was going to be in the panto with Kirsty he made her think he wanted a proper relationship.'

'Poor Ellie,' I said. 'So what's his alibi? Why is it shaky?'

'He says he left about eight o'clock, which does tie in with the crew members who were out the back – they'd finished by then and had come back inside, and were in the wings, out of the way. He says he went out the fire exit and then walked back to his car, which was parked a fair distance away in the top beach car park.'

'You mean the one car park in town that doesn't have CCTV cameras? That figures.'

'Yep. He says he didn't park near the theatre because he didn't want Kirsty to know he was there – he wanted to surprise her.'

'By bashing her head in? I'd say that would count as a surprise,' I said.

'Then he drove home, but as he lives towards Hatherleigh he didn't have to go through the town centre—'

'Avoiding the traffic camera.'

'Avoiding *all* the cameras. There's one speed camera on his route home, but so far we haven't been able to pick up his car passing it.'

'It was dark, though…'

'Yes,' said Nathan. 'Obviously if you break the speed limit and trip the camera, it flashes so we can pick up your license plate number. But if not…'

'So he *could* be telling the truth,' I said. 'I'm not saying he is, just playing devil's advocate, which is what any solicitor worth their salt would do. Even if it got past the CPS.'

'Yep. So although I'm pretty certain we've got our man, I don't have enough to charge him. Yet.' Nathan put his arm around me and I snuggled into him, feeling him relax. 'Oh yeah, you called me earlier, didn't you? Sorry I couldn't answer. By the time I could call you back I was just keen to get home.'

'I guessed as much. I didn't leave a message because it's a bit complicated.' I told Nathan about my conversation with Maeve Butler.

Nathan whistled. 'Bloody hell, there's a theory for you.'

'You don't think it's a possibility?'

'I don't know. It probably *is*, but... Jamie Westall still seems a lot more likely. Who would this tattooed man even be?'

'Well, I did initially think it could be Colin because he does have a tattoo, but of course he's got a pretty watertight alibi,' I said. 'You have corroborated that, I take it? I know you've got a lot of them to check.'

'Yes, we have. The bloke on the lighting desk and the old lady who runs the bar both confirmed they were with him at the time.'

'That's what I thought. I think you're probably right about Jamie,' I said, snuggling deeper into him. 'He's a nasty piece of work, the way he's treated Ellie. I know there's a difference between being a crappy boyfriend and being a killer, but he obviously only cares about what he wants, and who knows how he'd react if someone – Kirsty, in this case – told him he couldn't have it?'

'Wouldn't be the first time a jilted lover killed the object of their affection,' said Nathan. 'What do we always say? Look at the partner, or the ex, first.'

I yawned. 'Are you ready for bed?'

'Yes. It's been a long day today, and it'll be another one tomorrow.'

'Will you be able to make it to the carol concert at St Botolph's in the evening? I told Carmen we'd all go.'

'I'll do my best, but you know as well as I do – crime doesn't respect bank holidays or religious festivals…'

We went to bed, Germaine following us up the stairs and making herself comfortable on the duvet. Nathan fell asleep almost immediately, but I lay awake listening for Daisy to come home; Joe would be staying overnight (in the spare room, as far as I was aware, but since my recent conversation with Daisy I wasn't so sure), so I knew she'd get home safe, but I still couldn't do more than doze until I heard the front door go. I lay in bed thinking over what Maeve Butler had said to me, and about Colin and his tattoo – did he have any more that I hadn't seen? – and about Jamie. What sort of man would have sex in a cupboard (oh the romance!) with one woman, just to get access to another? Another woman, who had told him on multiple occasions that she wasn't interested in him. It wasn't *that* big a stretch to think that a man like that would lose his temper and lash out, after all. No, when all was said and done, Jamie Westall had the motive and the opportunity. It had to be him.

So why was I lying there thinking about tattoos…?

———————

Nathan was up and out early again the next day. I got out of bed to make him some breakfast before he left – I knew what he was like, he would get so involved in what he was doing that he'd forget all about food until he was absolutely starving, and I couldn't have him wasting away. But he ignored the plate of food on the table and grabbed a banana to eat in the car, kissed me goodbye and left, with a promise that he would pull out all the stops to be at Carmen's Christmas Eve carol concert later that night. I ate his scrambled egg on toast myself.

It was still relatively early – only about nine o'clock – when the front doorbell rang, sending Germaine into a frenzy of yapping, ready to repel foes and invaders. I had fortunately already showered and dressed (not always a given at that time of day when I'm not working, I'm ashamed to admit) so, after grabbing hold of the dog and shutting her in the kitchen, I answered. On the doorstep stood Tim and Maurice. I braced myself for another tirade from Maurice about the sheer audacity of Nathan dragging his beloved down the police station, but then I noticed that both of them – but particularly the mayor – looked somewhat sheepish.

Maurice held up a canvas tote bag. 'I come in peace,' he

said, handing it to me. I took a quick peek inside and spotted a whole lot of Christmas foodie stuff.

'You'd better come in, then,' I said, standing aside and showing them into the kitchen, where Germaine's defensive yaps had evolved into excited ones, as she recognised the voices.

'We—' began Maurice, but he started again after seeing Tim's raised eyebrows. '—I mean, *I* wanted to apologise for having a go at you on the phone the other day.'

'There's no need,' I said. 'You were worried, I understand.'

'Maurice has been feeling *awful*,' said Tim, gesturing to the bag. 'He's ordered half of Ocado, just to make it up to you.'

'So I see,' I said, emptying the contents of the tote onto the counter. 'M&S mince pies, stollen from Waitrose, proper French cheese… You really didn't need to.' *But since you have, you ain't having it back,* I thought. 'Tea? Coffee?' *Don't ask for coffee,* I thought. I only had instant, and going by the fancy stuff they'd bought me, they probably had a proper coffee machine at home. A cafetière, at least. Nescafé probably wasn't going to cut it.

Thankfully they were both happy with tea, so we sat down at the kitchen table with a brew.

'So you were right,' said Maurice. 'Nathan told us that Tim has been completely cleared and is no longer a suspect.'

'He actually said I was never really a suspect to start off with,' said Tim, and I nodded, although of course that wasn't what Nathan had said to me; Tim most definitely *had* been, based solely on what little evidence we – I mean, the police – had had at the time, it was just that Nathan hadn't wanted to believe he was any more than I or of course Maurice had. Nathan was obviously learning to be more diplomatic with our friends and neighbours.

'I hear they've got the real killer in custody now,' said Maurice, and I realised that this visit wasn't just an apology, it was an exercise in information gathering. It never failed to surprise me just how nosey everyone in this town really was.

'They do have someone, yes,' I said carefully. Tim nodded.

'Good to have an arrest so soon,' he said, 'and before Christmas Day, too.'

'He's not been charged yet,' I said, and then kicked myself, but the two men had already pounced on it.

'He? So it is a man, then?' asked Maurice.

'I heard it was her ex,' said Tim. They both looked at me. I shook my head and fixed them with a mock-stern gaze.

'You know I can't tell you,' I said, 'no matter how many nice things you've bought me.'

'I'll take my mince pies back,' threatened Maurice, but he was joking. I hoped. I was prepared to fight him for them, despite the fact he was at least twenty years older than I was. 'No, I know you have to be discreet.'

'It was that Jamie, though, wasn't it?' persisted Tim.

'Oh my God, I can't tell you!' I said, with an exasperated laugh. 'But… say it was…'

'Go on.' The two of them leant forward eagerly.

'Would you be surprised? I mean, you both seem to think it's possible, if not likely.'

'I would not be shocked, put it that way,' said Tim. 'Him *and* that Ellie.'

'You think Ellie had something to do with it as well?' Interesting. I had considered it, but not that seriously once Jamie's behaviour had come to light.

'She was convinced that Kirsty wanted him back,' said Tim. 'I only met him the once, when he was hanging around after rehearsals, but for the life of me I couldn't see the attraction. I mean, *obviously* he's young and fit—'

'Obviously,' said Maurice, with only the slightest hint of bitterness.

'—but he's got all the personality of the *Daily Mail* letters page. Classic narcissist. And Ellie's the classic narcissist's victim.'

'Victim, yes. But you think she could've had something to do with the murder herself?'

'What do you think would happen if the person you loved kept on and on taunting you about their relationship with someone close to you?' said Tim, getting into his stride as an amateur psychologist. 'Someone you saw every time you came to rehearsals. Someone who'd already taken the lead role you auditioned for, and now it looked like they were going to take your boyfriend as well.'

'You can't ask Jodie that,' said Maurice. 'She's got far too high an opinion of herself.'

'Thank you,' I said, not sure whether or not to be offended, 'I think.'

'It's a compliment,' said Maurice. 'You have too much self-respect to let some man treat you like that. You'd just dump his worthless *derrière* and move on.' *And scratch 'cheating wanker' down the side of his car,* I thought, but I didn't say it.

'That's true,' said Tim, 'but you know what I'm getting at. Ellie could have just snapped and bashed Kirsty with the lamp, although she'd have been better off thumping that horrible boyfriend.'

Daisy came into the kitchen in her pyjamas, yawning. She stopped short as she saw the three of us sitting at the table.

'What's going on?' she asked. 'I appear to have woken up in the low-budget Cornish reboot of *Only Murders in the Building*...'

Tim and Maurice left not long after that, and Daisy and Joe got themselves together and drove over to see a friend in Bideford, which just left me, Mum and the dog.

I knocked on the door of the annex – unlike her, I respected boundaries and didn't just barge in – and was greeted by my mother dressed in her finest.

'Where are you off to, your majesty?' I asked, taking in the skirt suit, the string of (fake) pearls and the carefully coiffured hair.

'Bob's taking me for a drive out towards Bodmin,' said Mum. 'We're going to have a walk around Lanhydrock

House – it's all done up for Christmas – and then have lunch there.' Was it my imagination, or was she blushing? 'He knew I was proper disappointed about the panto being cancelled, so he called me and said he wanted to take me out and cheer me up.'

'That sounds lovely,' I said. 'Bob's a really nice bloke.'

'He is,' said Mum. 'He's not your father, but…'

'No one could replace Dad,' I said, 'but that doesn't mean you shouldn't have someone else.'

'Do I have your blessing, then?' she asked, looking at me anxiously. I was surprised; my mum rarely does anxious.

'Of course you do, not that you need it. You've been on your own a long time now.'

'I have. I'm not that old. I still have needs—'

'—which we don't need to discuss in detail,' I interrupted, and we both laughed. I kissed her on the cheek. 'Go out and have a lovely time,' I instructed her. 'Don't do anything I wouldn't do.'

'I won't,' she said. 'Bearing in mind there's not a lot you wouldn't do.'

'Cheek!'

So now it was just me and the dog. I could see the day stretching ahead of me. I'd got everything I needed for Christmas Day tomorrow; I'd wrapped the last few presents the night before, while I'd been waiting for Nathan to come home. I could of course be one of those super-organised hostesses who preps all the veg for the big day ahead of time, but who wants to spend Christmas Eve peeling spuds, scrubbing carrots and cutting crosses into the Brussels sprouts, while being subjected to Michael Bublé on the radio? Not me.

'It'll be a nice thing to do, to keep Nathan and the gang's morale up,' I told Germaine, as I gathered together some of the goodies Maurice had just brought round and put them back into the tote bag. Germaine gave me a *pull-the-other-one-it's-got-tinsel-on* look. 'Yeah, I wouldn't believe me either,' I admitted. I got my big coat, my woolly hat, my scarf and my gloves on, clipped on Germaine's lead and headed out the door.

It was a fair walk into town, but it meant Germaine would get a good bit of exercise without us having to go on the beach, which also meant I wouldn't have to spend half an hour getting all the claggy sand out of her coat when we got home. We wound down the hill and up Fore Street, stopping to talk to a few people who were out getting last-minute presents, before reaching Penhaligon's. I didn't intend to go in, but Tony was outside, directing one of his staff members who was in the window, attempting to repair the display.

'All right, Tone? What happened?' I asked him.

'Morning, Nosey. You would not believe it, but a bloody seagull came in through the automatic doors and got into the window display,' said Tony. He turned back to the young man in the window and waved his arms about, trying to explain what he wanted, but the young man looked mystified. He gave up and turned his attention back to me. 'Of course, it was just before closing time last night and nobody noticed until about twenty minutes ago.

Laughing boy there went in to try and catch it, but not before the bloody thing had ripped the head off an elf, pooed all over Santa's hat, and tried to eat the star on top of the Christmas tree, which I reckon is why it's gone all lopsided. No, Ben—' this to the unfortunate member of staff in the window '—move it to the *left*! The other left!'

'I might just leave you to it,' I said. Germaine yapped her agreement.

'Go on, save yourself,' said Tony. 'Are you coming to the concert tonight? Carmen's worried no one will turn up.'

'What are you talking about? It's the highlight of the Penstowan Christmas season!' I said. 'We'll all be there.' Although with Mum out gallivanting, Daisy and Joe having fun with friends and Nathan desperately trying to close the case against Jamie, I knew the chances of the entire family being there were getting smaller and smaller.

'Thank you, she really needs your support. She's taken on this new verger to help her organise everything, but she's still convinced the church will be half empty.'

'Poor Carmen, stuck in a parish full of heathens,' I said, sympathetically. 'Tell her not to worry, most of Penstowan might be godless creatures but we all love a Christmas singsong. I've got her covered on the mince pie front too, remind her. See you later.'

I turned away, but then had a thought. I turned back. 'Did you know Colin's got a tattoo?'

Tony (reasonably enough) looked at me like I was mad. 'Colin Sweeney? A tattoo?'

'Yeah. Forget I mentioned it, it's probably not important…'

'He's got several, I think. One of the crew was talking about getting one, one of the younger blokes, and I showed him mine and told him how much it bloody hurt, and then Colin surprised us all by going, *'Call that a tattoo?'* and showing us his.'

'Can you remember where they were?'

'In the auditorium. It was during rehearsals—'

'No, you daft sod, where were the tattoos?'

'Oh, right. Hang on – Ben, just take the headless elf out of the window, for some reason it's upsetting the parents.'

'Don't you mean it's upsetting the kids?'

'Nah, the bloodthirsty little buggers think it's hilarious, it's their parents who are complaining.' He waved Ben out of the window and turned back to me. 'Let me think. There was one on his tummy, sort of here…' He waved a hand down his torso. 'He told us it looked better when he had a six-pack. I think it was a leaf or something.'

'A shamrock.'

'That's it! And then he had a couple on his arms – you know the ones that go all the way around, like a cuff? Really intricate tribal things. Looked like they were Māori or something. I was glad your Daisy weren't there, she would've called it cultural appropriation or something.'

'That does sound like my Daisy,' I admitted. 'Did he have any on his back?'

'I dunno, he was facing us.'

'Can you remember who else was there? Was Kirsty?'

Tony narrowed his eyes. 'What's going on? You do realise I've been subjected to a Jodie Parker interrogation before, right? I thought they had someone for the murder?'

'They do,' I said. 'Or Nathan thinks they do, anyway.'

'But you don't?'

'I don't know. I mean, everything's pointing to Nathan being right, but…'

'Yeah, but – *Colin*? They were really close. She was a real fan girl.'

'You said that before. What do you mean, she was a fan girl?'

'She wanted to know all about his career and how he ended up on telly, and then on the stage. I know he's had a few small TV roles again lately, but I've also heard rumours that he was about to be offered something big, so she was keen to find out all about that.' He wrinkled his nose in thought. 'She asked him about it, but he was a bit cagey about his early days. I got the impression he was embarrassed about *Mile End Days*, or about the way it ended, anyway. With him leaving cos he thought he could do better.'

'Yeah, he told me about that…'

Tony looked at me seriously. 'You don't really think Colin would hurt her, do you? Because I don't believe it. He genuinely liked her. I even heard him asking his agent about representing her.'

'Really?'

'Not in so many words, but he was definitely hinting

that she should. Looked like she was considering it, too, although I didn't hear her promise anything.'

'When was this?'

'Beginning of last week? One of the last rehearsals we did, anyway. She's been staying with him, so she came along to watch. I'm thinking now it was probably to have a look at Kirsty, see if she really was as good as he said she was.' Tony looked at his watch. 'Sorry, I need to get on. I've got loads to do and my boss is a right slave driver.'

'You're the boss, Tony.'

'Oh yeah, so I am.' He grinned at me and bent down to pat Germaine, who had been far too busy watching the elf-related shenanigans in the window to take much notice of him. 'I'll see you at the concert later. You're invited too, Germaine.'

'You might regret that,' I said, and walked on.

Chapter Eighteen

I made it to the police station without any further interruption. Desk Sergeant Sally smiled as we entered.

'Back again?' she asked. 'Are you sure you don't work here?'

'Well, sometimes, unofficially,' I said, holding up the bag, 'but today I'm delivering stuff.'

'I'll buzz upstairs,' she said, but just then Sunil came through the door into the foyer, bundled up in a thick padded jacket.

'Jodie!' he said, in surprise. 'Just who I wanted to see.'

'Really?'

'Yeah.' He turned to Sally. 'The guv and Matt are both still interviewing Jamie Westall. I'll take care of Jodie.' He gestured towards the door back out into the street, so Germaine and I left with him following close behind.

'Take care of me? That sounds ominous,' I said, and he grinned.

'I think actually it might be the other way round,' he said. 'I need someone to talk this over with. I'm not sure if it's important enough to interrupt the interview, though.' He looked around. 'Shall we sit in the car? It's freezing out here.'

'Okay,' I said, so we both got into Sunil's car. 'You looked like you were on your way out already,' I said. 'Were you coming to see me?'

'Not exactly,' said Sunil. 'I was going to see *someone*, but I wasn't sure if I should…'

'Go on,' I said, and Germaine gave an encouraging yap.

'I've been going over Kirsty's phone records,' he said. 'That's how we found out about Jamie more or less stalking her, harassing her over the phone.' I nodded; Nathan had told me that already. 'There were other numbers on there, of course, most of which I traced easily – they were listed in her phone, so friends or family – but there was one which I couldn't find. She called them on Friday morning and spoke to them for about twenty minutes, and then they called her back Friday night, just before the show.'

'Okay…' I said. 'That's not necessarily suspicious, but the timing could be significant.'

'That's what I thought. Anyway I finally found out who it was.' I looked at him, eyebrows raised. 'Hilary Beddows.'

'Hilary? Colin's agent, Hilary?'

'Yes.' He sat back, looking nonplussed. 'Why would they be calling each other, especially just before the show?'

'Were you thinking of going to see Hilary, to ask her about it?' I asked.

'Yes, although I wasn't sure if I was making a mountain out of a molehill.' I smiled at him steadily. 'Oh, you think I should?'

'Yep.' I turned and pulled the seat belt across my chest, buckling myself and Germaine in.

'Er… should you really be coming with me?'

'Yep. I'm a consultant, aren't I? Nathan's used me loads of times. Besides, she's staying at Colin's cottage and it's a bit hidden away. You haven't lived here that long, you'll never find it.'

'I've got a satnav…'

'You'll never find it without a local,' I said firmly, and he grinned and turned on the engine.

'Lucky you're here, then.'

We drove over to the harbour, then slowly wound our way up to the harbourmaster's cottage. Sunil parked up on the grass verge outside and we all got out. Well, the humans did – I settled Germaine onto the back seat to wait for us.

'Stay here, sweetheart,' I said, 'we won't be long.' I bent down to retrieve the canvas tote bag of goodies from the passenger footwell, thought for a moment, then just took one thing out. Sunil watched, bemused. I held up a Christmas pudding.

'My excuse for coming along with you,' I said, and he nodded.

We rang the doorbell. There was no answer for a while, and I had begun to think that there was no one in when suddenly the door opened and Hilary stood in front of us. She looked very surprised to see us.

'Oh, hello,' she said. 'If you've come to see Colin, I'm afraid he's not here. He's down at the theatre, picking up some of the props.'

Sunil held out his warrant card.

'I'm Detective Constable Bakshi, and I think you've already met Jodie. It's you we've come to see, Ms Beddows,' he said politely. She looked even more surprised.

'Me?'

I held up the pudding. 'And to drop off a thank-you present for Colin,' I said. 'The panto might have been cancelled, but Mum and Daisy really enjoyed working on it with him.'

'Oh, that's very nice of you,' she said, smiling, but she still didn't invite us in.

'Could we come in?' asked Sunil. 'I promise we won't take up too much of your time.'

'It is a bit nippy out here,' I said, hopping from one foot to the other to emphasise just how bloody freezing it was.

'Of course,' she said, standing aside and waving us in. 'Go through to the kitchen.'

We walked down the hallway, Sunil taking in the framed photos that were hung along the walls. He stopped in front of a picture that I hadn't noticed before, which showed a much younger Colin and Hilary, wearing loose, colourful robes, standing in front of a teepee.

Hilary saw what we were looking at and stopped too. 'That was a long time ago,' she said.

'Where was that?' I asked.

'That's where I first met Colin. 1993. It was a spiritual

retreat in Ibiza,' she said. 'Much more Colin's thing than mine. He was a few years into his *Mile End Days* contract and having a wobble. I was there under completely false pretences, with an ex-boyfriend of mine who I was hoping, naively as it turned out, to win back. We spent two whole weeks wafting around in kaftans, trying to "find ourselves".' She sounded thoroughly sceptical. 'At least it was sunny.'

'You weren't his agent when he started *Mile End Days*?' I asked.

'No. I had a couple of clients, but no one of Colin's stature. When he told me he was thinking of sacking his agent and throwing in the towel on his acting career, I swooped in and rescued him before he did something he could regret.' She smiled. 'The only time I've come back from a holiday with a souvenir worth keeping. The ex-boyfriend certainly wasn't. Shall we?' She gestured for us to move on and we went through to the kitchen, which felt warm and cosy and rather less cramped than the last time I'd been in there. I thought about what Nathan had said – *a woman scorned* – as I followed her into the room.

'You and Colin look very close in that photo,' I said, and she scoffed.

'Is this your way of asking me if there's more to our relationship than just agent and client?' she asked.

'Is there?'

'You sound like my ex-husband. You miss *one* wedding anniversary because you're busy schmoozing a Hollywood producer at Cannes, and suddenly it's all "you care more about your clients than your marriage".' She sat down at the table. 'Although to be fair, he wasn't entirely wrong. But no, Colin is a close friend and one of my oldest clients, and that's all. I would never get romantically involved with any of my clients, or indeed any actor. They're all far too self-obsessed.' She waved to us to take a chair each too. 'So how can I help you? I'm assuming it's about that poor girl.'

Sunil opened his notebook. 'What did you think of Kirsty?' he asked.

'What did I think? I didn't really know her, but she seemed like a nice girl.'

'You didn't know her, but you had a twenty-minute telephone conversation with her the morning before she was murdered,' said Sunil. Hilary looked surprised again, and not pleasantly so, but quickly covered it up.

'She did call me, yes,' said Hilary.

'Can you tell me what the conversation was about?' Sunil looked up from his notebook, his pen poised to take notes. Waiting. I'd seen Nathan do it in the past, and it always seemed to work; people saw the pen, saw that he meant to get an answer and was prepared to wait for as long as necessary until he got one. He wasn't just there for a chat. It was funny to see Sunil do it, too, and I wondered if he'd learnt it off Nathan.

Hilary smiled. 'Of course. I only didn't mention it before because it didn't seem relevant. In fact, it just feels rather sad now.'

'Go on,' I said.

'She knew that Colin had told me how much he rated

her as an actor. I'd been along to one of the rehearsals earlier in the week, as I had a few last-minute things I had to discuss with Colin and with him being so busy with the panto, it was just easier for me to come along and talk to him whenever he had a spare moment. Plus it was nice to see what he was working on.'

'You weren't there to watch Kirsty?'

'Not initially, no. People are always telling me who I should sign up, tipping me off about who the "next big thing" is, and they're never right. Most people don't understand that it's not enough to be pretty, or talented, or even both – there has to be something *else*, that spark that makes this performer special.'

'A star, not just another actor,' I said, and she nodded.

'Yes. It's completely indefinable, which is why it's so hard to spot. Kirsty – well, she didn't *quite* have that spark, but she had *something*, and I did think that with a little more work under her belt, a little more experience of something more, shall we say, *worthy* than an amateur panto or two on her resumé, she might just end up with that quality.'

'Did you tell Colin that?'

'No, in fact I discouraged him somewhat, because I wasn't sure what I could do to help her, and I wasn't sure I wanted to.' She looked at me, and then Sunil. 'I'm sorry if that sounds harsh, but the number of times people have asked me for favours in this industry and they've come back to bite me on the backside, well…'

'So how did she have your number?' I asked. Hilary shrugged.

'I honestly don't know. Maybe Colin gave it to her? But she could just as easily have got it from my website. My mobile number is listed on there as I don't like to miss calls when I'm out of the office. I normally do a better job of screening them, but for some reason I didn't look at the number and just answered it.'

'Still, you had a long conversation,' said Sunil. 'What did you talk about?'

'She basically asked me to represent her. Now, I'm normally very good at saying no to people—' Hilary smiled, and it was the sort of insincere, surface-only smile that made it very easy to believe that she was good at letting people down, gently or otherwise '—but again, for some reason, I couldn't bring myself to turn her down. Because I suspected she *could*, one day, be worth representing. So we had quite a long conversation about what I thought she needed to do, to increase her chances of success, and I told her a little bit about the realities of being a jobbing actor, because this industry can be rather cutthroat at times. I half wanted her to change her mind, but if anything she became even more determined to impress me and take her on as a client.' Hilary looked thoughtful. 'I was almost tempted to sign her up there and then.'

'But you didn't,' I said, and she shook her head.

'So what was the brief phone call later on about?' asked Sunil. 'Kirsty would have been preparing for the performance, so it seems like a bit of an inconvenient time. What was so important it couldn't wait until after the show?'

'I had a change of heart,' said Hilary. 'I was preparing for a Zoom meeting with a production company in LA, about a big role Colin was up for – I believe Colin's told you about this, Jodie? Anyway I was looking through the casting materials they'd previously sent me, and I spotted a very small role that I thought Kirsty would actually be perfect for. I didn't think they'd cast the smaller parts yet, so I decided to mention Kirsty to them and if they were interested, I would take her on and represent her. Obviously I had to get her permission before I talked to them about her, so no, it couldn't wait until after the performance.' She sighed. 'She was so excited, although I did have to remind her that there was no guarantee they would even audition her, let alone give her the part.'

'Which production company?' asked Sunil. 'Can you tell me who you spoke to?'

Hilary looked openly annoyed now. 'Is this really necessary? I would rather not drag my business contacts in LA, who have nothing whatsoever to do with any of this, who haven't even *heard* of Cornwall, to say nothing of Penstowan, into a murder investigation. How do you think that would make me look? How unprofessional? You might even be putting my client's reputation, *and* his part in this TV project, in jeopardy.'

Sunil remained calm and firm. 'The name of the company and who you spoke to, please, Ms Beddows.'

Hilary gave a hmmph of irritation but gave him the name and contact details of the people she'd had the Zoom meeting with. Sunil got to his feet, and I followed suit.

'Thank you very much for your time, Ms Beddows,' said Sunil. 'We may need to talk to you again, so please let us know if you're planning to go back to London.'

We headed outside and back into the car, where Germaine went wild with joy. The poor thing had been abandoned for all of fifteen minutes, after all. She'd have been on the phone to the RSPCA, if only she'd had the opposable thumbs required to work a mobile.

'So what do you think?' I asked Sunil, as we pulled away.

'It sounds like a reasonable explanation,' he said, 'although I will of course check with these people in LA and see what they say.'

'Yes...' I said, thoughtfully.

'You don't think it sounds reasonable?'

'I don't know. I was talking to Tony earlier, and it kind of chimes with what he told me – he thought that Hilary was at the rehearsal to watch Kirsty. She says she wasn't, but obviously she *did* watch her, and she was reasonably impressed. But then Colin told me yesterday that when he mentioned the possibility of her representing Kirsty she brushed it off, she wasn't interested. So it seems quite a big turnaround, her going from not interested to mentioning her to a TV producer in LA.'

'True... but maybe she said that to Colin before she'd had a chance to watch her perform?' Sunil turned the car back towards the town centre, stopping to let a van go by. He looked at me. 'Are your Spidey senses tingling?'

I laughed. 'That's what Nathan calls them,' I said.

'I don't know. I'm usually pretty good at reading people, but I can't get a read on Hilary. I think maybe I just don't like her. She's a bit cold, isn't she? Like it's all about business.'

'There are a lot of people out there who are like that,' said Sunil, 'but they're not all murderers.'

'No, true, that…'

'Hopefully the LA people will clear up what exactly she said to them,' said Sunil. 'That should prove or disprove her story.'

'I suppose so,' I said.

We drove the rest of the way back to the station in silence, both deep in thought. Even Germaine, now that we'd un-abandoned her, had settled into a pensive mood, or as pensive as it's possible for a Pomeranian to get. As much as I hadn't warmed to Hilary, I could hardly use that as an excuse to accuse her of murder. I had a sneaking suspicion that one of the reasons I didn't like her was because she reminded me of my ex-mother-in-law, who I could quite easily have imagined shoving crippled children out of her way and drowning puppies (no, we hadn't got on). Hardly fair to punish Hilary for that…

We drove into the station car park. Sunil switched off the engine and turned to speak to me, but then his eyes widened as he saw something behind me. 'What the…?' he muttered. I whirled around in my seat to look.

Nathan was standing outside the police station, holding the door open, and walking – no, *sauntering* through that door was Jamie Westall, followed by a smartly dressed man

I didn't know, and Matt, who was glaring at him so hard I wouldn't have been surprised to see the back of Jamie's head melt under the ferocity of it. Sunil and I exchanged looks and leapt out of the car.

'Don't leave town,' said Matt to Jamie. Jamie smirked.

'How's that going to work? I live in Kilkhampton. I've got to leave town to go home,' he said. Matt took a step forward but Nathan inserted himself between them.

'You know full well what we mean. Don't go too far as we may need to speak to you again,' said Nathan.

'Yes, to apologise no doubt,' said the smartly dressed man, who I guessed was Jamie's solicitor. Matt scoffed but didn't say anything.

'Merry Christmas,' said Jamie, sarcastically. 'I hope Santa brings you a clue.' The solicitor snorted in amusement and led his client away.

'What's going on?' I asked, hurrying over to Nathan. 'Why have you let him go?'

'Because there's no forensic evidence to tie him to the murder,' said Nathan, grimly. 'The results came back on the Widow Twankey dress. The blood on it is Kirsty's, as we thought, but there's only the tiniest traces of other DNA on it, including Tim's, because he wore the costume at the dress rehearsal and tried it on for fittings, and a couple of unidentified female traces, which I'm assuming will be Li and other cast or crew members – there're several people who could've handled the costume, so that DNA could belong to any one of them. What it doesn't have, however, is any DNA from Jamie Westall.'

'Bugger,' said Sunil, which was the strongest cuss word I'd ever heard him use. 'But everything else points to him, doesn't it?'

'Yes, it does,' said Matt stubbornly, but Nathan shook his head.

'Without the DNA evidence, the rest of it is circumstantial,' he said. 'We can put him in the right place, possibly at the right time, although we can't prove that he was still there when she was murdered. The only witness we have saw someone in the Widow Twankey costume, and it's covered in the victim's blood, so the killer definitely had it on. If Jamie is the killer, he somehow had enough time to completely erase any of his DNA from that dress, which seems unlikely as there's other people's still intact on it.'

'But most likely, he never had it on,' I said. 'So he's not the murderer…'

'No.' Nathan sighed in exasperation and ran his fingers through his hair. He looked exhausted. He turned to Sunil. 'What have you and my missus been up to?'

Sunil told him about identifying Hilary's phone number and our subsequent visit to the harbourmaster's cottage.

'Okay. See if the LA people can confirm her story, but—' he looked at his watch '—it's only just gone twelve, so it'll be the middle of the night there, I think. Plus it's Christmas Eve, so that might make them even harder to get hold of. Do your best.'

'I'll go through the witness statements one more time,' said Matt. 'There must be something we've missed…'

'Concentrate on the timeline,' said Nathan. 'But don't

spend all day doing it. Go home and get some rest.' He yawned, and looked at me. 'What are you up to now? Are you heading home?'

'I don't know,' I said, 'I'm playing today by ear. Although Germaine looks almost as knackered as you do, so maybe we should head back.'

'Good idea. I'm coming with you. I need some lunch, and I need to get out of that building for an hour or two…'

We drove home in Nathan's car. He could barely stop yawning, now that the adrenaline of interrogating Jamie had worn off.

'You look worn out, babe,' I said, as we neared the house.

'I am.' He pulled into the driveway but didn't get out. 'I didn't sleep very well last night. This one's really got to me.'

'The murder? I thought you'd be used to them by now.'

'I am, but this one feels close to home. Daisy was right there, for God's sake.' He reached over and took my hand. 'I know I'm not her real dad, but I feel like I am. I want to get the scumbag who did this off the streets, so I can make sure she's safe.'

'Oh, bless you,' I said, leaning over to kiss him. 'You're a better dad than her "real" one ever was.'

Chapter Nineteen

I realised once we were inside that I was still clutching the canvas tote bag of goodies (and the dog), so I unloaded everything onto the kitchen table again (apart from the dog), grabbed a couple of plates and told Nathan to tuck in. After a couple of posh organic pork and caramelised onion relish sausage rolls, a brie and cranberry filo pastry pinwheel, and a big chunk of stollen, Nathan began to look more awake. I popped the last pastry pinwheel into my mouth and smiled at him.

'Better?'

'Better. I just needed to get out of that bloody interview room…' He gave a big stretch and then sat back in his chair. 'I was so convinced it was Jamie Westall. I need to rethink everything.'

'You said there was female DNA on the dress,' I said. 'Could that be from Ellie?'

'I don't think so,' he said, shaking his head. 'Obviously

we did wonder if it was her, taking out her rival, but during the murder window she was either on stage or with the rest of the chorus getting changed. Plus Jamie admits it was his idea to have a little bit of pre-show hanky panky in the cupboard, not hers.'

'He's a charmer, isn't he?' I said. 'I've found that people who work with animals are usually really nice, but not him.'

'According to Matt he's a terrible vet as well,' said Nathan with a laugh. 'Apparently his dad called the vet out when one of their goats was ill, and he turned up. Mr Turner senior was not impressed.'

'How was the goat?'

'It lived, but no thanks to Jamie, according to Matt…' Nathan dabbed at a crumb of stollen. 'Can't charge him for being crap at his job, though. More's the pity.'

'So what now?'

'I don't know. Maybe a mince pie…'

'I meant with the investigation.'

'I know. And I don't know. Do you think it's too late to write Father Christmas a letter?'

'What, like, "Dear Santa, all I want for Christmas is a signed confession from Kirsty's murderer"?' I began to clear away the lunch stuff. 'That would be nice, wouldn't it?'

'It certainly would. Leave the mince pies…'

'You'll get fat,' I warned, but without much conviction because Nathan was one of those annoying people who could eat like a horse and never put any weight on. I left the mince pies anyway, because I fancied one myself. I spend the whole of December addicted to mince pies, and the whole of January going cold turkey. And often *eating* cold turkey, because we always had too much. 'What about the lipstick on the fabric from the wardrobe? Did anything come of that?'

'Not really. Forensics couldn't get enough DNA from it to be useful, but they did match it to the lipstick you took from Eesha. So we know it probably came from the shop in Fore Street. Matt talked to the owner and unfortunately that colour was really popular over the summer, in fact it had sold out by the end of September and she's been pestering the woman who makes it to give her more, but she's been away to visit a sick relative and hasn't been home...' Nathan rolled his eyes. 'Matt got the full story and believe me, it was a *very* full story. But basically, whoever bought it did so before the end of September. And ninety per cent of people pay cash in her shop, so she can't trace customers.'

'Dead end, then.'

'Probably. Forensics did say the smear was probably left on the fabric fairly recently, within the last couple of months, because they would've expected an older smear to have dried out more, but they can't narrow it down any further than that. And even if we did track down the person who left it on there, it doesn't mean they had anything to do with the murder.'

'But the blood spot was Kirsty's?'

'Yes. Doesn't mean the lipstick ended up there the same time as the blood though, does it?'

'No, I suppose not…' I mused. 'Shame there's no lipstick on the Widow Twankey dress…'

'Yep. That might actually be helpful.'

'So if it wasn't Tim, because there are witnesses who confirm he was in the green room and he doesn't have any kind of motive, and it wasn't Jamie, because there was no DNA evidence on the dress, and it wasn't Ellie, because she was on stage – who does that leave?' I asked. 'Because obviously there were loads of other people around who *could* have had the opportunity. Who else had motive?'

'No one, as far as we can make out,' said Nathan. 'And there aren't even that many people who had opportunity, because they were either on stage or with other people.'

I reached out for a mince pie, allowing myself to give in to the temptation, reasoning that in a month the shops wouldn't be stocking them anymore so it didn't matter if I ate a load of them now.

'What about Mark Matheson?' I asked. 'I know we ruled him out because he said she'd done him a favour, and he's now got a better job and a fiancée, but everyone's still talking about him here. She might not have ruined his entire life, but she ruined it in Penstowan, and he's still got family here.'

'True, but killing her wouldn't stop the gossip, would it?' Nathan pointed out. 'And anyway, he called me the day after we spoke to him and told me he stopped at the petrol station and bought a pint of milk on his way home from the theatre. There's CCTV footage of him there during the murder window.'

'So definitely not him.'

'Nope. Even without the CCTV, it was still unlikely because he was sitting next to Maggie right up until the interval, and then he went out the front door, so he wouldn't have had much time to somehow get back inside, go backstage without being seen and then kill Kirsty.'

'One other thing that's been puzzling me – how did the killer get hold of the murder weapon? Where was the lamp and how did they get hold of it?'

'Jocasta cleared that one up for me,' said Nathan. 'I was wondering about it myself. In Kirsty's final scene before the interval, she runs off stage with the lamp, because Aladdin is supposed to be saving it from Abanazar by hiding it with Widow Twankey. She was meant to leave it on the props table in the wings, but Jocasta said she always forgot to leave it in rehearsals and just headed off to the green room with it still in her hands. So she must've had hold of it when the killer came across her.'

'Right.' I frowned. 'But *where* did the killer come across her?'

'In the wardrobe room,' said Nathan. 'They argue, it gets physical and in the fracas – possibly – the killer gets lipstick on the dress on the floor. Or maybe they didn't and it has nothing to do with the murder. Anyway – Kirsty ends up on the floor, injured, maybe knocked out, but not dead because there wasn't enough blood, just that one spot, which could've come from the cut above her eye.'

'Okay. So how did she end up in the storage room?'

'There were panto costumes in the wardrobe room, so

the killer wouldn't have to be a genius to work out that people would be coming in and out of the room during the performance. They knew that she'd be discovered quite quickly if they left her there. So they slip on the Widow Twankey dress to disguise themselves, and drag her out into the storage room, knowing there's a cupboard in there they can shut her in. Maybe they didn't even intend to kill her, just shut her in there so she missed the rest of the performance.'

'So Ellie, the understudy, could take over?'

'Hmm, maybe, but we know it *wasn't* Ellie because she was on stage or with other people.'

'Her uncle might've wanted to give her a shot,' I said, but again Nathan shook his head.

'Except her uncle is Matheson, who we just ruled out because there's footage of him at the petrol station.'

'Aargh!' I groaned in frustration. 'This case is infuriating.'

'Tell me about it,' said Nathan mildly. 'Anyway, they're in the storage room, maybe they always intended to kill her, or maybe they didn't, but she starts coming round and the killer bashes her in the head with the lamp, then tries to roll her up in the rug and stuffs her in the cupboard. Then they hot-foot it out through the fire exit, dump the dress in the recycling bin, and then…'

'And then?'

'Well, depending on who it is, they either slip back into the theatre through the fire exit, which they propped open, or they go in through the front entrance, unnoticed because there are people in there at the bar, and it would only take about six people standing in there for it to be crowded, and go back to their seat in the audience. Or of course they go home.'

'If they went home, it would have to be someone not connected to the panto,' I said, 'because otherwise people would notice they were missing.'

'Yes,' said Nathan. We stared at each other for a few seconds. 'Okay then. Who did it?' We stared at each other again, and then burst out laughing.

'I don't have a Scooby Doo,' I said. 'Not a clue. Except there probably are *loads* of clues, I just don't know what to make of them.'

'Glad it's not just me,' said Nathan, with a rueful smile.

'What about Maeve Butler's theory? About the tattooed man?'

'The only person who really fits her description – without knowing about tattoos, of course – is Colin, who has an alibi.'

'He has an alibi for *Kirsty's* murder, yes. But does he have one for her grandfather's?' I asked. Nathan groaned.

'Please don't give me another murder to investigate, especially not a decades-old cold case, not on Christmas Eve.'

'I'm not, I'm just saying... I don't actually know what I'm saying. And then there's Hilary, I can't put my finger on it but there's something about her I don't like...' I wasn't going to admit to Nathan it was because she reminded me of my ex-mother-in-law, and besides, surely it wasn't just that?

Before he could reply, Nathan's phone rang. 'Sunil, what's up?' he said, answering. He listened for a moment, then— 'Hang on, I'm putting you on speakerphone so Jodie can hear.'

'Hi Jodie,' said Sunil, sounding awkward.

'Hi Sunil,' I said.

'So I was just saying to Nathan, I checked on Hilary Beddows's alibi and it all checks out.'

'That was quick,' said Nathan. 'But it's, what, four o'clock in the morning in LA, how did you manage that?'

'I emailed the production company, and it was seen by some poor intern who's pulling an all-nighter, trying to clear a backlog of scripts,' said Sunil. 'He called me back and confirmed that Hilary spoke to his boss on Friday, at one-thirty in the afternoon LA time. And better still, they recorded it. Apparently they've had legal issues in the past when someone's agent has claimed they offered more money during the call than they put in the contract, so they record everything now *and* transcribe it. He's sent me the footage and the transcript, although I've not had a chance to look at it yet.'

'Okay. Can you send it to me? I'll have a look at it here before I come back to the office.'

'I'll send it right now.'

'Thanks, Sunil. Anything else going on?'

'Not really. Matt's gone home for a break.'

'Okay. Finish whatever you're doing and head home too.'

'Are you sure, Guv?'

'Yes. Make the most of it, because you could well be on your own tomorrow.'

'Okay. Thanks, Guv. Bye, Jodie.'

'Bye!' I said. As the call clicked off I said, 'Is he down to cover Christmas Day, then?'

'He offered. He's Hindu, he and Eesha don't celebrate it so they try and treat it like any other day. Although I did think all of us would be in, finishing off Jamie Westall…'

'At least it means I'll have the pleasure of your company for Christmas dinner,' I said.

'True. Definitely a silver lining.' Nathan checked the emails on his phone. 'So you were saying about Hilary?'

'It doesn't matter now. Her alibi checks out.'

'We've not watched the recording of it yet,' said Nathan.

'I know, but she was back at Colin's cottage on a Zoom call during the murder window, so it hardly matters what they talked about, does it?'

'Probably not.' He held up his phone. 'But Sunil's sent me the transcript of it too. It was a very brief meeting…'

We looked at the transcript on his phone.

'Here we go… "Transcript of Zoom meeting between Peter Goldberg, head of streaming content, Goldberg Brothers Productions, and Hilary Beddows, The Impressive Talent Agency, Friday December 19, 2025 at 1:30pm Pacific Standard Time.".'

'Not very gripping so far,' I said. 'Can we cut to the chase?'

Nathan laughed. 'Okay. Hilary thanks him for agreeing to the Zoom...' He scanned the words in front of him. 'Goldberg formally offers Colin the part, asks if he found the terms outlined at an earlier meeting are acceptable, she says yes...'

'Did she mention Kirsty?'

'Yes, right at the end. She asks if they've started casting the smaller parts yet, as she's just taken on a new client who she thinks would be perfect for the role of Diogenes's servant Aaryssa. Goldberg agrees to take a look at her.' Nathan looked up at me. 'She must be talking about Kirsty, yes?'

'That tallies with what she told us, so yes.' I sighed. 'Poor Kirsty. If she'd got that part, her whole life could've changed. But she never got the chance.'

'No, she didn't... Anyway, the Zoom only lasted about five minutes.'

'An important five minutes for Colin, and it would've been for Kirsty too,' I said. 'Did the tech guys get into Kirsty's laptop?'

'Yes, Sunil had a quick look at it but there wasn't anything that leapt out at him as unusual or suspicious,' said Nathan. 'He did find a few old interviews with Colin that she'd downloaded, where he's talking about how he got into acting, but we were kind of expecting that, after what we've heard about her being a fan of his. It got put aside, to be honest, once we got Jamie in custody. We'll need to take a deeper dive into it now.'

'I could have a look, if you like…' I said. Nathan smiled.

'I can't let you have her laptop, but I'll send you links to some of the stuff she downloaded when I get back to the office,' he said. 'It's mostly things like old interviews from the *Radio Times*, articles about *Mile End Days*, that kind of thing. Not sure any of it'll tell us anything.'

'I've got nothing else to do this afternoon,' I said. 'I've got some mince pies to bake for the carol concert later, but I've already got a batch in the freezer, they just need to go in the oven. Do you think you'll be able to come, now you've had to let Jamie go?'

'Sadly, yes. Not sadly because it means I'll have to listen to Shirley singing her version of "We Three Kings"…'

'We three kings of orient are, one in a taxi, one in a car—' I sang, and he laughed.

'Not that it's not very entertaining, of course. But I would rather be putting the finishing touches on a watertight murder charge.' He shook his head. 'At the moment it feels like that would be a Christmas miracle.'

'Poor babe. Do you really *have* to go back to the office this afternoon? I could let you unwrap one of your presents early, while we have the house to ourselves…' I smiled seductively at him, although I did have filo pastry crumbs down my top and probably a bit of stollen stuck between my teeth.

'That's a tempting offer, but…' Bless him, he looked like he really was quite torn, but then I am a bit of a catch, even if I say so myself. 'No, stop it, you sexy Christmas minx, I need to go back and man the phones just in case the killer decides to ring up and confess. But I'll be back by six.'

'What if they ring up to confess after six?'

'They can leave me a voicemail. It's Christmas Eve, I'm not hanging around all night waiting for them…'

So Nathan abandoned me and drove back to the office. Germaine, who had soon realised that this particular human lunch was far too good for dogs and she was destined to be disappointed if she was hoping for crumbs, had decamped to the living room, where she was stretched out on a rug in front of the fire. It wasn't a *proper* fire – it was a gas one, although it did have realistic-looking coals in it – but it had a big enough mantelpiece to hang five colourful stockings on it (including one for the dog), and they dangled there cheerfully but (obviously) emptily. With fairy lights strewn along the top of the fire surround, and the Christmas tree in the alcove, covered in baubles and with a big pile of presents underneath, it looked so cosy that it would have been easy to forget that there was a murderer in our midst…

Chapter Twenty

Nathan was as good as his word and emailed me the information (or the links to it, anyway) that Kirsty had found on Colin. As I tapped into my laptop I realised that she hadn't really had to dive too deep to find stuff; a quick Google search brought up many of the same articles. There were one or two, however, that took a bit more digging; interviews that went back years, as Nathan had said, right back to the days where Colin Sweeney was just becoming a household name on one of the nation's newest and most popular TV soaps.

There was an interview with Terry Wogan on the Wogan Show, along with several other cast members. It was 1989 and *Mile End Days* had only been on air a year or so at that point, and it wouldn't be inaccurate to say that EVERYONE in the country was watching it. It was quite unlike anything anyone had seen before: gritty and realistic (apart from the fact that there seemed to be rather a lot of dodgy gangsters living in that one particular square in East London, and none of them used any swear words stronger than 'flipping heck', which from my own days in the Met seemed unlikely), but still with a strong vein of humour running through it. Loves were lost and found, friends betrayed, babies were born (but raised by their grandparents, not finding out until years later that their 'big sister' was actually their mum), and an inordinate number of people appeared to not have washing machines in their houses, because they all used the launderette, which was a hotbed of gossip and deceit. In other words, it was a bit like real life, but on steroids. Everything that *could* happen *did* happen at some point, and Colin Sweeney was one of the pioneers of this new 'heightened realism'. This was in the days before 'scripted reality' TV shows like *Made in Chelsea* and *Real Housewives of...*, of course, so it really was groundbreaking stuff, particularly because a lot of the cast had no previous acting experience (and with some of them, it showed). What they did have, however, was life experience; experience of living somewhere like that, or with people like that, or even *being* people like that. Which was where Colin came in.

Terry Wogan, the genial Irish host whose twinkling eyes and soft voice hid a sharp, perceptive mind and fierce wit, was asking Colin about his life before becoming a TV superstar, and how it had prepared him for the role of bad boy Ewan McCafferty. Colin looked rather different to how he did now: well-built and muscular, and, it had to be said, pretty hot.

'Well, Tel, I grew up in Deptford, in a big London Irish family just like the McCaffertys,' said Colin, leaning back in his seat. He was very confident, to the point of being a bit cocky. He seemed as unlike the Colin Sweeney I knew today as it was possible to be.

'But of course the McCaffertys are, how can I put this, not unfamiliar with the inside of the auld clinker, are they?' said Terry, in his gentle Irish lilt. 'Are ye leading me to believe that your own family have a similar reputation?'

Colin laughed. 'That's a diplomatic way of putting it. Yeah, me dad and me brothers used to get into all sorts of trouble, you know, drinking and getting into fights, stealing cars...'

'Not you, though? You were the white sheep of the family?'

Colin laughed, clasped his hands together in prayer and assumed a saintly expression, which quickly crumbled as he and the audience laughed again. 'Nah, not quite. But I weren't that bad. I was a bit of a tea leaf and I had my fair share of run-ins with the police, but I weren't never up to Ewan's level.'

I paused the video. Colin had grown up in Deptford? That was right next to Bermondsey, where Kirsty's mum and grandparents had lived, right up until the fateful day when someone had shot her grandfather in the family's post office.

I clicked on another link, this time a newspaper article from a few years later. According to the article, Colin's character Ewan had just taken part in a major storyline in

Mile End Days, where Ewan had been forced to take part in an armed robbery by his older brother Callum – Callum was blackmailing him into it, after catching him in bed with their *other* brother Joe's wife. Joe would kill him if he ever found out (which meant he *would* find out at some point in the future, the storyline kept in reserve until the writers started to run out of plots), so Callum was holding that over Ewan to make him comply. But of course the robbery had not gone smoothly, ending up with a hostage being taken and Callum being shot, supposedly accidentally, by the reluctant Ewan in a bid to free them.

In the article, Colin talked about how his own background, growing up in a poor part of London and being around people who thought nothing of breaking the law, had helped inform not just his own performance, but also the script – because he'd talked to the writers about his own experiences. Just how closely did the storyline follow Colin's own life, though?

I looked at the date of the article: April 1993. Not long before Colin had gone off to the spiritual retreat where he'd met Hilary. Where he'd been having what Hilary had dismissed as 'a wobble', but it had been a big enough wobble to make him seriously consider quitting acting. Had something really bad happened in Colin's past, something he'd suppressed for years, but then, as his acting skill grew, he'd channelled it into his performance? And in doing so, he'd unleashed feelings of – well, depending on what this bad thing was, guilt, or fear, or remorse, or grief? And bringing all that up to the surface had brought on this 'wobble'?

Come off it, Jodie, I thought. What you're really asking is, did Colin – or maybe one of his large, lawless family – shoot Kirsty's grandfather, Alan Butler, during an armed robbery? Or, even if he hadn't been involved, had Kirsty suspected he had? Had she seen a tattoo on his back, one that she'd only ever heard about before from her nana?

I rang Nathan.

'Hi babe,' I said. 'You know you didn't want me to give you another murder to investigate?'

'The thirty-year-old cold case?'

'Yeah, except it's actually forty years old. Well…' I ignored his groan. 'I think we need to get a look at Colin's back.'

'Seriously?'

'Yes, seriously. It could be nothing – it probably is – but it turns out Colin grew up not far from the Butlers, and he would've been about twenty-two at the time, which fits Maeve's tattooed man theory—'

'In as much as she can give us a description,' pointed out Nathan. 'But go on…'

'Okay, well, he told Terry Wogan that he grew up in a family full of lawless reprobates—'

'Those were his words, were they?'

'Not as such, no. But he admits they were into drinking and fighting, and that he was a bit light-fingered himself and he got involved with the police too. So forgetting the intervening forty years, if you'd been investigating Alan

Butler's murder and Colin had been on your radar, would you have pulled him in for questioning?'

'I don't know about that, but I might've looked into him.'

'Okay. Anyway, a few years later, according to the *Radio Times*, he took a tragic event from his past to inspire the writers of *Mile End Days*, and they used it to write a storyline where Ewan is reluctantly involved in an armed robbery that goes horribly wrong, where he shoots someone by accident. Possibly.'

'Possibly?'

'I think the "possibly" is dramatic license, rather than what actually happened in real life. Because of course Maeve said that the bloke who shot her husband had obviously been unhappy when the other one grabbed Maeve's daughter and put a gun to her head, and that during the struggle his gun had gone off – accidentally, she thought. Sounds pretty close to that soap opera storyline, doesn't it?'

'Yeah…' Nathan groaned. 'You might've solved a murder, but it's the wrong one.'

'It's not the wrong one if you're Maeve Butler,' I said. 'It doesn't matter how long ago it happened, her husband was murdered, and he deserves justice.'

'You're right, of course,' said Nathan. 'But we need a bit more than two ancient press interviews to reopen the case. It's not like we can get Terry Wogan to testify, is it? Not unless Jocasta can commune with the spirit world.'

'I wouldn't put it past her,' I said. 'But like I told you, we need to see Colin's back…'

'Yes…' Nathan sounded doubtful. 'Not sure I can get a warrant forcing someone to take their top off…'

'No, I suppose not,' I said. 'We need to get it off by other means.'

'Not sure how I feel about my wife discussing how to get another bloke half naked,' said Nathan. 'I'm also not sure, as a police officer, I should know what you're planning.'

'I'm not planning anything yet,' I said. 'Although I bet Mum would have some ideas…'

'Please don't let her do anything that means I'd have to arrest my own mother-in-law on Christmas Eve,' said Nathan, and I laughed.

'Yeah, you might have a point there. We'll play it by ear… Anyway, I'll leave you to it. Love you.'

'Love you too.'

'You're in the office on your own, then?'

'No, I'm just not ashamed to let people know I love my wife.'

I disconnected the call with a warm, fuzzy feeling inside, and then went to put some mince pies in the oven.

Daisy and Joe came home not long after, faces flushed with the cold and with young love (aww!). I heard them giggling together as they came through the front door. It absolutely warmed the cockles of my heart that my daughter had learnt from my mistakes with her father and found herself someone who genuinely seemed to actually *like* her, not just fancy her. They always seemed to have such a good time together, and they supported each other's dreams without having to get too involved. Daisy was happy for Joe to pursue his musical career, and during the school holidays she did sometimes go with him when he played in different parts of the country (chaperoned by his mum, Flo), but she wasn't always desperately hanging around him – she trusted him. And for his part, he encouraged her interest in photography, suggesting places they could go where she might get some good photos, and using some she'd taken of him in press releases and online.

'Ooh, can I smell mince pies?' said Daisy, coming into the kitchen where I was taking a batch out of the oven.

'Yes you can,' I said, slapping her hand away from the oven tray with an oven gloved hand, 'but you can't have one. They're for the carol concert.'

'They look amazing,' said Joe. He never knew what to call me. He'd started off calling me 'Mrs P', but of course I *wasn't* Mrs Parker. 'Miss P' made me sound like a spinster, and 'Ms P' sounded just plain weird. After the wedding, he'd tried out 'Mrs W', but I hadn't changed my surname, so that wasn't right either. One day – probably after they'd been married for ten years and had a couple of kids – he might call me Jodie, like I'd told him to, but for now he just avoided calling me anything.

'Well, I might have made a couple extra, for quality control purposes,' I said, and Daisy snorted.

'Is he getting one just because he complimented your pies?'

'Of course. You should know that flattery works on me by now...'

Mum came in, her face wreathed in smiles and a slightly dreamy look in her eyes as she struggled to take her coat off. Joe rushed over to help her and I thought, *That's TWO mince pies for you, my boy.*

'Nice outing?' I asked, and she nodded.

'Very,' she said, and we all waited for more. But she was uncharacteristically quiet, although her smile spoke for itself.

'Well? Where have you been?' demanded Daisy.

'On a date, if you must know,' said Mum.

'So it *was* a date, then?' I asked, putting the kettle on. I knew the application of tea would help tease the details out of her.

'A date? No!' Daisy looked shocked. 'Did you finally give in to Bob?'

'I thought he'd earnt it,' said Mum, sniffily, but she looked very happy. 'He's been hovering around me ever since Grandad died.'

'He's a nice man,' I said. 'I'm glad you had a good time.'

'We did,' said Mum. 'We saw all the Christmas decorations and had a little walk around the gardens, but it was a bit too cold for that, so he bought me lunch at a nice pub down the road.'

'You should've brought him in,' I said. 'I could've asked him if his intentions towards you were honourable.'

'Oh God, I hope not,' said Mum. 'At my time of life I need a *dishonourable* man! I want some fun before I pop me clogs.' Daisy made barfing noises. 'What? You think you young 'uns are the only ones with needs? And you don't have to worry about getting up the duff at my age.'

'And on that note,' I said, cutting off the conversation before anyone could go too far, 'the second batch of mince pies are done, and I need you to eat a couple of the cooler ones to make room for them…'

As predicted, the lure of a mince pie was enough to shut down the topic of Mum and her 'needs' (which I suspected could end up hospitalising poor Bob if she wasn't gentle with him). The mince pie filling was still a little too hot really, but at least it kept everyone quiet for a bit. Honestly, my whole family (and Joe) are addicted to mince pies, probably because I can't be bothered to make my own mincemeat and you can only really buy it around Christmas, so they have to make the most of it when it's available.

The rest of the afternoon passed quickly enough. I thought about telling the others what I'd learnt about Colin, but decided against it. Daisy was quite fond of him, despite his tendency to bang on about his chakras and all that malarkey, and I didn't want to upset her unnecessarily, because I *could* be wrong, although I didn't think I was. And Mum – well, if I told her I needed to find a way to get a bloke's top off, with her still riding the high from her date, there was no telling what she'd come up with, and probably no stopping her either. Nathan's warning, about not letting her do anything that could constitute harassment, sexual or otherwise, rang in my ears; it probably would put a bit of a downer on Christmas if my husband had to arrest my mum on Christmas Eve. Because, although I hadn't worked out how, I was determined that today – what remained of Christmas Eve – would be the day I found out once and for all if Colin Sweeney really was a killer. And the ideal place for that to happen would be the carol concert.

'Sorry, Carmen,' I mumbled, as I packed up the mince pies.

Chapter Twenty-One

If you're ever invited to a carol concert in the UK, in December, in a church – especially at night – wrap up warm. Thermals, two pairs of socks, gloves, hat, scarf, and big coat. You'll need them all.

St Botolph's was a beautiful little church, with a view across the fields and down to the sea that could make even a heathen like me believe in God – almost. It was dark now, of course, so the view was pretty much obscured, but it was dotted here and there with lights; from the windows of nearby houses, and in the distance the fairy lights that led along Fore Street, culminating with the huge Christmas tree that had been put up in the square outside the library, the big illuminated star on top shining in the darkness. There were even the lights of a solitary ship out at sea; I wondered if the sailors on board would make it home for Christmas Day. The church itself was quaint and full of character but, like most other seventeenth-century buildings, a tad draughty. The stained-glass windows, while inspirational works of art, were not double glazed, and the flagstone floor did not have underfloor heating. There were a few portable heaters dotted around the building, but most of the heat drifted straight up into the vaulted ceiling, as if in a hurry to join God up there.

'I feel like the Michelin Man in this puffer jacket,' moaned Daisy, stamping her feet to keep warm as we waited outside the church. Joe pulled her in for a hug and she buried her freezing face into his chest. Germaine, who had her own little coat on, tried to join the love-in by burying her own cold little nose into Daisy's legs.

'Cold enough for you?' Tony appeared behind us from the church, blowing into his hands.

'I *hate* that saying,' I growled. 'What makes you think I want it this cold?'

'Er – I don't know, it's just one of those things people say, innit?' He grinned at me. 'You'll feel better with some of my hot mulled wine inside you.'

'Where? Where is it?' I pleaded. 'I need it now.' He laughed.

'Patience, young Padawan... Carmen's just setting everything up with the verger. I was trying to help them, but I felt like I was just getting in her way.'

'I've got her mince pies here,' I said, nodding to the box at my feet.

'You'd better take them in and hand them over to Mary.'

'Who's Mary?'

'The new verger. I made some joke about it almost being

time for her to give birth, although she'd be hard pushed to find three wise men round here, and she looked like she wanted to kill me. I wasn't saying she was fat, it was just – her name's Mary – it's Christmas Eve… She hates me.'

'Who could possibly hate you?' I asked, in a tone that suggested it would be only too easy to imagine it. Tony laughed.

'Don't you start on me, it's Christmas.'

I took the box of mince pies inside. It wasn't a lot warmer indoors than it was outdoors, but at least the thick stone walls blocked the slight chill breeze that had ruffled the grass in the church yard. There were lit candles along the edges of the pews – those LED ones, not real ones, as that many naked flames in an old building full of wood with no purpose-built fire exits would have been very festive and spiritual, but also a Health and Safety nightmare – which gave the building a lovely, soft glow.

Carmen was standing at a table towards the back of the church, along the wall to the left, with another woman who I couldn't see properly. There were two large hot water urns and a big catering-sized lidded saucepan – one of mine – on a portable dish warmer, which I assumed had Tony's mulled wine in. There were several other plates of food, like mini chocolate yule logs and cupcakes with Santa faces on them, all donated by parishioners, along with lots of plates, mugs, teabags, coffee and milk. Carmen looked up as I walked over, an expression of relief crossing her face.

'Jodie—' she started. The other woman – the verger – whirled around and stared at the box in my hands. She was,

I couldn't help noticing, heavily pregnant. *Oh Tony, you absolute muppet*, I thought.

'Are they the mince pies? Put them here,' she said.

'Oh – yeah, okay…' I put the box down. Mary immediately opened it and started putting the pies on plates, as if I wasn't there. She had to stretch an arm around her baby bump in order to reach the table.

'Thank you, Mary,' said Carmen. 'You are a treasure, what would I do without you?'

'Put the food out yourself? Or get that boyfriend of yours to do it?'

'Er – yes. I'll leave you to it…' Carmen gave me a *help-me-escape* look.

'I'd just like to talk to you about something, if you have time, Vicar?' I asked.

'Yes, of course Jodie. Let's talk over here…' Carmen led me away and we sat on a pew, about as far from Mary as we could get without actually leaving the church. 'I am *so* sorry about her, she's normally very sweet but tonight she's turned into an absolute monster.'

'Maybe Tony's joke about it being almost time for her to give birth might have something to do with it,' I said.

'Oh dear God,' said Carmen. 'That's not something you say to someone who's already two weeks overdue.'

'Oh no, really? Poor woman must feel like she's about to burst. Daisy was a week late, and I was ready to buy some forceps and pull her out myself.' I looked around the church. 'Um, should she really be here tonight? Tony was an idiot to say it, but – it *is* Christmas Eve, and her name *is* Mary…'

'She insisted,' said Carmen. 'If the worst comes to the worst, one of my regulars is a midwife, and we've got plenty of hot water.' She waved her hand towards the urns. I hoped she was joking. 'So, was there something you wanted to talk to me about, or were you just helping me get away from Moody Mary?'

We both sniggered, but then I shook my head. 'No, poor Mary. Her hormones will be going *crazy*. Actually, I do have something I want to talk to you about. Do you know Colin Sweeney?'

She snorted. 'Do I know Colin? Oh yes, I know Colin.'

'Hmm. I'm getting some definite vibes here… You don't get on?'

'I wouldn't say that, exactly. I do a class on comparative religions every Wednesday morning, you know, concentrating on what we have in common with other religions? Like Jesus, or Isa, being a figure in Islam. Colin takes great delight in coming along to the class most weeks, and talking at length about Buddhism and Shinto.'

'Yes, I can imagine Colin enjoys talking at length,' I said.

Carmen laughed. 'Don't get me wrong, he's a nice man, and we've had some very intelligent discussions, but… It feels to me like he doesn't quite believe in any of it. It's like he's taken a pinch of Hinduism, a touch of Bahá'í, a sprinkle of Jainism, and mixed it all together into some big spiritual smoothie.'

I looked at her, agog. 'You mean all Colin's spiritual stuff is bullshit? Sorry.' I glanced over at a nearby statue and gave an apologetic bob of the head at Jesus, in case he was offended by the word 'bullshit' – I considered genuflecting but I wasn't entirely sure how to do it. 'Do you mean Colin is faking it all?'

'No, not at all. I think Colin is *desperate* to find something that fills a hole inside him. I think he truly wants to believe in something, and until he finds the right fit he'll keep trying everything.'

'That's a bit sad,' I said, not sure if I felt better or worse for having sniggered about his chakras so many times. 'What would drive someone to be like that, do you think?' *A guilty secret from the past, maybe?*

'Could be anything. Unhappy childhood, past trauma, grief, loneliness – trying to find somewhere you fit in, maybe. Or even just boredom.' She shook her head. 'I don't know. Jocasta thinks he's lost.'

'She does?' I was surprised – Colin seemed to share a lot of Jocasta's beliefs – but then Daisy had said that even she found him a bit much.

'Yes. I know I shouldn't really gossip about my parishioners, but… She thinks losing his wife completely untethered him. Which is understandable.'

'Yes… Or… what if you'd done something really bad in the past, and you felt guilty about it because you'd never been punished for it?'

'That would probably do it…' She looked at me. 'Is this a hypothetical question, or…?'

'We should probably start letting them in now,' said

Mary, appearing right in front of us. 'It's cold out there, I wouldn't be surprised if some of them have given up and gone home.'

'It was you who thought they should wait outside,' muttered Carmen, under her breath. She stood up. 'Let the merriment begin!'

Everyone was very happy to come into the church, although they soon quietened down when they realised it was almost as cold inside as out. I was relieved to see that a lot more people had joined the throng while I'd been talking to Carmen, including Mum's new fancy man Bob, and my old fancy man, Nathan, who despite his earlier promise hadn't made it home by six.

'You made it! Good.'

He leaned in and kissed me. 'Sorry I'm late. Would you believe there was a last-minute crime spree in Penstowan, and there was hardly anyone left at the station to deal with it?'

'Not really, no.'

He laughed. 'Okay, it wasn't quite a crime spree, but bloody Joey Trevally parked his tractor in the Co-op car park again and stopped all the last-minute Christmas shoppers getting in to buy their sprouts. There was practically a riot. Poor Chrissie needed help controlling the angry mob.'

'She's here as well, I see. And Matt.'

'Well, you said Carmen was worried about the turnout, so I corralled as many people as I could along here.' He grinned at me. 'I also thought we should have a few officers on standby, in case Shirley gets Colin's top off and all hell breaks loose.'

'That would be terribly inappropriate in a church, even for Mum...'

'Welcome, everybody, thank you for coming,' said Carmen, standing in front of the congregation. 'I know it's cold tonight, but a few carols will warm us up, not to mention Tony's mulled wine! I hope none of you are driving.' There were a few chuckles and more than a few longing looks towards the pan of hot wine. 'Let's start with a favourite carol of mine, just to get us all in the mood.' She nodded towards Mary, who was doubling up as the organist although she could only just reach it because of her belly, and the first strains of 'Once in Royal David's City' filled the church.

I'm not much of a singer, but I am better than Mum, who couldn't carry a tune in a bucket, and Germaine, who yapped her way through the first verse and chorus before settling down under the pew. A few other people had brought their dogs with them, and they joined in with the odd bark or whine too. Jocasta, who had met us outside the church, sat next to Mum, drowning her out somewhat with her own very pleasant voice, although with her untamed hair and boho scarf I could better imagine her singing something like 'I'd Like to Teach the World to Sing'. Nathan somehow managed to have a stronger Liverpudlian accent when he was singing than when he was talking, which was bizarre but also quite sweet. I couldn't hear Matt, but I suspected he wasn't singing at all, just miming, which was exactly what I used to do at school assemblies.

A few pews further down, Colin and Hilary were also singing, Colin belting it out like it was a show tune rather than a hymn. Hilary was dressed much too nicely for a carol concert in a Cornish church, where the ubiquitous Christmas jumpers were out in full force, but then she was a stylish woman; she always seemed to be well groomed, even when Sunil and I had caught her unawares at the harbourmaster's cottage. She was wearing a fur hat, and when she took it off her hair was smooth and sleek, no sign of the frizzy bed head look I always end up with when I take my beanie off. I recognised a few of Colin's pantomime cast and crew, including Sarah, who'd played Princess Jasmine, and of course Tim and Maurice, Maurice looking even more like the actor Terence Stamp than usual – Terrence Stamp in a spy movie though, rather than 'Priscilla, Queen of the Desert'. Which would've been inappropriate for church, even at Christmas.

The song finished and everyone sat down. Carmen took to the pulpit and looked at everyone, smiling.

'As I look around the congregation this evening, it's so nice to see so many different faces, including lots I don't normally see here in church—' There were a few guilty murmurs and a bit of foot shuffling at that, and she laughed. 'I'm not calling you out for not being here much in the past, but more to say that even those of you who positively avoid all things religious, even those of you who steer clear of us "God botherers", are welcome here at

St Botolph's. Because Christmas transcends Christianity, it even transcends Jesus—' Here she turned and looked up at the stained-glass window that represented Jesus at the sea of Galilee, talking to the fishermen. 'Sorry, Boss,' she said, and everyone laughed. 'So many people recognise Christmas as a time not just to celebrate the birth of Christ, but to celebrate family and friends, to come together and share food and warmth and love. And I think Jesus would heartily approve of his birthday being co-opted for that purpose. What better reason is there to come together, but to share love?'

'Amen to that,' said someone a few pews along. Carmen nodded and continued.

'Our friend Jocasta would no doubt tell you that it was Christianity that co-opted Christmas in the first place, and that it was originally a pagan festival, which came about to bring light and joy into people's lives at the harshest, darkest time of year, the winter. This is why we light candles and string fairy lights up, to bring back the sunshine, and baubles and holly, to bring back the fertile days of spring, which at the moment feel so far away. And maybe this is true. But what better symbol of sunshine and fertility, of light and hope, than Jesus Christ? In Him we are all born and reborn, given a second chance to make a difference and bring light into the dark places. This is His gift to us. During the next couple of days, when you're unwrapping presents and carving the turkey, find if you can just a few quiet moments to think about what *your* gift to the world is. It doesn't have to be massive, because the little, everyday things are often what make the biggest difference. How can you make it a better place? How can you make a difference to someone's life? What can you do that would be the perfect gift back to Jesus?'

Next to me, I heard Nathan's tummy rumble, and he clapped a guilty hand over it, like that would muffle it.

'And now let us sing "O Little Town of Bethlehem"...'

After that we went straight into another carol, and then it was time for some refreshments. Everyone gathered around the table and tucked into the mince pies and chocolate yule logs, but what they were really after was the mulled wine. A few sips of that warmed us all up and got the vocal cords ready for another song. I watched Colin as discreetly as I could, sending him *get-suddenly-hot-and-take-your-top-off* vibes, but it was no use. If only he was a perimenopausal woman, he'd have been stripping off in no time, although I could feel my own hot flush coming on and that just made the temperature more pleasant. I was going to save a fortune in central heating over the winter.

Appetites maybe not satiated but at least tempered for the moment, we all headed back to the pews for some more songs. But as we retook our places, there was one person missing: Mary.

I went over to Carmen. 'Where's Mary?'

'She went to the loo a couple of minutes ago. I thought she'd come back...' We exchanged worried looks.

'I'll go and check on her,' I said, but just then the verger reappeared.

'Oh Mary, thank goodness, we were getting wor—'

started Carmen, but Mary interrupted her with a groan. She was clutching her bump in a most alarming fashion. *Oh shit, Tony was right,* I thought.

'I think my waters have broken,' she said, panting a little. 'I went to the toilet but it felt weird…' Carmen and I both grabbed an arm and half carried her over to a seat. The rest of the congregation had noticed by now that something was happening, and a few people rushed over.

'Where's the midwife?' I asked Carmen, who looked around. She went pale.

'She's not here. She did say she was on call…'

On the chair, Mary groaned in pain again. 'I need to call my sister, she's my birthing partner.' She fumbled about under her black cassock, bringing out a mobile phone. She held it up. 'There's no signal.'

'Unlock it,' said Nathan. 'I'll take it outside where there's a signal and call her for you.' She nodded and handed him the phone.

'It's Sophie,' she said. Nathan patted her on the arm and hurried outside.

'Okay,' I said, 'I think the concert is over. Is there a back room or an office or somewhere we can take her until her sister gets here?'

'The vestry,' said Carmen. 'Can we get some help here? I don't think I can carry her all the way in there.'

Matt and Tony both stepped forward to help. Mary looked at Tony through narrowed eyes.

'Don't you say a bloody word,' she said, and Tony hesitated.

'I've got this,' said Colin, taking his place. He hoisted Mary on to her feet and, very slowly and gently, he coaxed her across to the door at the back of the church, letting her walk at her own pace. Carmen and I followed even more slowly, along with Jocasta.

'What shall I do?' asked Tony. Carmen glared at him and didn't answer. Mum patted his arm.

'Make yourself useful and tell everyone to go home. Unless there's anyone else here who can play the organ?'

'It's playing the organ that got her into that situation in the first place,' said Tony. Daisy rolled her eyes.

'That's a double entendre worthy of Nana. Well done.' She turned round. 'Okay everyone, let's give them a bit of space. Everyone outside for some a cappella carol singing…'

Confident that between them Daisy, Mum and Tony could sort it out, I followed Mary into the vestry. There was a padded leather office chair in front of a desk, which Colin deftly manoeuvred the pregnant woman into.

'Your sister's on her way,' said Nathan, entering behind me. 'She says she'll be about ten minutes. Not long now, Mary!' He lowered his voice. 'Is she okay? Is she going to last ten minutes?'

'Well,' I said, 'it took me twenty-seven hours to have Daisy, so I think we'll be fine. But you never know… You ever delivered a baby?'

'You are joking, aren't you?'

'I bloody hope so…'

On the chair, Mary groaned again. She began to slither

down in the seat, the shiny material making it difficult for her to stay upright. Nathan looked alarmed.

'Okay sweetheart,' said Jocasta. 'Let's get you down on the floor, where you'll be more comfy and can't hurt yourself.' Carmen quickly grabbed a couple of cassocks from a nearby cupboard and laid them on the floor.

'Nooo,' moaned Mary, 'I can't ruin your clothes...'

'Please do, they're getting old and if you give birth on them the Bishop won't be able to refuse me the money to buy some new ones,' said Carmen with a smile. 'You're doing me a favour.'

Nathan and I grabbed Mary under the arms and guided her down on to the floor. She managed to sit upright, but she looked very uncomfortable.

'Hang on,' said Colin. He took off his puffer jacket and, seeing what he intended, Nathan and I both followed suit, removing our coats and folding them up to form a cushion for her to lean back on. Mary sank into them gratefully as Carmen wheeled a portable heater closer.

'Comfortable?' asked Jocasta.

'As much as I can be.' Mary grimaced and sucked in her breath as another contraction hit her. They were coming quite fast already.

'Okay, I'm going to take you through a pain relief meditation I learnt in Guadeloupe,' said Jocasta. I caught Nathan's eye and he grinned. The last thing I'd have wanted when I was in labour was a bloody Guadeloupian meditation, but in the absence of drugs I supposed it was better than nothing. I was just glad that Daisy and Mum weren't in here, because they'd have gone into hysterics.

But before Jocasta could start chanting (I could see Colin was itching to join in as well), the sound of voices from outside the church reached us. And immediately the tension in the room began to dissipate, although not completely disappear, of course.

> *Silent night,*
> *Holy night,*
> *All is calm,*
> *All is bright.*
> *Round yon verger mother and child,*
> *Holy infant so tender and mild…*

'That's beautiful,' I whispered, feeling a bit teary at the emotion of it all. Mary spoilt it a bit by moaning again, but I had to cut the poor woman some slack; she was in labour on the stone floor of a church vestry, after all. She took a breath in and then managed a smile herself.

'That's so lovely,' she said. 'I wish Greg was here. My husband. He's in the Army and he's away…' Her breath hitched in her throat, but whether it was from pain or the tears that had started to stream down her face I couldn't tell. 'He's back next week, I was hoping…'

Carmen and I squatted down next to her. I took one of her hands, while Carmen stroked the hair away from her face.

'He'll be home soon,' she said softly, 'and you'll both be here to greet him.'

'Your sister will be here in a moment,' said Nathan. 'Everything will be okay.' He turned to me. 'I'll go and wait outside so I can show her where to come.'

'Good idea,' I said. Apart from anything else, the poor woman deserved a bit of privacy, not a handful of strangers (and her vicar) staring down at her.

'That was quick,' I heard Nathan say. 'This way.'

'Mary! Oh my God, Mary!' A young man in an Army uniform burst through the door and dropped to his knees in front of her, followed by another woman, who I guessed was her sister, Sophie, and Nathan. The rest of us looked at each other, all thinking, *what the—*

'Greg? What are you doing here?' Mary looked amazed but very, very happy.

'I thought I was going to miss the birth,' he said. I scrambled out of his way so he could take her hand. 'I begged them to let me start my leave early, but this was the earliest I could get here. I was going to surprise you, but you weren't home so I went round to Sophie's and then you called.'

'I think you should take Mary to the hospital,' said Jocasta. 'Her contractions are already coming on quite strong. Are you going to the maternity unit at Truro?'

'Yes,' said Sophie, helping her sister struggle to her feet. 'It'll take us about an hour to get there, so we'd better go now. Are you okay to walk to the car, sis?'

'I am now,' said Mary, smiling at her husband. And with

her sister on one arm and her husband on the other, we watched the three of them slowly make their way out of the church, following them out of the vestry and calling after them.

'Take care, love.' 'Give the baby a cuddle from us.' 'Best Christmas present ever!'

We watched them go, and then all five of us simultaneously let out deep sighs.

'Wow,' said Carmen. 'That is *not* how I expected tonight to go.'

'Tony did,' I said, and she laughed. 'Right, I need my coat, I'm bloody freezing. I hope there's no bodily fluids on it...'

Colin headed back into the vestry and we followed him.

'What a night,' I said to Nathan.

'Just a bit. I never—' he started, and then his words died in his throat. Because in front of us, Colin had bent over to pick up the coats from the floor. His jumper had ridden up and there, in the small of his back, was a black Celtic tattoo.

Chapter Twenty-Two

I turned to Nathan, my eyes wide, and opened my mouth, but he gave a very slight shake of the head.

'Well I don't know about you, but I think I'm done for the night,' he said. Colin laughed.

'Me too! I didn't expect such excitement. And so lovely to see her reunited with her husband just in time,' he said. 'It made me feel quite emotional.'

'Yeah, it's a real Christmas miracle,' I said. 'We'd better go and find Mum and Daisy…'

'I need to find Hilary. She's so squeamish, she's probably halfway home by now,' said Colin. 'You probably wouldn't expect it of her, but she can't handle blood or gore, or any hint of pain, really.' He laughed. 'Although she *is* a talent agent, so she's quite used to handing it out.'

'I can imagine,' I said. 'Well… Merry Christmas, Colin, or whatever you pagans call it.'

'Ha ha ha, Merry Christmas to you too!' He slipped his coat back on and headed outside, while I pretended to struggle into mine. When he'd gone, I whirled round to look at Nathan.

'You saw it, didn't you? The tattoo?'

'Of course I saw it! Is it how Maeve Butler described it?'

'Yep, almost exactly, even though it's been forty years since she last saw it.' I went over to the door and peered out, to where most of the carollers had come back inside and were milling around, chatting excitedly. There was Colin, heading for the big wooden door out into the churchyard, stopping on route here and there to exchange a few brief words with people before moving on. 'So what do we do now? Should we follow him?'

'Why would we do that? We know where he lives, he's probably going home…'

'Shouldn't you arrest him?'

Nathan shook his head. 'No, not yet. We need to make sure we have enough to charge him first, and we need to see how – or if – this fits in with the investigation into Kirsty's death. Because even if she did suspect him, even if she told him she suspected him, he didn't kill her.'

'No… No, he didn't. But it must be linked? That must be why she was murdered.'

'We can't know that for certain until we know without any doubt that he killed Maeve Butler's husband all those years ago. The evidence we have, especially now with the tattoo, is looking pretty good, but we can't rush in and make a mistake that means he gets away with it for another forty years, or that warns Kirsty's killer that we're onto them.' Nathan peered over my shoulder into the church. 'Come on, Daisy's waiting out there. We need to go home and think this over.'

'But—'

'There's no hurry. Colin doesn't know that we're onto him. It was so long ago, as far as he's concerned it's all in the past, so why would anyone be looking into it now?'

He had a good point, so we left the vestry and went to find Daisy and Germaine, Joe and Mum, who we discovered chatting with Maeve Butler and her granddaughter, Lesley, and a man who I assumed was Kirsty's dad. Nathan nodded to him solemnly.

'Mr Dunwoody,' he said. 'How are you holding up?'

'Fine, as long as I don't think about it,' said Mr Dunwoody. 'I take it you don't know who killed my daughter yet?'

'Dad!' Lesley scolded him. 'You have to let the police do their job.'

He scoffed. 'Pardon me if I don't have a lot of confidence in them,' he said, 'but there have been two murders in this family and neither of the killers have faced justice.' Behind him, the crowd moved and parted slightly, and I realised that Colin was standing right next to us, his back to us, as he spoke to someone else in the congregation I didn't recognise.

'David, stop it,' said Maeve Butler. 'They're doing their best.' She smiled bravely at me and Nathan. 'This has been a terrible time for our family, but we've got over tragedy before and we'll do it again.'

I took her hand. It felt terribly frail and cold. 'It doesn't get any easier though, does it?' I said gently.

'No, it doesn't. I lost my husband to violence, and my daughter to cancer. To lose a grandchild as well, well, it's heartbreaking.' Her voice trembled, and so did her hand in mine, but she carried on. 'But we will get through it, because what other choice do we have?'

'Nathan is doing his best to see justice is served,' I said, desperate to tell her that we might just have found her husband's killer, if not her granddaughter's, but as the suspect was standing not three feet away from me I decided against it. Nathan looked up suddenly and saw Colin.

'Colin, do you know Kirsty's family?' he said, and I almost gasped. What was he doing? Colin turned round and smiled sympathetically at them.

'We haven't met,' he said. 'I'm Colin Sweeney, I was Kirsty's director, and I like to think her friend and mentor, too. She was a wonderful actor, and a lovely girl. I am so sorry about what happened, such a great loss to us all.'

'This is Kirsty's dad, David Dunwoody,' said Nathan, making the introductions. 'Lesley, her sister, and this is Kirsty's grandmother.'

'Maeve,' said Maeve, holding out her hand. I felt the hairs on the back of my neck stand up as Colin reached out and gently took her hand.

'I wish we were meeting under better circumstances, Mrs Dunwoody,' he said, sincerely.

'Oh, it's not Dunwoody – I'm on her mother's side. It's Butler,' said Maeve. Was it me, or did Colin's eyes widen in shock for a moment?

'Butler? Oh, I see,' he said. He'd either recovered quickly, or I'd imagined it. Would whoever killed Alan Butler all those years ago even remember his name? Unless they were a complete psychopath with a massive body count, I thought, yes, they would. That sort of thing would surely stick in your memory.

'You're not from round these parts,' she said. 'You're an incomer, like me. How long have you lived down here?'

'Oh, a couple of years, on and off. You?'

'I moved here forty years ago. Still treated like an outsider!' she cackled. 'Only another couple of generations until they class us as local, although of course the girls' father is Cornish through and through. London?'

'Yes. You?'

'Bermondsey, do you know it?'

Colin definitely looked uncomfortable now. 'Not really. I lived in Islington before I moved down here,' he said, and I thought, *Yeah, but you grew up in Deptford, just down the road…*

'Anyway, I'd best go and find Hilary – she's staying with me for Christmas, so I'd better not lose her! I'm so sorry again for your loss.' Colin turned and practically ran for the door. Nathan looked at me, eyebrows raised, and I nodded. Colin had been momentarily surprised by Maeve's surname, but plenty of people were called Butler, so what were the chances they would be *those* Butlers? But then finding out where they'd moved from – that they *were* those Butlers? He couldn't have looked more guilty, to me anyway, if he'd tried, although *'He looked a bit shifty, m'lord'* was unlikely to hold up in court on its own.

'What a nice man,' said Maeve, looking sad. 'I'm glad Kirsty had so many people around her who appreciated how special she is.'

'Yes,' I said. 'Everyone on the panto thought so highly of her.' But it hadn't stopped someone killing her…

We left Maeve and her family, and headed out to the car, Nathan and I both deep in thought. When we got home we left Daisy and Joe saying goodbye out on the doorstep – Joe was spending Christmas Day with his parents, so he had to drive back to his home in Exeter – and headed for the kitchen, Germaine waddling in front of us; she was pleased to be back in the warm. Mum was chattering away about her day out with Bob, which was lovely to hear, but neither of us could really concentrate on what she was saying.

'And then we climbed up onto the back of a giant llama, which sprouted wings and flew us to Truro,' she said. 'Where Bradley Walsh made us a curry.' Nathan and I both looked at her. 'Oh, you were listening, then?'

'Yes, Mum. Sorry,' I apologised, 'it's just something's come up related to the case and we're both a bit distracted.'

'You know who killed Kirsty?'

'Not exactly…' said Nathan. 'But I think we're getting close.'

'Good.' Mum patted him on the arm. 'I'll let you off not listening to me going on, then. Just this once, mind.'

'Thanks, Shirley,' said Nathan. 'You want a cup of tea?'

'Nah. I think I'll go and sit in bed and watch telly,' she said. 'I'll make me own once I'm in me nightie. Been a long day.'

I gave her a hug and kissed her on the cheek. 'Night, Mum. I'm really glad you had such a lovely day today. Bob's a nice bloke.'

'I'm glad you like him, because I invited him round for Christmas dinner tomorrow,' she said. 'Night, sweetheart.'

'You did wh—' I started, and then stopped as she winked at me. 'I wouldn't mind, actually, but it would be better with more notice.'

'Next year,' said Mum, and then she headed off to her annex, leaving me and Nathan alone in the kitchen.

'Well, what do you make of that?' I asked him.

'Bob's a nice bloke—'

'Not *that*, I mean what do you make of Colin? I couldn't believe it when you called him over.'

'Oh that, I just wanted to see how he would react.'

'Guilty as sin,' I said. 'Only now, surely he knows we're onto him?'

'I don't see why,' said Nathan. 'Introducing him to Kirsty's family, when he was standing right to next them, was a perfectly natural thing to do. And you know what it tells us?'

'What?'

'That he had no idea Kirsty had made the connection between him and her grandfather's murder.'

'No?'

'No. Look at how surprised he was, when he realised who Maeve Butler was. If Kirsty had told him she knew who he was, and she'd accused him of murder, he wouldn't have been so shocked, would he? He would already have known that the Butler family moved down here forty years ago.' Nathan poured boiling water into a couple of mugs and stirred. 'Which completely removes any motive he might have had for killing her.'

'But you do agree that he killed Alan Butler?'

'It's certainly looking that way. I'll email Matt and Sunil all of this, so they're up to speed, and then we can decide how to progress. I don't think there's any need to go blundering in until we've got a proper case against him.'

'And it means you can enjoy Christmas,' I said, and he laughed.

'Well, yes. Sunil will be in tomorrow anyway, so I'll get him to dig deeper into Colin's background, his family – because they sound right dodgy – see if we can find out where he was living in 1985 or whenever the murder was.'

'Sounds like a plan,' I said.

We went into the living room and sat on the sofa, drinking tea. Nathan emailed Sunil and then sat back, dog snuggled into his lap and me snuggled into his side, to enjoy some well-deserved downtime.

Only it didn't last very long. My phone rang; it was Tony.

'Jodie, can you do us a favour?'

'Tone, it's almost ten o'clock on Christmas Eve...' I groaned. 'The presents are wrapped, the elves are hooking

Rudolph up to the sleigh, and Daisy's getting Santa's cookies and glass of milk ready.'

'No I'm not!' called Daisy, but I ignored her.

'We're just about to go to bed.'

'I know. But Colin's just knocked on the door of the rectory and confessed to a murder...'

Chapter Twenty-Three

'Well this is a proper turn up for the books, innit?' Tony greeted us on the doorstep of the rectory, Carmen's pretty stone cottage not far from the church.

'Indeed,' said Nathan. Tony peered at us closely.

'Except you already knew, didn't you?'

'We suspected. Where is he?'

'In the living room. Carmen sat him down, made him a cup of tea, and then he just unburdened himself...' Tony turned and led us down the hall and into the cosy reception room.

Colin was slumped in an armchair, a mug of tea by his side. Carmen was perched on the edge of hers, and she looked up at us as we entered, an expression of relief on her face.

'Hello, Jodie,' said Colin, flatly. He seemed to have no energy left in him, exhausted perhaps by getting everything off his chest.

'Hi, Colin,' I said, taking a seat on the sofa opposite him. Tony hovered uncertainly as Nathan grabbed a footstool and pulled it up close to Colin's chair.

'Okay, Colin, do you want to tell us what's going on?' he asked gently. Some criminals need a firm hand; they need to know you're in charge and you're not going to take any of their shit, so there's no point lying. But others – like Colin, who looked shellshocked – need more careful handling.

'Are you here in your official capacity?' asked Colin. 'I only came to confess to the vicar…'

'Well, that depends on what you have to tell us,' said Nathan. 'At the moment, it's just you and me. Jodie and the vicar are here to support you.'

'And I'm here to make the tea,' said Tony, which earnt him a flat smile from Colin.

'Colin, tell Nathan what you told me,' urged Carmen, leaning forward and reaching for his hand. 'You want to do the right thing, that's obvious. That's why you let Tony call him. What did you say to me? "I want to make the world a better place", just like I talked about in my sermon this evening. You know how you can do that. By taking a family's pain away.'

Colin took a deep breath. 'I killed someone. Forty years ago.'

'Alan Butler,' said Nathan, and Colin looked at him in amazement.

'You knew?'

'Jodie worked it out, the bare bones of it anyway. Why don't you tell us what happened, Colin?'

'It was in 1985. I was twenty-three and I already felt like my life was over. I had no job, no prospects, and I was stuck living at home with my family.' He sighed. 'My family weren't great, to put it mildly. My dad and my brothers were all heavy drinkers and gamblers, they got into fights, they robbed people – I knew it was wrong, but it was the only way I knew to get money. I let myself get dragged into whatever they were up to – normally robbing people's houses, but that wasn't enough for my brother Sean, who decided that armed robbery would get us more money for less effort.' He shook his head. 'I knew it would escalate. I knew once he got his hands on a gun, there was only one way it was going to end, but he wore me down and I was too weak, too stupid, to say no.'

'You robbed the Butler family's shop and post office in Bermondsey,' said Nathan. Colin nodded.

'Yes. Sean had watched the place for a couple of weeks, and he told me that the time we were planning to rob it was best because it would be quiet, and there'd only be the two of them working in the shop. But when we got there, their kid was with them.'

'Tessa,' I said. 'Kirsty's mum.'

'Yeah, I guess so. I told him we should call it off and go back another day, but he said he'd always intended to do it while she was there, because it would scare the parents more and they'd do whatever we told them to do. He said it would be quicker and easier that way.'

'But it didn't work out like that, did it?' asked Nathan.

'No. Bloody Sean. The dad – Alan Butler – he was

terrified. He couldn't open the safe because his hands were shaking too much. So Sean dragged him out and put the gun to his daughter's head, and then told the mum to do it. We argued – I didn't want him using the girl like that – and then Butler threw himself at Sean. I turned round to see what was happening, and then somehow my gun went off, and…'

'And Alan Butler got a bullet in the head,' said Nathan.

'Yes.' Colin was pale, shaking, as if reliving that day was traumatising him all over again. 'I didn't know what to do. We just ran, we didn't even take any money or anything from the shop. I just wanted to get away from the sound of that girl and her mum screaming.' He looked up at us, eyes pleading. 'I never meant to kill him. I never meant to hurt anybody. I didn't even want to be there.'

'But you didn't go to the police afterwards,' I said.

'No. I wanted to, but Sean and my dad both threatened me, because I couldn't give myself up without dropping my brother in it, and my dad was the one who got us the sawn-off shotguns, so…'

'So he'd have been in big trouble too,' I said. 'What did you do, then?'

'I just lay low. I couldn't come to terms with what I'd done. I felt sick every time I thought about it. I still do feel sick, telling you about it now. For about six months I barely left the house, and by the time I did I'd buried it so deep, it almost felt like someone else had done it.'

'And then you got the part in *Mile End Days*,' said Tony. I'd almost forgotten he was there, lurking. 'How did that come about?' Typical Tony, to ask something about his acting career. Maybe he was still holding out for a part in *Penstowan Days*.

'I auditioned almost by accident,' said Colin. 'I was determined to go straight, so I got a job as a bike courier. I'd only been doing it a couple of weeks, when I had to cycle over to some TV producer's office in Soho with some documents. When I walked in, there was a group of people at the reception desk, arguing over head shots, and then the producer looked up and saw me and went, 'That's who we need! Someone who looks like that. You! Can you act?' So I said yes, of course, and the next thing I knew they were giving me a screen test. Couldn't believe it when I saw the part they wanted me to try for, it was almost like my real family.'

'Who else knows about the murder of Alan Butler?' asked Nathan. 'Did Kirsty know?'

'What? No, of course she didn't! I didn't even realise they were related until earlier this evening, when you introduced me to Maeve.' Colin looked at Nathan, realisation dawning. 'That's why you introduced us, isn't it? To see if I gave myself away.'

'You're certain Kirsty didn't know?' I asked. 'Or at least suspect?'

'I am. At least, I hope she didn't, because I genuinely cared about her, and to think that she might've known about it, and hated me...' Colin's face dropped, and he looked now like he was about to cry. 'She would've felt so betrayed. What makes you think she knew?'

'Just some things we found on her computer. Old interviews with you, for instance. And she asked her grandmother about the tattoo she'd seen on the killer's back, all those years ago.'

'She saw my tattoo? Oh God…' Colin slumped down in his chair. 'She must've hated me.'

'You must see what we're asking you here, Colin,' said Nathan, gently but firmly. 'If she knew you'd killed her grandfather all those years ago, what would you have done to stop her telling everyone?'

'What would I…?' Now he looked horrified. 'Wait, you don't think I killed her, to keep her quiet? But I didn't even know she suspected anything! And I've got an alibi for the night she was murdered.'

'So who else knows?'

'Well, Sean and the rest of my family, obviously,' said Colin. 'No one else. I didn't even tell my wife – I couldn't – oh…'

'Who?' Nathan leaned forward. We *all* leaned forward.

'Hilary.'

'How did she find out?' I asked.

'We met at this spiritual retreat in the early 1990s. I don't know what she was doing there, but I was in the middle of a nervous breakdown, basically.'

'This was after you had that big storyline in the soap, which you admitted at the time was based on real life experience, although of course no one could've known just how much of it was real,' I said. He nodded, surprised. 'I read an interview you gave the *Radio Times* about it. You thought it would be a good idea to use all of that for a soap opera storyline, and it gave you one of your finest performances, but you didn't realise how much reliving it on screen would bring back all the guilt and trauma.' I gave a thin smile. 'Hilary said she met you when you were having a wobble.'

'A wobble? It was like all of it had happened yesterday,' said Colin. 'I thought it would be cathartic, but it just brought everything back. All the guilt. I wanted out.'

'Of the soap opera?'

'Of life. So it was a bit more than a wobble. I'd fired my agent and I was about to quit acting altogether, but then I got talking to Hilary, who recognised me, of course. We had to find partners to share our trauma with.' He laughed, bitterly. 'Hilary doesn't do trauma, but luckily I had more than enough for both of us. I ended up telling her everything.'

'So she knows about the murder?' I asked, glancing over at Nathan.

'Yes. I wanted to go to the police after I'd told her, but she persuaded me not to. She said what was done was done. The old Colin Sweeney, the one that pulled the trigger, was dead, and I should let him be. She persuaded me to reinvent myself, to stop talking about my shitty family and my horrible childhood and concentrate on being Colin Sweeney the successful actor. And of course she took me on as a client.'

'Hilary's been with you ever since then, hasn't she?' I asked.

'Yes. She's always been completely loyal.'

'Is Hilary in love with you?' asked Nathan.

'What? No!' Colin was so surprised he half laughed. 'No, God, no. Hilary's fond of me as a friend, but the only thing she's in love with is the money I earn her. Although I'm assuming my big TV comeback is off now.'

'So what happens now?' asked Carmen. 'Do you have to take him in?'

'I'm afraid so, yes,' said Nathan, getting to his feet. 'I'm sorry, Colin. I don't doubt that you very much regret what happened, and that it's haunted you ever since, but a cold case is still a case. A murder is still a murder, even forty years later.'

'I know,' he said, rising too. 'It's almost a relief to finally give myself up.' Carmen stood up and quickly embraced him.

'Well done, Colin,' she said. 'I'm very proud of you. This will help ease that poor family's pain, like you wanted.'

'I only wish I knew who'd killed Kirsty,' he said. But I had the sneaking suspicion that we already did know, we just had to work out how.

Nathan drove Colin to the station, where he would be kept in a cell overnight while Nathan worked out what to do with him. By rights the case belonged to the Met police, so tomorrow a call would be put in and, more than likely, someone from the department who had originally investigated the robbery and murder would drive down to take Colin back with them. Carmen offered to call Hilary, to let her know what was going on, but Colin had left after she'd gone to bed, so Nathan told her to leave it to the police to let her know in the morning.

Tony gave me a lift home, and he was uncharacteristically quiet all the way.

'You all right?' I asked him.

'Yeah, I was just thinking… Poor Colin. I know he's a murderer and that, but he's a nice bloke.' He laughed gently. 'Hark at me, calling a murderer a nice bloke! But you know what I mean. He made a mistake, one that I reckon he's paid for several times over, but it's going to ruin the rest of his life.'

'The sad thing is, if he'd followed his heart at the time and given himself up, he'd have served prison time and been let out years ago,' I said. 'Not coming clean for all this time will hurt his case. And he might not have meant to kill Alan Butler, but he still went in there, armed with a sawn-off shotgun, so he knew the risks. He knew what could happen, and unfortunately, the worst did.'

'You're proper stern, you, aren't you?'

I laughed. 'Just had more experience dealing with people like Colin than you have,' I said. 'Loads of criminals aren't evil, they're just stupid or lost or easily persuaded. Still, it's harder to say no when it's your own family, isn't it?'

'Yeah, I reckon.' We pulled up outside my house. 'Anyway, happy Christmas, Jodie.'

'Happy Christmas, Tony.'

Chapter Twenty-Four

It was almost three in the morning when Nathan finally got home and crawled into bed next to me.

'Is that you, Santa?' I asked sleepily, rolling over to snuggle into him. 'Have you got a present for me?'

'That depends. Are you a good girl?'

'Sometimes. Other times, I can be very naughty…'

Nathan laughed quietly. 'In that case, I definitely have a present for you, but it'll have to wait until the morning because I'm knackered.'

I was desperate to ask him about the case, or if Colin had said anything more that might incriminate Hilary or shed light on anyone else who might know about his past, but I could hear in his voice exactly how worn out he was. It could wait until the morning, along with my present.

We both must've fallen deeply asleep within seconds, because it seemed like I'd barely shut my eyes again when I was woken up by a tap at the door, followed by 'I hope you're decent because I'm coming in!' from Daisy. I opened my eyes and looked at the clock: it was already almost eight thirty.

Germaine rushed through the bedroom door and leapt up onto the bed, tail wagging excitedly as if she knew it was Christmas Day. Daisy came in a bit more sedately, bearing a tray with three cups of tea on it. She set it down on the chest of drawers before going out again, reappearing a few seconds later with four Christmas stockings.

'What's all this?' I asked, sitting up in bed. Nathan reached for a cup of tea and passed it to me, before getting one for himself. Daisy sat on the end of the bed with the stockings.

'I heard you saying to Nana that you missed the days when I used to run in at five o'clock in the morning, shouting that Father Christmas had been,' she said. 'So I thought I'd do it again this year.'

'But with tea and at a better time of day,' said Nathan.

'Yeah, I ain't getting up at five for anyone,' said Daisy. 'I didn't think you'd mind a lie in.'

I reached out and grabbed her hand. 'Aww, thank you, sweetheart. You're lucky I can't reach you for a cuddle or I'd start getting all soppy.'

'*Start* getting soppy? You mean you stopped at some point?'

So we sat and drank our tea, and opened all the daft presents in our stockings. Germaine was particularly taken with the squeaky dinosaur we'd bought her, although I was already starting to regret it as the squeak was louder and more annoying than anticipated. Nathan was very happy with the pocket multi-tool shaped like a lobster (bottle opener in one claw, screwdriver in the other, and pocket knife in the tail), and Daisy loved her *How to Communicate Telepathically With Your Dog* guidebook. As for me, the high point of any Christmas stocking has to be the chocolate orange at the toe, and as Christmas is one of the few days where it's not just acceptable but mandatory to eat chocolate for breakfast, I'd soon unwrapped it and tucked into a couple of segments.

Stockings exhausted, we all got up and headed downstairs to see Mum, apart from Nathan who headed into the shower. We laughed at the contents of Mum's stocking (which included a magnetic photo frame with a picture of Bradley Walsh in it, to stick on her fridge) and then I made a proper, non-chocolate breakfast, although sticking some croissants into the oven to warm up probably doesn't really count as 'making' anything.

Nathan came down just as I was putting the plate of croissants on the table, along with butter and strawberry jam. He was smartly dressed.

'Are you going into work?' I asked him.

'Yeah. Only for a couple of hours, though. I'll be back for lunch and then I'm yours for the rest of the day.' He smiled ruefully. 'Probably.'

'What do you have to do? Can't Sunil do it?'

'He can, but it's probably best if I'm there too for a bit. I emailed the serious crime unit at Bermondsey last night, but

I need to follow it up with a phone call. And I want to check on Colin, too.'

'Will he get out on bail? They surely won't keep him in on remand, will they? It could take months for the case to come to court, after this many years.'

'I'd be happy to let him out on bail, because he's not a flight risk, and I think if anything coming clean now has been a relief. But I can't really do that until I hear from Bermondsey nick and see how they want to proceed.' He took a croissant and pulled it apart, spreading jam on it and eating it, still standing up. 'I'll get Sunil to dig a bit deeper into Hilary's alibi, too. I've read the transcript of her meeting, but I haven't watched the recording, so I'll get him to do that. Otherwise it's back to square one.'

'It can't be square one – the murder of Kirsty's grandfather must have something to do with her own death?'

'Not necessarily.' He finished his croissant in super quick time, then bent down to kiss me. 'I will be as quick as I can, I promise. I'm not missing Christmas lunch for anyone. Did you make that chocolate tiramisu…?'

'Yes I did, especially for you as you don't like Christmas pudding, so you'd better be here for it!' I kissed him back. 'Go on, then, get out of here so you can come back quicker.'

The rest of the morning was spent prepping lunch. I thought about peeling the potatoes, but veg is actually healthier with the skin left on (as long as you wash it properly), so I just washed and chopped them, then scrubbed the carrots and chopped them up too. I'd been quite prepared to forgo the sprouts, but Mum had insisted, so I gave her the job of rinsing them and cutting little crosses in the top to help them cook. I had put my foot down and swapped out the turkey for a free range, corn-fed chicken, because every year we had far too much meat and ended up having turkey for the whole Christmas and New Year period – and none of us even liked turkey that much…

Nathan was true to his word. He was home again by twelve-thirty, clutching a Tupperware container.

'Chocolate barfi, from Eesha,' he said. 'I have no idea what they are, but they smell amazing.'

'Oh my God,' I said, sniffing the small Indian sweets, 'they smell of saffron, and something else…'

'Cardamom, apparently,' said Nathan, reaching in to take one.

'Just one! Leave room for your lunch!'

'Yes, Mum.' He grinned at me, his cheeks bulging. 'I'll just get changed and then I'll be back to help.'

I put the kettle on and sat at the kitchen table, nibbling one of the sweets. Mum and Daisy were in the living room, watching *The Muppet Christmas Carol* (best Christmas movie EVER, and a tradition in our house), with Germaine curled up across Mum's lap. The chicken and the roast potatoes had just gone into the oven, the stuffing was ready, and the veg was poised to go on the boil. There wasn't much else to be done, other than setting the table with our least chipped crockery and putting a couple of candles in the centre, surrounded by artfully draped holly from our back garden. I'd gone with candles that apparently smelt of Christmas spices, having been dissuaded from buying the one that said 'Light this candle, because burning stupid people is illegal' on the grounds that it didn't really fit the festive spirit.

Nathan returned, looking far more relaxed in jeans and a hoodie. I put a cuppa in front of him and we sat at the table, enjoying the peace and quiet.

'Go on, ask me,' he said, after a couple of minutes of contemplative silence.

'Ask you what?'

'About this morning. You must be bursting to.'

I laughed. 'Well, yes, but I was being thoughtful and letting you have the afternoon off before I started interrogating you. But if you're ordering me to... Did Sunil watch Hilary's Zoom?'

'We both did. It's time stamped and it all matches up with what she told us. She was talking to LA for the first ten minutes or so of the murder window, and she didn't have enough time to get from Colin's cottage to the theatre to kill Kirsty.'

'Dammit! I've been going over it in my head, and her being the killer is the only thing that makes sense.'

'Do you want to watch it? It's on my laptop. Maybe you can pick something up that Sunil and I missed.'

I looked at the clock. 'I've got half an hour before I need to do anything with the dinner,' I said. 'Might as well.'

Nathan got his laptop, and we sat down together to watch.

'Hmm,' I said, a few seconds into the recording.

'What?'

'Hilary's wearing bright red lipstick…'

Nathan smiled. 'Yes, Sunil noticed that too. I think he's become a lipstick aficionado.'

'Impossible to tell from this, but it's very similar to the one on the fabric. Did Forensics ever get anything from that lipstick smear?'

'Only that it was left by a woman. A biological one, rather than a pantomime dame.'

'Okay…' We carried on watching. Behind Hilary was a large bookcase, full of books and plants and ornaments. 'The background's sort of weird, isn't it? It doesn't look like Colin's house.'

'Is it not his study?'

'I don't think so. Obviously I've not been in every room in his house, but… look at how tall that bookcase is. The ceiling's really high, like in a Victorian or Georgian house. The ceiling in his little cottage is a lot lower than that.' I peered closely. Hilary sat very straight and upright in her seat – awkwardly so – and didn't move much, but when she did the background warped around her. 'She's using a backdrop,' I said. 'I bet that's her office at home.'

'I think you might be right,' said Nathan, leaning closer to the screen. 'But a lot of people do that, don't they? They want to project a professional image. Maybe Colin's cottage didn't look professional enough for her.'

'Hmm,' I said. Something was lurking in the outer reaches of my brain. Yes, lots of people *did* use backdrops – I remembered when I'd video called Mum once, before we'd moved down here, and Daisy had been fiddling about with the settings on my laptop. I'd spent most of the call trying to remove the underwater kingdom behind me, because the fish swimming in and out of the background had kept distracting my mother.

On screen, Hilary sneezed, and in that instant I saw a flash of something, but it was gone before I could tell what it was.

'Rewind and freeze that bit!' I cried. Nathan reached out and rewound it, stopping just as Hilary moved. 'There! What is she sitting on? That's a weird-looking chair. That's not the sort of chair you'd have in an office, is it? And while we're at it, the angle of this whole thing is all wrong. The camera's up here—' I waved a hand in front of my face. 'It's not where you'd have your computer or laptop camera if it was sitting on a desk.'

'Holy shit,' said Nathan, and we looked at each other as the answer came to both of us. 'She's not sitting at a desk at all, she's sitting in her car!'

'Which could have been parked outside the theatre, giving her time to finish her call, slip inside the theatre and shut Kirsty up.'

'How did she get in? We're back to that question.'

'Not really. Jamie Westall slipped out the fire exit, and maybe he didn't shut it properly? Those doors are heavy, and they take a while to swing back into place.' I visualised it in my head. 'Maybe she got lucky. Or maybe she'd arranged to see Kirsty before the interval, and so Kirsty knew she'd be waiting and let her in when she came off stage.'

'The telephone conversation they'd had that morning...' said Nathan, and I could almost hear the cogs in his head turning. 'Kirsty realises that Colin killed her grandfather. She's been struggling with what to do – maybe she doesn't believe it, because she genuinely liked him, like everyone's said – who knows Colin best? Who's known him long enough to know if it's true or not?'

'His agent.'

'Exactly. So she calls Hilary and tells her what she knows, and that she's thinking about going to the police; what should she do? Hilary pretends to be shocked, and tells her to hold off. She tells her they should meet up and discuss it first.'

'Hilary must be cursing Kirsty, because she's just got this deal for Colin for his TV comeback,' I said. 'She's about to get a big payout, she doesn't want some small-town wannabe actress to spoil everything. So she's wondering how to shut her up...'

'Yes!' said Nathan. 'That's why she mentions Kirsty to the LA producer. She wants to bribe Kirsty, pay for her silence with the lure of a role in a big production, and hopefully fame and fortune will follow. Killing her is the last resort.'

'Hilary tells Kirsty to meet her before the interval, because she knows Colin won't be around backstage at that point, so they can speak privately.'

'They talk in the wardrobe. Hilary offers her a shot at the big time, but only if she keeps what she knows about Colin to herself. It gets heated, one or both of them get knocked over, leaving Kirsty's blood and Hilary's lipstick on the fabric. Hilary knows her chance of buying Kirsty's silence has gone, so she disguises herself in the Widow Twankey costume and drags her off to the storage room, but Kirsty is only briefly knocked out. She comes round, and Hilary bashes her in the head, several times to make sure, and kills her. She rolls her up in the carpet and shoves her in the cupboard.'

'Yes!' I said. 'She knows the body will be discovered fairly quickly, but she doesn't need long, just enough time to get back to the cottage before anyone starts asking questions.' I looked at Nathan. 'I take it Hilary now knows that Colin is under arrest for Alan Butler's murder?'

'Yes. I told her not to leave town, as we might need her to post his bail.' He grinned. 'I also told Uniform to park down the road from his cottage and keep an eye on her. If she leaves we'll know about it...' He stood up. 'Babe, you know what this means?'

'You're going to miss Christmas dinner. I know. But it'll keep.'

Chapter Twenty-Five

One of the frustrating things about not being a copper anymore is that you don't always get to be present when the bad guy (or girl) is confronted with the evidence against them. I was fairly certain that Nathan and I had worked out the mechanics of what had happened, but whether it could be proved sufficiently to satisfy the Crown Prosecution Service was another matter. A confession always helps, but would a woman like Hilary ever admit to murder?

The answer, it seemed, was yes.

Nathan got home at eight o'clock that evening. We'd had dinner, but there was plenty left for him, and I dished him up a plate and warmed it through as he sat, worn out but looking pretty pleased with himself, at the kitchen table. I presented him with the plate and a Christmas cracker, poured us both a glass of wine, then sat down opposite him, trying not to look expectant but failing miserably.

'I have been dreaming about this dinner,' he said, spearing a piece of chicken and stuffing onto his fork.

'Sorry we couldn't wait for you,' I said.

'I didn't expect you to. I actually thought I'd be there a lot longer, but Hilary caved.'

I looked at him in surprise. 'You what? She confessed?'

'Yes. She and Colin "accidentally" passed each other in the corridor as he was being taken into an interview room by a DS from Bermondsey, and I may or may not have previously let slip to him what she'd done…'

'I think you might be on the naughty list next Christmas for that little stunt,' I said, and he laughed.

'That's just between you, me, Colin and Santa,' he said. 'The important thing is we got a result. He asked her what on earth she thought she was doing, and she shouted at him that it was her job to protect him and that's exactly what she'd done.'

'Oooh, she sounds like a bit of a bunny boiler,' I said. 'So she admitted killing Kirsty? Did we get it right with our scenario?'

'Pretty much, except killing her wasn't a last resort at all. She never intended to get Kirsty a part in the TV project, she just mentioned it on the call to strengthen her alibi and make it look like she was on Kirsty's side. She guessed that the phone calls between them might come out, so she needed to make it look like they were about Kirsty's career, not her suspicions about Colin.'

'Wow, she really is a piece of work…'

'Everything else, though, spot on. She was going to

message Kirsty to get her to come outside, but then she saw Jamie Westall slipping out through the fire exit and managed to get through it herself before the door closed. She surprised Kirsty in the wardrobe room, where she threatened her, but it was obvious she wasn't going to change her mind about going to the police, so Hilary had to kill her. She managed to knock her out, but she realised there would be people coming in to get changed in the wardrobe during the interval, so she disguised herself, did a quick recce and found the storage room, dragged her in there and finished her off before she came round again.'

'She was completely cold-blooded,' I said. 'And what about the lipstick? After all Sunil's work on that, don't tell me it wasn't hers?'

'Oh no, it was. Colin bought it for her for her birthday in the summer. He thought "Sunset Boulevard" was an apt name for a lipstick for her, given the movie connection.'

'The only close-up she's going to be ready for any time soon is a mugshot,' I said. 'Poor Colin. I shouldn't feel sorry for him, but I do. If he hadn't met Hilary at that retreat, maybe he'd have gone to the police back then. I don't think he's a bad person, he's just been surrounded by the wrong people for a lot of his life.'

Nathan nodded. 'First his family, and then Hilary.'

'And poor Maeve! I hope knowing who killed her husband will help her get closure.'

'I'll be recommending they get involved in the restorative justice programme,' said Nathan. 'If they're agreeable to it, Colin and Maeve will be able to sit down together and talk about what happened. I think it could help them both come to terms with it.'

'That's a good idea,' I said. 'And we've got justice for Kirsty, too. Good work, DCI Withers.'

'Couldn't have done it without you, Consultant Parker.' He raised his wine glass and we toasted each other.

Nathan finished his dinner, and then we wrapped up warm to take Germaine out for a last walk before bedtime. It was too cold to go over the cliffs, so we headed towards town, where we could see the fairy lights criss-crossing Fore Street all lit up. In the windows of the houses around us, Christmas trees sparkled, lights twinkled, and in the distance we could hear the bells of St Botolph's church ringing. We passed others out for a walk, coming home from the pub, working off their Christmas dinner or, like us, with dogs. We smiled and greeted each other with 'Happy Christmas', then walked on. Somewhere, someone was drunkenly singing 'We Wish You a Merry Christmas', but as it wasn't Mum (for a change) we just smiled and walked on.

We found a bench overlooking the beach and sat down, letting the lead out to its full length so Germaine could sniff around almost to her heart's content.

'Oh, I heard from Carmen earlier,' I said. 'The verger, Mary, had a baby girl. They're calling her Eve.'

'That's a good name,' said Nathan, smiling. He put his arm around me. 'I haven't given you your present yet, have I?'

I laughed. 'What, out here? It's a bit cold for that sort of thing…'

'Not that! You're insatiable, woman. You can have *that* when we get home. No, your main present.'

'I thought the jumper was my main present?'

'Nope. It's a nice jumper, but that's a boring present.' He put his hand in his coat pocket, but kept it there for a moment. 'You told me ages ago about a charm bracelet your nana had, that you used to play with when you were little.'

'Oh, yes. Nana Gwen. She had tons of charms. She never left Cornwall, so other people used to bring charms back for her from faraway places. I always felt a bit sad that the charms were all about other people's adventures, not her own, but she was happy.' I smiled, remembering Nana Gwen, who had been just like my mum – daft as a brush, but warm and funny. She'd smelt of Lily of the Valley talcum powder, and always had a lace hanky tucked up the sleeve of her cardigan and a packet of mints in her handbag. She'd died of pneumonia when I was eight. 'Nana always told my mum she would get the bracelet, and Mum was going to pass it on to me, but after she died Grandad needed the money, so he flogged all of her jewellery apart from her wedding and engagement rings.'

Nathan brought his hand out of his pocket, clutching a small, beautifully wrapped box. 'Your present. You can probably guess what it is now,' he said, grinning. I took it from him and quickly unwrapped it.

Inside the box was a thick silver chain bracelet. I took it out and held it up, to better see the charms dangling from it.

'I've started you off with a couple,' said Nathan. 'That one—' He pointed to a dog charm. 'Pretty obvious who that's supposed to be, although I think it's a Scottie rather than a Pomeranian. That one—' He pointed to another, which was shaped like an old-fashioned police helmet. 'That one's because once a copper, always a copper.' He took the bracelet from my hands, undid the clasp and then slid it over my wrist, fastening it again. 'And this last one—' a cupid, with a bow and arrow '—this one is because you are the love of my life.'

'Oh babe, it's beautiful,' I whispered, holding up my arm to look at it. I turned to him and kissed him hard. He smiled.

'And the best thing is, there's lots of room for more charms. We need to have a few more adventures, so we can get some more charms.'

'Adventures?' I smiled. 'I can guarantee you lots more of *them*.'

Thanks and Acknowledgements

I have always thought it must be so much fun being in a pantomime. I've done amateur dramatics in the past, but a part in a panto has (so far) eluded me. I'd be even more keen to do one now; as I'm well past the age for being cast as Cinderella, I could definitely bring something to the part of the Wicked Stepmother...

But the unsung heroes of any production are not the ones who get the plaudits and standing ovations; they're the people who work tirelessly backstage to make sure the show goes on and the stars look good. So in honour of those people, and continuing my tradition of making this bit fit in with the rest of the book, here's my tribute to everyone who contributed to *The Cornish Christmas Pantomime Murder*.

CAST AND CREW

The Evil, Megalomaniacal Queen – Fiona Leitch
(mwah ha ha ha haaa!)

The Good Fairy – Lina Langlee, who has helped make so many of my writing dreams come true

Supporting Cast – Nina Kaye, Sandy Barker, Andie Newton, Carmen Radtke and Jade Bokhari, a group of wonderful ladies and fellow writers who have given me more support over the years than a push-up bra

Director – Jennie Rothwell, editor extraordinaire

Costume Designer – Lucy Bennett, who makes sure the whole series is well dressed

Line Prompts – Tony Russell and Caroline Scott-Bowden

Voice Coach – Zara Ramm, who does top notch work on the audiobooks

Catering – Dominic and Lucas Leitch for providing tea, biscuits and occasionally sympathy during the creation of this work, and for being willing guinea pigs for my recipes. You guys have eaten far more trifle (all in the name of research) than is probably healthy, and I love you for it!

Decadent Chocolate Orange Trifle

A wise woman (not me, obviously) once said, 'There are two types of people: those who like chocolate, and bit@#es.' While I won't go *quite* as far as that, I honestly cannot conceive of anyone not liking chocolate.

The Mayans and the Aztecs believed that chocolate was a gift from the gods, and I reckon they had a point. They used it in religious rituals, gave it to brave warriors returning victorious from battles, and used it as currency – it was literally worth more than its weight in gold. These days, we might not reward warriors with it, but we do use it to treat ourselves. Bad day? A bar of Dairy Milk* will make it better. Celebrating? Get yourself a box of those chocolate and praline seashells**. Lunch on the run? Meal deal with a cheese sandwich, a packet of crisps and a KitKat***, bish bash bosh, sorted. And of course nothing says Christmas like a tin of Quality Street**** in front of the King's Speech and a Terry's Chocolate Orange***** in the heel of your stocking.

Basically, what I'm saying is, this book's recipe involves chocolate. A *lot* of chocolate. So if you're a chocolate hater

(I won't call you a bit@#), I apologise, although you could probably swap out the chocolate bits for other flavours.

It also involves a favourite of British households up and down the nation (certainly my household): Jaffa Cakes. If you're not a native of these isles, let me tell you about these delicious delicacies which are so ingrained in the British psyche that they should really have their picture on the £10 note (Jane Austen is currently on it, so maybe we need to tweak the picture and have her tucking into one). The first thing you need to know is that, strictly speaking, they're not *really* cakes (or are they?). They're small circles of sponge, topped with a smaller circle of orange jelly, topped in chocolate. Despite the name, they're packaged and eaten more like biscuits. In the 1990s they had to go to court to prove that they *were* cakes, because items classified as biscuits are subject to VAT (Value Added Tax) while cakes aren't. Thankfully for us Jaffa Cake devotees (some may call us addicts), they won their case, and we can still enjoy our favourite treat without having to pay VAT on them.

On to the recipe. I make this as alternative to Christmas pudding, because not everyone likes the traditional dessert but they still deserve something a bit fancy to end the festive feast. It's more of an assembly job than actually having to cook stuff – it's Christmas, you want to spend it with your family, not be stuck in the kitchen (although of course it's sometimes nice to have an excuse to get away from them…). You can make this the day before – in fact, it's probably best to make it the day before, to give it time to set properly.

other chocolate bars are available.
**no, OF COURSE it doesn't have to be this type of chocolate.*
  Obviously. I just said as much.
***just leave it now, for the love of God!*
****okay you're making it weird.*
*****I can't even with you right now.*

Enough asterisks, let's get on with it... This makes one big
trifle, or you can make individual ones if you prefer. I made
four individual ones with this recipe and it was a bit too
much, especially after a big Christmas dinner – I have a
second stomach just for dessert, but even I couldn't eat it all.
I think I'd probably make six smaller ones if I was doing
individual trifles again.

A note about the layers: you can actually play about
with the order you put these in, leave some out, or add
different things in. If you're making individual ones, you
can make them all slightly different. For example, Daisy
hates jelly so I left that out of hers and just put some
mandarin orange segments in instead.

Ingredients and measurements are in UK metric but I've
attempted to add US measurements and equivalents in
italics.

1. Melt **100g/1/2 *cup* plain/*dark or semisweet*
   chocolate** in the microwave (do it in short bursts,
   stirring in between) or in a bowl over a pan of
   boiling water. Let it cool for (but not enough to
   set again!) and then whisk it into **500ml/2 *cups***

ready-made custard until fully combined (you can make your own custard, of course, but see my earlier point about it being Christmas; chances are you'll already be spending a heap of time in the kitchen, you've probably got a turkey to stuff, spuds to peel, presents to wrap and alcohol to drink, so make life easier for yourself and buy ready-made). Set the mixture aside.

2. Add the zest of **1 orange** (depending on the size – if they're small you might need a couple) to **300ml/1 1/4 *cups* of whipping/*heavy* cream** and whisk until the cream is thick and fluffy.

3. Line the bottom and sides of a serving bowl (or individual bowls) with **Jaffa Cakes** (if you can't get these where you are, brownies would also work well, or chocolate sponge or swiss rolls). Don't worry if the ones lining the side fall over, we're going to stick something in the middle next which will keep them standing up!

4. Fill the well in the middle of the Jaffa Cakes with something orangey… This can be either **orange jelly** (pre-make it the day before, or use ready-made, and spoon it inside) or maybe **tinned mandarins** (if you use these, you'll probably need a couple of tins). Or go wild and use jelly with

mandarin segments in it (that's what I used, and it was *lush*).

5. Spoon the chocolate custard over the top.

6. Top with **whipped cream**. Decorate with more orange zest (if you like), more mandarin segments, and segments of **Terry's Chocolate Orange**. If you can't get that where you are, grate over dark or orange-flavoured chocolate. And it's Christmas, so if you want to go wild add some orange jellies, a few sprinkles, or even some **Orange Matchmakers** (another chocolatey Christmas favourite). Maybe a chocolate Santa or two!

7. Put on some elasticated waist trousers (pants!), throw away your calorie counter, and tuck in.

Have you read the rest of the
Nosey Parker series?

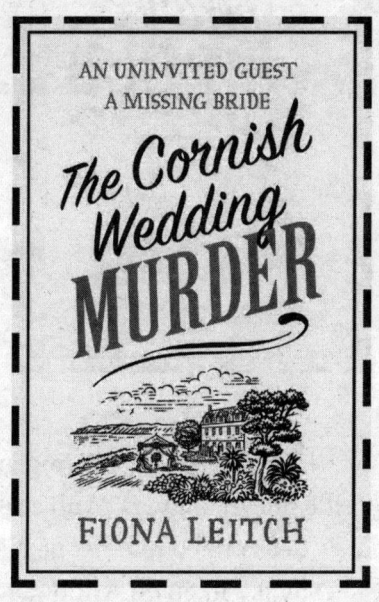

Still spinning from the hustle and bustle of city life, Jodie
'Nosey' Parker, is glad to be back in the Cornish village she
calls home. But with a missing bride on her hands, murder
and mayhem lurks around every corner…

A BODY ON A BEACH
A VILLAGE FULL
OF SUSPECTS

The Cornish Village **MURDER**

FIONA LEITCH

When a body turned up at her last catering gig it certainly put people off the hors d'oeuvres. With a reputation to salvage, Jodie's determined that her next job for the village's festival will go off without a hitch.

But when chaos breaks out, Jodie Parker somehow always finds herself caught up in the picture…

Can she find the killer before the village faces another brush with death?

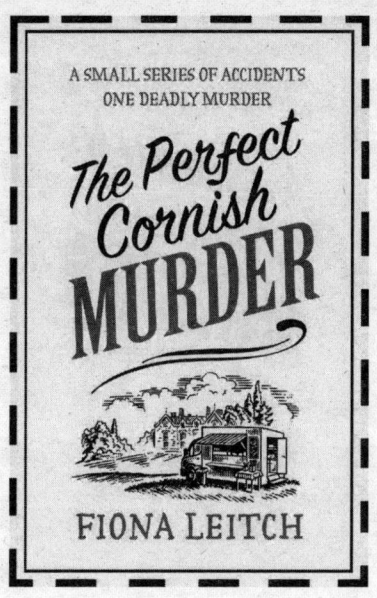

A SMALL SERIES OF ACCIDENTS
ONE DEADLY MURDER

The Perfect Cornish **MURDER**

FIONA LEITCH

A film company is coming to the Cornish village of Penstowan, and the whole community turn up to be cast as extras, even Jodie 'Nosey' Parker.

But right on cue, the company's caterer is sabotaged and Jodie must step up. It soon becomes clear that someone is out to spoil the filming… With actors behaving out of character and the house literally being brought down, breaking a leg is the least of their worries.

Can Jodie save the day once again, or will it be their final curtain call?

TWELVE GUESTS
ONE SNOWSTORM

A Cornish
Christmas
MURDER

FIONA LEITCH

A PINCH OF PARANOIA

It's three days before Christmas, and detective-turned-chef Jodie 'Nosey' Parker is drafted in to cater an event run by a notorious millionaire at a 13th-century abbey.

A DASH OF DECEPTION

Things get more complicated when a snowstorm descends, stranding them all…

A MURDER UNDER THE MISTLETOE

Secrets mull in every corner – can Jodie solve the crime before the killer strikes again?

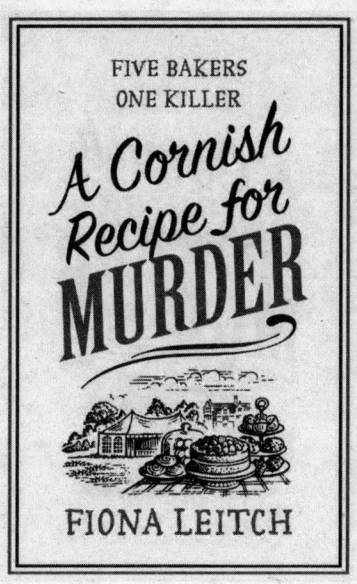

FIVE BAKERS
ONE KILLER

A Cornish
Recipe for
MURDER

FIONA LEITCH

When 'The Best of British Baking Roadshow' rolls into town and sets up camp in the grounds of Boskern House, former police officer Jodie 'Nosey' Parker finds herself competing to represent Cornwall in the grand final.

But with a fellow contestant who will stop at nothing to win, Jodie discovers that the roadshow doesn't just have the ingredients for the perfect showstopper cake, but also for the perfect murder…

Can Jodie expose the culprit? Or will the murderer become the real showstopper?

AS THE TIDE GOES OUT
SECRETS ARE REVEALED

A Cornish Seaside
MURDER

FIONA LEITCH

A Siren's call… to murder

While tourists and locals alike are falling under the spell of
the annual mermaid festival with its captivating legends of
Sirens luring fishermen to their deaths, Jodie and Nathan
fear they may have found themselves in the middle of a
very real – and very dangerous – turf war.

As the casualties start to stack up, they must face the
likelihood that something sinister has been going on under
their noses for some time…

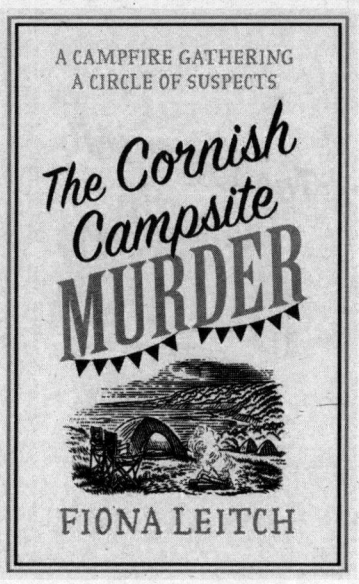

A CAMPFIRE GATHERING
A CIRCLE OF SUSPECTS

The Cornish
Campsite
MURDER

FIONA LEITCH

A campfire gathering. A circle of suspects.

Just along the coast from Penstowan, the local festival has
filled the area. Former Met police officer Jodie 'Nosey'
Parker has agreed to step in and help run the Pie Hard food
truck, along with her reluctant fiancé, DCI Nathan Withers.

As they prepare for a weekend of camping, Jodie hadn't
bargained on witnessing a fight between members of the
lead band. But when the body of one of the band members
is found not far from the campsite, Jodie finds it hard to
believe it was an accident. Especially when the other
members had so much to gain…

A WEEKEND AWAY BUT SOMEONE
IS GUILTY OF MURDER

The Cornish
Castle
MURDER

FIONA LEITCH

Could the murderer be on the guest list?

The time has finally come for former Met police officer Jodie 'Nosey' Parker to wed her fiancé DCI Nathan Withers, But their long-anticipated wedding doesn't quite go to plan…

As their guests descend on a luxurious Cornish castle for a weekend of activities, celebrations grind to a halt when they find the body of a young woman floating face down in an ornamental pond. With the champagne chilling and canapes assembled, and an old London adversary brought in to investigate, it's up to Jodie and Nathan to uncover the killer, before they strike again.

ONE MORE CHAPTER

YOUR NUMBER ONE STOP
FOR PAGETURNING BOOKS

The author and One More Chapter would like to thank everyone who contributed to the publication of this story...

Analytics
Imogen Wolstencroft

Audio
Fionnuala Barrett
Ciara Briggs

Contracts
Laura Amos
Inigo Vyvyan

Design
Lucy Bennett
Fiona Greenway
Liane Payne
Dean Russell

Digital Sales
Laura Daley
Lydia Grainge
Hannah Lismore

eCommerce
Laura Carpenter
Madeline ODonovan
Charlotte Stevens
Christina Storey
Jo Surman
Rachel Ward

Editorial
Rosie Best
Kara Daniel
Charlotte Ledger
Jennie Rothwell
Tony Russell
Sofia Salazar Studer
Caroline Scott-Bowden
Helen Williams

Harper360
Emily Gerbner
Ariana Juarez
Jean Marie Kelly
emma sullivan
Sophia Wilhelm

International Sales
Peter Borcsok
Ruth Burrow
Bethan Moore
Colleen Simpson

Inventory
Sarah Callaghan
Kirsty Norman

Marketing & Publicity
Chloe Cummings
Grace Edwards
Katie Sadler

Operations
Melissa Okusanya
Hannah Stamp

Production
Denis Manson
Simon Moore
Francesca Tuzzeo

Rights
Ashton Mucha
Alisah Saghir
Zoe Shine
Aisling Smyth
Lucy Vanderbilt

Trade Marketing
Ben Hurd
Eleanor Slater

**The HarperCollins
Distribution Team**

**The HarperCollins
Finance & Royalties
Team**

**The HarperCollins
Legal Team**

**The HarperCollins
Technology Team**

UK Sales
Isabel Coburn
Jay Cochrane
Sabina Lewis
Holly Martin
Harriet Williams
Leah Woods

**And every other
essential link in the
chain from delivery
drivers to booksellers
to librarians and
beyond!**

ONE MORE CHAPTER

One More Chapter is an
award-winning global
division of HarperCollins.

Subscribe to our newsletter to get our
latest eBook deals and stay up to date
with all our new releases!

signup.harpercollins.co.uk/
join/signup-omc

Meet the team at
www.onemorechapter.com

Follow us!

@onemorechapterhc

Do you write unputdownable fiction?
We love to hear from new voices.
Find out how to submit your novel at
www.onemorechapter.com/submissions